THE DREAMING TEAM

CHRIS WALLACE

In the spirit of reconciliation, Round Lake Publishing acknowledges the Traditional Custodians of country throughout Australia and their connections to land, sea and community. We pay our respect to their Elders past and present and extend that respect to all Aboriginal and Torres Strait Islander peoples today.

Copyright © Chris Wallace 2023
The moral right of Chris Wallace to be identified as the author of this work has been asserted.

All rights reserved. Without limiting the rights under copyright above, no part of this publication shall be reproduced, stored in or introduced into a retrieval system, or transmitted in any form or by any means (electronic, mechanical, photocopying, recording or otherwise) without the prior permission of both the copyright owner and the publisher of this book.

Published by Round Lake Publishing
Book design by Rainsford from the painting, Possum Dreaming, used by permission of the artist Nyrulla Possum Burns.
Back cover photo by Brett Tucker

ISBN: 978-0-6459687-0-5

First, this book is dedicated, with deep respect for their strength and resilience, to all Aboriginal Australians, and through them to all Indigenous people the world over, past, present and future. And second, it is dedicated to the good people of Australia, black, white and brown, for accepting me as one of them.

FORWARD

I expect it will be said that this Yank has some nerve, writing a book about, not just an event in Australian history, but Aboriginal history to boot. To which I reply, I have thought the same thing myself, despite having lived as an Australian citizen for thirty years.

For a number of years going back to the mid-20 teens, I was involved in a peripheral way with this story. So, I've known about it in some detail since then. I've always thought it was too important not to be made available to the general public. During these intervening years, no one else in the creative community (of which I number myself) has told this story. I was reluctant to write it for the obvious reasons already articulated. But as I began to think seriously about writing it, I concluded that it might be an advantage being an outsider. I can tell the story in a freer way, still respecting the truth but using my own voice as an observer.

For better or for worse, that has been my motivation and I make no apologies for it. It has been my goal to portray these characters as real people and to let them speak for themselves. Only you, the reader, can determine if I was successful or not.

Contents:

Chapter One   -   Unaarrimin

Chapter Two   -   Pine Hills Station

Chapter Three   -   The Search

Chapter Four   -   The First Eleven

Chapter Five   -   A White Man's Game

Chapter Six   -   The Tour

Chapter Seven   -   Lawrence to the Rescue

Chapter Eight   -   The Vast Beyond

Chapter Nine   -   The Tour (Take 2)

Chapter Ten   -   Back to the Real World

Chapter Eleven   -   Aftermath

Chapter Twelve   -   Return to Country

Acknowledgements

About the Author

Chapter One – Unaarrimin

"But, Mum, he's all alone. He doesn't have anyone."

"That's not our worry, Alice. Now, help me hang this washing."

Alice takes one side of the washing basket while her mother takes the other.

As they peg the laundry onto the clothes line, Alice keeps up her protest. "And besides, he's my age. We grew up together. He's like a brother to me."

"Alice, stop it! I don't have time for this nonsense. We've given him a job and food and a place to sleep while he was growing up. That's more than a lot of people would do."

Alice has never been one to give up easily on anything. When she was a little girl, her mother insisted that Alice's hair grow long enough so she could braid it. Alice didn't like wearing braids. Her mother braided it anyway. Alice protested. Her mother ignored the protests. Alice got hold of some scissors and cut all her hair off.

"Well, I don't care what you say. I like him and he's my friend. He's the only friend I have. He's my *best* friend! I guess I'll have to talk to Dad about it."

"Don't you dare. And besides, I've already talked to him. Listen to me, Alice. It was one thing when you two were little. But you're getting to be a woman now. And don't pretend you don't know what I'm talking about. I just don't think it's a good idea to spend so much time with Black Johnny. Things happen. And I'm not going to let things happen to you. It's already decided. He's going and that's the end of it."

* * * * *

As he wanders away and into the dense Australian bush, Unaarrimin looks back at Mullagh Station. The brick house and its veranda, along with the sheds and pens, had been the only things he could identify with for these many years. They had been his everyday surroundings, as were the dogs and horses he looked after and the sheep he sheared. The land on which Mullagh Station sits had also been his ancestral home going back thousands of years. This is his country. It provided his Jardwadjali people with everything they needed. It took care of them and they took care of it. This dot on the earth had been his everything, his every place, his only place. Then the white settlers came and made the land do things that were unnatural to it after brutally displacing the people who had lived there for thousands of years. They introduced new animals and ripped down the trees and plants that had stood there since the beginning of time. They plowed up the earth and sowed new plants that this land had never known. They built new structures that belonged on another continent. They said they owned it now. Unaarrimin knew that nobody can own the land. It is the earth. People cannot own the earth. All anyone could do is to be part of it – be at one with it, as the Jardwadjali have been since the Dreaming. But now, he is no longer even a part of this new version. Now, his attachment to the land is in his soul, not in a geographic location.

He walks deeper into the bush. Little by little he finds it more and more familiar, not by way of recognition, but as a concept, as an organic existence. With each step, he goes farther away from the station and closer to his roots. He stops by a stream. Without thinking about it, he takes off his "white man" clothes and fashions a loincloth from one of his old work shirts. Then he kneels down for a drink of the fresh water. As he gazes down at his reflection, his mind wanders back to a day when he was at his father's side, drinking from this same stream.

"Try it again," his father says, as he hands the boomerang to Unaarrimin. "Hold it like this.. Throw from your shoulder." The boy takes the boomerang. It is nearly the size of his arm. "Now make yourself calm," his father continues. The boy tries to relax but feels the pressure of wanting to please his father. His father senses this and says in a softer, more encouraging voice, "Be calm, son. You must be still inside. Stillness is the key. You can do it." The boy lets out a big breath and his shoulders relax. He steps away from his father and hurls the weapon into the air. It whirls around in a wide arc with a velocity that belies the boy's size, coming to rest on the ground in front of his father. Unaarrimin beams up at him.

"Now do it again," says his father, suppressing a slight smile.

After some time has passed, being driven off Mullagh Station doesn't feel as much of a hardship for Unaarrimin. He is at home in the bush. In his genetic memory, he knows that everything he needs is here. He grazes on berries and bush tomatoes as he strolls along. As the afternoon sun bears down, he decides to have a rest. No reason to hurry. No place to hurry to. He finds a spot in the shade of a gum tree and stretches out with his hands behind his head. Before long, he is in a deep, peaceful sleep.

It is late afternoon when he is awakened by birds in a pre-dusk conversation, announcing their presence to one another from all around the canopy of trees: brilliant crimson rosellas, double banded plovers, fairywrens. Their presence sparks his recollection. These are birds he has known from his childhood, albeit by different names. Each bird adds a different voice to this familiar symphony. He sits up to listen. He realizes that he's smiling. Then he hears another bird emit three sharp, penetrating screeches which immediately grab his attention. This is a call he knows very well. Looking up through the trees, he spots the Black Cockatoo, his totem. He hears his father's voice, *"This is your totem, your brother. Our people have known this bird since our beginning. It will protect you. You must respect and protect it too. We are one with the Black Cockatoo. Never forget this." Unaarrimin looks up at the bird and nods to his father. "I will remember, father." "Always." "Yes, father, always."*

Unaarrimin can't recall the last time he wandered in the bush without a destination or purpose. He knows he will eventually have to find employment somewhere. The bush can no longer really be his home. White men have pieces of paper that say they own it. But at least for the moment, he is free. He continues wandering aimlessly, looking at the sky, listening to the wind, feeling the cool evening air begin to embrace him. He'll need to find a place to camp soon. When it gets dark here in the bush, it gets dark. Moonlight and the stars are the only light source. On moonless nights, it's only the stars. On cloudy nights, there is nothing.

Just at dusk, he comes upon a billabong. He gathers some brush and broken limbs and builds a satisfactory lean-to against a huge blue gum. He rolls out his swag and picks a place to build a fire. In a few minutes, it is glowing and throwing sparks into the night air. Soon some of the night creatures begin serenading from the darkness. He hears the haunting sigh of the brush tail possum. Then, the screeching rumble of the Soot Owl. The fire casts flickering shadows onto the surrounding vegetation. Unaarrimin stares into the fire and listens to this night music. His mind wanders.

The corroboree is in full swing. They come from three different groups: the Jardwadjali, the Gunditjamara and the Wotjabaluk people. It is already well into the night. Fires blaze. Sparks fly up into the sky. The sound of didgeridoos and clap sticks fill the night air, along with the sound of bare feet beating against the earth. The adults are dancing and singing and telling stories of the Dreaming. The festival is also a chance to catch up with old friends. The girls steal surreptitious glances at the boys who are trying to impress one another with their physical skills. Later in their lives, these same boys will be known by "white" names: King Cole, Bullocky, Sugar, Jellicoe, Dicky Dick, Redcap, Johnny Cuzens, Neddy, Tarpot, Sundown and Peter. Even Unaarrimin will be called by another name. But for now they are busy challenging one another. A ball made of possum skin is suspended from a limb. In turn, each of them jumps as high as he can in an attempt to dislodge it. Tiny Johnny Cuzens leaps and leaps while the others have a hearty laugh. Finally he gives up and laughs with them. "One day," he says. "'One day.'" Bullocky's thick body barely leaves the ground when he tries to jump. Jellicoe comes closest, but still falls short. Finally, it's Unaarrimin's turn. Before he jumps, he quiets himself. Stillness is the key. Then he springs into the air and grabs the possum ball with both hands before landing lightly on the balls of his feet. The others whoop and howl in celebration. He always outdoes the others in these games. They are used to it and they would be disappointed if he didn't. Dicky Dick tells Unaarrimin to put it back up there. He wants to have a go. Unaarrimin tosses the possum ball up into the tree. Dicky Dick stands beneath it. He sizes it up from one angle. Then he looks up at it from another. With great drama, he looks over his thumb to calculate the height. He is finally ready. Then he runs to the tree's trunk and scampers up with the agility of a koala. He shinnies out onto the limb and retrieves the ball, before dropping to the ground. The others, including the girls, applaud and laugh as he bows in all directions. The fruit bats banging around in the trees above him bring Unaarrimin out of his reverie. He banks the fire and lies on his back looking up through the trees until he falls asleep.

He wakes up as the new day dawns and has a full throated yawn and a leisurely stretch. He gathers some wood and refreshes the fire. After fetching some water in his billycan, he carefully sets it at the edge of the flames and tosses in a handful of tea. He sees a tall tree trunk a short distance away. He climbs up to the top and looks down inside the hollow. Just as he thought, there is a duck nest in the bottom with four large, white eggs resting in it. He takes two from the nest and leaves the others. Breakfast. He returns to the billabong and finds wattle ferns and grinds the seeds into flour between two rocks. Then he adds water and salt, shapes it into a loaf and puts it on the coals to become damper, bush bread. A feast at his fingertips.

Two more days pass in this same, relaxed, unhurried way. By now his day has a familiar routine. After he has had his morning tea, he goes out looking for food. The variety is limitless: one time he'll trap a possum, another time he'll catch a fish. Each day, he digs up some tubers, picks some leafy plants or collects nuts. One of the days, he feels especially daring. He climbs a tree and with the greatest delicacy, using a long stick, steals some honey without being attacked. He tries to imagine what it would be like to live by this billabong forever.

But on the morning of his fourth day, as he eats his morning meal, his mind feels unsettled. He is not focused on anything in general or anything in particular. But the euphoria of being free and on the land, which had so powerfully embraced him these past days, begins to fade. Something is bothering him. He knows he has to still himself. Whatever it is will reveal itself once he is still. It is the way he solves all problems. He closes his eyes and lets out a long breath. As he feels himself calming, he begins unconsciously humming a song. Finally, he is where he is, focused, present. He suddenly becomes aware of the song he is humming. Alice had sung this song when they were children. Like a tidal wave, an enormous sorrow washes over him. He begins weeping shamelessly, the tears of a heartbroken child. It was only four days ago. It seems like an eternity.

Mr. Buckingham has asked Black Johnny to come into the shearing shed. They stand together, both uncomfortable for different reasons. Unaarrimin wonders if he's done something wrong. He has always tried to be a good worker. Never complained about anything. Was happy just to be there on the station. What could he have done? In the very back of his mind, he wonders if it has anything to do with Alice but dismisses the thought as soon as it comes. Mr. Buckingham is uncomfortable because he doesn't like confrontation. And especially this one. He is perfectly happy with Black Johnny, finds him easy going, cooperative and good at his job. It's only because of his wife that he is in this position. After a few more awkward minutes, Buckingham clears his throat and begins. "You know . . . Um . . . You see . . . If it was up to me . . . Well . . . Er . . . The Missus has a bit of ah . . . Oh, damn it, I'm going to have to let you go. That's the size of it. You'll have to leave the property. I've arranged some provisions for you, tea and sugar, salt, a blanket, a billy, matches, a good knife. But you'll have to go." Unaarrimin can only look at this man dumbfounded; this man who has been his guardian since he was orphaned as a little boy. "What have I done?" Unaarrimin asks. "Well, that's just it, you see. It isn't that you've done anything. It's more like . . . um . . . look, Johnny, let's just leave it that the Missus would rather you weren't here anymore. Like I said, if it was up to me, we wouldn't be having this talk. But you've got to go. Here, take this letter with you. It'll help you get a job somewhere else. But she wants you off the property tomorrow. Early."

Alice and Unaarrimin had been inseparable when they were children. She claimed him. She taught him to read. As she learned them, she taught him manners. They hiked all over Mullagh Station together. He taught her how to live in the bush, showing her what plants were edible; how to make bread, how to build a proper fire. They got into all manner of mischief together, stealing honey from Mrs. Buckingham's cupboard and tobacco from Mr. Buckingham's pouch. One time Unaarrimin twisted his ankle jumping from the roof of the shed because Alice dared him. When they saw that he was alright, they rolled on the ground together in fits of laughter. He remembers how infectious Alice's laugh is. It's like a melody, like music to him. He would always do anything to make her laugh. And she always did. One day he was teaching her how to throw a boomerang. "Hold it like this,' he says. "Throw from the shoulder". Alice cranks her arm for a mighty toss and cracks Unaarrimin in the nose. She starts laughing her magical laugh. Even when it starts bleeding, she's still laughing. And by now, he is laughing too. Alice takes a handkerchief from her pocket and begins dabbing the blood. Then she gives it to him so he can apply enough pressure to *stop the bleeding. All the while they are laughing uncontrollably.*

But there is no laughter now. Now, he is filled with sadness as he empties the remains of the billy onto the fire and rolls up his swag. Where is he to go? What is he to do? He ambles away from the billabong, no longer conscious of freedom, but thinking of what he has lost, wondering if he'll ever see her again.

* * * * *

It is late afternoon. He hears men's voices coming from a clearing up ahead. As he approaches the clearing, he puts on his trousers. A group of men are in a paddock. They are playing a game of some kind. One of them throws a ball in the direction of another who is holding some kind of stick. Others are standing around the paddock. These men are both black and white and are having fun together. The man with the stick hits the ball that is thrown at him and it comes flying in Unaarrimin's direction. An Aboriginal man is chasing the ball. Unaarrimin steps into the clear and the ball comes to a stop at his feet. He's wondering if it is alright to pick it up and toss it to the man running toward him. But before he can act, he hears the Aboriginal man shout out his name.

"Unaarrimin!" the man calls.

Now he looks more carefully at the man coming toward him and recognizes him from corroboree days. King Cole is on him and grabs him by the shoulders for a mighty hug. In language, he says, "Hello, my brother. I am happy to see you."

It takes a moment for Unaarrimin to remember. Then he says, "Bripumyarrimin?"

"I am called King Cole now."

"King Cole?"

"Yes. It is because none of the white fellas can pronounce my name. What are you doing? Why are you here? Last I knew you were over at Mullagh Station."

"They ran me off."

"Why would they do that? What happened? What did you do?"

"Nothing. I think Mrs. Buckingham was afraid of what I might do. I don't know."

"So, you are free? Do you have work?"

"I am as free as a cockatoo."

"You have to come with me. The Edwards run Pine Hills and they are good people. You'll meet them and I'll make sure they give you a job here. Murrumgunarriman and Boninbarngeet are here too."

"They are?"

"Yep, but like me, they have "white" names too."

"What are they called?"

"Two Penny and Tiger."

Chapter Two – Pine Hills Station

Pine Hills Station is owned by Mr. Edwards. On it he runs a few thousand sheep and several hundred cattle. The homestead is newly built with bluestone exterior walls and a large, inviting veranda across the front and around one side. Its shearing shed and other out buildings are also relatively new. Like the station, Edwards is a progressive man. Egalitarian. Hard working and fair. His wife, Felicity, shares his philosophy and looks after the men who work for them as if they were her sons. The Edwards' only child, a daughter named Nell, is married to Jake, Edwards' head stockman and right hand man.

The cricket game is finished. The men are putting the cricket gear back into the shed and Mr. Edwards is on his way to the homestead when King Cole calls to him. "Hey, Boss."

Edwards looks back.

King Cole takes Unaarrimin by the arm and pulls him along. "This is an old friend from corroboree days, Boss. His name is Unaarrimin. This is Mr. Edwards."

"Nice to meet you, young fella," And to King Cole, "What can I do for you, King?"

"I want you to meet my friend. Maybe you can find a place for him here at Pine Hills."

Edwards looks Unaarrimin up and down and likes what he sees, but still says, tentatively, "Oh, well, we're not really looking for anyone now."

"He's a real good worker, Boss. He can outwork ten men, maybe twenty." These are the most words and the most enthusiasm Edwards has ever heard King Cole express. It is so uncharacteristic that Edwards is taken aback.

"Well . . . um . . . Sorry. What did you say his name is?"

"He's called Unaarrimin, Boss,"

"Mu . . . An . . . Say it again."

"Unaarrimin."

"Right. Well, where did you come from, Um – ari - man? Did I say it right?"

King Cole starts to correct Edwards.

Unaarrimin cuts him off. "I been working at Mullagh Station since I was a little boy."

"He's a good worker, Boss," King Cole quickly adds.

"Mullagh Station. That's Buckingham's, isn't it?"

"Yes, sir."

"Why did he let you go?"

Unaarrimin exchanges a glance with King Cole. Then, thinking quickly, he reaches into his pocket and says, "I got a letter here from Mr. Buckingham." He hands the letter to Mr. Edwards.

As he peruses it, Edwards says, "Hm. He seems to think a lot of you. It looks pretty good. So, why did he let you go?"

Unaarrimin turns to stone. What can he say? He doesn't know why he was let go. He didn't want to go. He won't lie and he doesn't know what the truth is.

Edwards senses something. Perhaps a kind of pride or dignity. Something. He decides not to pursue it further. He can always find out from Buckingham next time he sees him. "Well, it doesn't matter. Buckingham thinks you're all right. Says you're a good worker. That's enough for me." He thinks for a moment. "Can you look after horses?"

"Yes, sir. I like animals. That was one of my jobs at Mullagh Station."

"We might be able to use a groom. I could use the fella who's doing that somewhere else. We'll put you on as a groom, then."

"Thanks, Boss," King Cole says. "You won't be sorry."

"I hope not," Edwards replies. "Why don't you look after him. Tell Jake I've hired him. Show him where he can sleep and put his things. And say your name once more for me."

"Unaarrimin." "I'm not sure I can get my tongue around that. Is that what Buckingham called you?"

"No, sir."

"What did he call you?"

"Black Johnny."

"Hm. Well, we'll call you Johnny too. We've got another Johnny here though. I know. How about this? Since you're from Mullagh Station, we'll call you Johnny from Mullagh, Johnny Mullagh. Is that all right with you?"

Unaarrimin smiles his first smile at Pine Hills Station. "That suits me. From now on I'll be Johnny Mullagh."

* * * * *

It isn't long before Johnny Mullagh feels very much at home at Pine Hills. One afternoon, Mr. Edwards calls out to the workers that it's tea time. Mrs. Edwards always has fresh scones and jam for them. As they are sitting around having their tea, Edwards says, "Listen, lads, who's for taking the rest of the day off and playing a little cricket?" He knows what the answer is before he asks the question. "We're all right to do that, aren't we, Jake?"

"I reckon we can have a hit," Jake answers in his laconic way.

Two Penny and Tiger go to the shed. This is a routine they're familiar with. Two Penny grabs the bag that contains the stumps and bails, while Tiger grabs the bats and balls. They take them out to the paddock where Jake and Mr. Edwards set up the wickets. This is one of the perks of working for Edwards. He's an avid cricket fan and loves to play. Any excuse he can find to have a bat in his hand is excuse enough. Mrs. Edwards just smiles and shakes her head as she says to herself, "They're all just a bunch of overgrown boys."

King Cole calls to Johnny Mullagh. "Come on, Unaarrimin. I mean, Johnny Mullagh. We're in the field."

"I don't know this game," Mullagh answers. "Let me just watch."

"You didn't play at Mullagh station?"

"No. There weren't so many of us there and Mr. Buckingham didn't like to waste time."

Mr. Edwards calls out, "Are you going to join us, Johnny . . . Mullagh?

King Cole answers, "No, Boss. He's feeling a little crook." Mullagh looks at him quizzically. King Cole says, "It's better than saying you don't want to play. The Boss loves his cricket."

For the next couple of hours, the men at Pine Hills Station become the boys Mrs. Edwards predicted. Arguing about nothing. Teasing each other without mercy. Puffing out their chests when they can and slinking away when they have to. All this time, Mullagh watches with keen focus and interest. Studying how they move strategically; how they hold the bat and move their feet. He watches the way the bowler releases the ball from a kind of side arm position, how he twists his wrist to make the ball move in different directions on its way to the batsman. By the time they finish their game, Mullagh has figured out the fundamentals. He is certain that his athletic skills can be applied to this sport. But for now, he prefers to watch.

*****

A few weeks have passed. Johnny Mullagh is now truly a part of Pine Hills Station. He has a natural way with the horses and the dogs, and something in his bearing and character inspires the other men to look up to him. Both Edwards and Jake are satisfied that this was a good decision.

Late one afternoon, as the work day is winding down, he goes to see Jake.

"Jake, I was wondering if it'd be all right if I knock off a little early today."

"You feeling crook?"

"No. I'm feeling fine. It's just I got a little business I got to take care of."

"I don't see no reason why you can't take off a little early. But if I was you, I'd try to be back for tea. Mrs. Edwards made some of her famous lamb stew. You don't want to miss that."

"I should be back by then. But if I'm not, save me a bowl if you can."

Jake gives him an index finger salute and Johnny Mullagh walks away.

As soon as he is out of sight of Pine Hills, he starts trotting toward Mullagh Station. He hasn't stopped thinking about Alice. However dangerous it may be for him, he has to see her again. On his way, he stops for a drink of water at the same stream. Eventually, he approaches Mullagh Station. He is extremely cautious and when he is close enough to have a view of the homestead, he steps into some brush for concealment. He has been clutching the handkerchief Alice gave him for his bloody nose for the entire journey. He never returned it. It is now their only connection. He peers through the brush up toward Alice's room on the upper floor. It is a room he knows well from all the times they played there as children.

'Unaarrimin, I have a surprise for you," Alice says, "but you can't tell anyone I gave it to you. Do you promise?" "I promise." "All right. Close your eyes and hold out your hand." He does. "Don't peek." "I'm **not**." "Okay, are you ready?" "Yes. I'm ready." "Okay, here it is." Alice plants a kiss on his cheek. "There. Did you like it?" She laughs her Alice laugh. "It was nice," he says, "but I was hoping it was lollies." She punches him on the shoulder.

There doesn't appear to be any sign of life anywhere at Mullagh Station. Where could everyone be? His first thought is that something may have happened. His imagination begins to cloud his better judgment. He wants to get closer to the house and maybe have a look around the side or in the back. He decides to go closer. Just as he shifts his weight to stride out, one of the white stockmen comes out of the shed. Johnny Mullagh quickly ducks back behind the brush. The stockman is looking in his direction, as if he saw something. He takes a few steps forward and stands there for a few moments, his gaze fixed on the brush, looking for any movement.

Mullagh dares not breathe. The stockman finally decides it is nothing and goes on about his business without further inspection. Johnny Mullagh unfreezes and goes back to Pine Hills.

* * * * *

Augustus Harriman is a neighbor. His station is the next one west of Pine Hills. Like Edwards, he is also a cricket enthusiast bordering on fanatic. Like most of the station managers, Harriman has men who love playing cricket. It's the one unanimously approved activity in the Western District. This doesn't make it unique though. All of Australia is cricket mad. It is everyone's sport of choice.

On a particular afternoon, when things are quiet at his station, Harriman rides to Pine Hills to see Edwards. As he trots up to the homestead, Mr. Edwards comes out of the house.

"Thought I heard a horse," he says.

"G'day, mate." Harriman responds.

"G'day, Gus."

As he dismounts, Harriman asks, "How's the Missus?"

"She's just fine, thanks." They shake hands and Edwards motions him toward a chair on the veranda. "Fancy a cuppa?"

"I don't mind."

Edwards calls in to his wife to tell her they have a visitor. She comes out. "Well, look what the cat dragged in. Hello, Augustus. Now, you just sit tight. I'll just fetch us some tea." She goes back into the house.

"How's your Missus?" Edwards asks.

"She's just fine. Thanks for asking."

"The young ones?"

"Getting bigger."

"So, what brings you this way? It has to be something. You never visit us this time of day. Everything all right?"

"Oh, yeah. Just fine. But I have been thinking about something for a while now and this is the first chance I've had to come over and find out what you think of it."

"What's that?"

"Well, I've been thinking about cricket."

"You came all this way to tell me that?"

"Not just that. I've got an idea."

"Let's hear."

"Well, I can get the local grounds for a match. Your boys play cricket. My boys play cricket. So, I was thinking we could have a friendly match there, your station against mine. What do you reckon?"

Edwards looks out across the wide yard. "Hmm, that sounds like it could be interesting." Then, as casual as he can make it sound, Edwards glances back at Harriman and says, "I suppose there'd have to be a little wager attached."

"Why, I hadn't thought of that," Harriman says without much conviction.

Mrs. Edwards comes out with a tray of scones, jam and cream. "You gents can get started on this. The tea's coming."

Edwards blurts out, "Gus wants to challenge Pine Hills to a cricket match."

Mrs. Edwards looks from one to the other. "Do tell. What's the purse?" she asks.

"Purse? Why, Felicity, I just thought it might be a little fun," Harriman says.

Mrs. Edwards laughs. "That'll be the day." To her husband, she says, "Well, I'm sure you're going to turn him down. You wouldn't want to waste your time and money on anything as frivolous as cricket, would you?"

Edwards looks at Harriman. "She knows me too well, this woman. She knows I'll do anything to get a bat in my hand."

"And make a bet," she adds. She smiles to herself as she returns to the kitchen. "They're *all* just a bunch of overgrown boys, every one of them."

"What are you thinking, Gus?"

"Well, I reckon Sunday week. That is, If it suits you."

"No. I mean how much?"

"Oh, something easy. Let's say the loser shouts drinks at the pub afterwards." Then he adds, "Be sure and bring some money with you."

"I don't reckon I'll need any, but let me check with Jake and see if it's okay with him. Sure hate to see you ride all this way just to end up putting your hand in your pocket, though."

Mrs. Edwards comes out with the tea. Again, she looks from one to the other. "Looks like you boys have decided something. You're too quiet."

* * * * *

The next evening, King Cole and Mullagh have had their evening tea and are sitting together on a wooden bench outside the shearing shed. King Cole is whittling.

"What are you making?" Mullagh asks.

"Oh, I just carve these little boats. Jake's boy, Timmy, likes 'em." Takes 'em down to the creek and floats 'em. He always loses 'em though. I can barely keep ahead of him."

They are quiet for moment, just taking in the evening sounds. King Cole then says, "Say, you heard what the Boss said about playing cricket against Harriman's mob, didn't you?"

"Yep. I heard."

"You're gonna play with us, aren't you?"

"Thinking about it. Not sure," Mullagh says.

"Well, think good. It's fun to show these white fellas up at their own game."

"What do you mean?"

"They don't reckon anybody but them can play this game. You should see them strut around. They think being white makes a difference. All it is is throwing, catching and running. We been doing that since The Dreaming."

Mullagh thinks a moment. "You gotta bat too, don't you?"

"Well, that's different. Everybody has trouble with that." After a beat, he implores, "Come on. You gotta play. Some of the Black fellas from old times will be playing for Harriman's mob. It'll be fun."

"We'll see."

* * * * *

The Sunday of the match rolls around. A good sized crowd has gathered for this match, some standing along the boundary, others seated in the stands. Harriman's boys come out of their change room dressed in not-quite-matching blue shirts. This is as close as they'll get to looking like a team. When Edwards' team comes out, they are wearing yellow sashes that Mrs. Edwards whipped together for them. This constitutes the entirety of *their* uniforms.

As the Black fellas from both teams recognize one another, they shout out their "G'days" and congregate in a bunch on the edge of the pitch. Johnny Cuzens is still small compared to the others. Bullocky is still stout. But the atmosphere is raucous with their enthusiasm at being together. It's like a new kind of corroboree. The white fellas on both teams don't seem as enthusiastic to see one another, or so many Aboriginals, for that matter. A few are even scornful of the Blacks having such a good time. This isn't a party. It's a serious cricket match.

When the match gets underway, it is clear from the beginning that Harriman has prepared his team. Edwards' boys bat first. One of the openers is out for two. It looks like they're going to have a long afternoon. King Cole comes in and manages to stay at the crease a little longer. But he too is soon out for five. The fourth batter on Edwards' team has a reputation as someone who can hit anything. He is the only one who seems to be able to stay at the crease. Wickets continue to tumble around him. When Tiger is bowled out for a duck, Two Penny pulls Mr. Edwards aside before going to the crease.

"Hey, Boss, I reckon you ought to give Johnny Mullagh a go."

"He's never played cricket. And it looks like we're in too deep to take chances."

"He was always the best athlete of all us Black fellas back at the corroborees."

King Cole overhears this conversation. "Yeah, Boss. He can't do no worse."

"Well, you go ahead out there, Two Penny, and I'll think about it."

Two Penny manages to survive a few overs before he is also dismissed like the others.

Edwards scratches his head, then turns toward Johnny Mullagh. "Reckon you'd like to have a go, Johnny?"

"If you want, Mr. Edwards."

Edwards says, "All right, grab a bat and get out there. Let's see what you've got."

Mullagh picks up the cricket bat and feels the weight of it. He swings it back and forth from hand to hand to get its balance. As he walks out to the crease, he lets out a big breath. Stillness is the key. Like all the other Aboriginal players, he is barefoot when he takes his place. The white players on Harriman's team are already taunting the new guy. *"You know which end of the bat to use?" "Ever been hit by a cricket ball?"* None of them is expecting much. The Black fellas are quiet as they exchange knowing glances. The bowler starts his run up, picks up pace and lets fly with a perfect pitch. Mullagh watches it closely, sets himself and decides to let it pass. It just misses the stumps. No one on either team would have imagined this first-timer would have this much cricket awareness. Most expected him to swing at anything that came at him. The bowler approaches again. It's almost as if he is insulted by Mullagh's nonchalance. As the ball comes toward him, Mullagh adjusts his stance ever so slightly and cracks the ball through a mid-on that carries all the way to the boundary for four. All the Aboriginal players on both teams laugh and applaud. They nod to each other with smug *I-told-you-so* expressions.

Mr. Edwards looks out onto the pitch with wonder. *Where did this come from?* He keeps his enthusiasm under control for fear it was a fluke.

The bowler once again reaches the top of his mark and begins his run up. There is menace in his approach this time. He lets fly a ball fully intended to hit Mullagh in the chest. Mullagh doesn't flinch. Instead, he deftly sidesteps it and effortlessly glides this one through the covers. It rolls for another boundary and four more runs.

Now, everyone is taking notice. Before he is retired, Mullagh scores 16 runs. But in the end, even he is bowled out and Edwards' team has only totaled 37 runs.

When Harriman's boys go to the crease, it is clear that they have come to play. They pummel Edwards' bowlers mercilessly and before long have surpassed their opponents to claim the win.

* * * * *

At the pub Harriman is all smiles. "Drink up, boys. Edwards is paying."

Only white players are inside the pub. All the Aboriginal players are congregated outside. They are less concerned with who won or lost. They're enjoying being with old friends. They bring one another up to date on who is where now. On the latest gossip. But there is an undertone, like an anger that everyone feels whether it is articulated or not. When they are together in a group like this, they know who they are. They are men. They aren't relics or savages or any of the other things the white settlers describe them as. And, clearly, they can hold their own at this white man's game. They know they have worth as human beings, a quiet confidence. They all sense it and feel it and silently share it.

"You're still the best," Johnny Cuzens tells Mullagh.

"Where you learn how to bat like that?" Bullocky asks.

"I watched you," Mullagh says.

"You never saw me bat before today." He thinks a second. "And you batted before I did."

"Oh, it must have been some other chubby bloke," Mullagh says. They all laugh.

Their laughter is heard inside the pub. Some of the white fellas look out that way. One of them, a large Scot, looks like he wants to do something about it, as if their laughter was some kind of insult to him personally.

Before the Scot can move, Harriman senses the situation and goes over to him. "Easy now, Angus. They're just having a little fun. They're not hurting anyone so let 'em laugh." Angus puffs up as he stares out the door, then he looks at Harriman. Harriman has a no nonsense expression on his face that can't be mistaken. Angus decides to re-focus his attention on his pint.

Harriman returns to Edwards at the bar. "Sometimes some of my boys get a little aggressive with the darkies. I've got to watch them. Your boys do that?"

"Not so much. All our boys seem to get along pretty well. Oh, there's an occasional flare up, but I think that's more boys being boys than anything else."

Harriman takes a long swallow of his beer, then says, "You know, some of those Black boys weren't too bad out there today."

"I'll tell you, when Johnny Mullagh hit those two boundaries right off the bat, I didn't know what to make of it. He has never even played with us on the station. I've never seen him hold a bat before. I don't know where in the world that came from."

"Mate," Harriman says, "You just gave me an idea."

"How much is this going to cost me?"

"Not a penny. Well, not yet anyway."

"What's your idea?"

"A couple of my boys play acceptable cricket. And a couple of your boys do. There must be some other Aboriginal boys at some of the other stations in the District that can play. What if we put together an all Aboriginal team? We could challenge all the other stations with them."

"Hm. That'd be a novelty, all right. Gus, there are times I reckon you're some kind of genius. That's a very interesting idea."

"And it could be a money maker too," Harriman adds.

"Well, I'm not so interested in making a business out of it. But I definitely like the idea."

"Good. I'll go around to the other stations and see what I can find out. I might need you to talk some of the other managers into letting their boys off so they can play. Are you game for that?" Edwards nods. "Yep."

Chapter Three – The Search

It is getting late. Many of the cricketers are draining their glasses of the last few drops when John Duff, the local carpenter, comes running into the pub. He is frantic. His eyes are wild. "My god. You've got to help me," he cries out.

Edwards and Harriman go to him. "What's the matter, John?"

"It's Isaac, Jane and Frank. They're lost. I been looking for 'em since sundown and can't find 'em. They went to cut some heath for brooms. They done it plenty of times before. They went out this morning and ain't come back yet. I'm worried sick. The wife . . . "

"Settle down, John," Edwards says, "We'll find your children."

"Do you know which way they went?" Harriman asks.

"I tried to track 'em but it was gettin' dark and I couldn't see my hand in front of my face, so I come back."

Edwards tries to reassure him, "We'll organize a search party and head off first thing in the morning. Nobody would be able to find their tracks at this time of night."

By now all of the others have crowded around Duff, trying to console him. *"We'll find your kids, John." "Don't you worry, mate." "We'll go out at first light."*

* * * * *

The next morning more than thirty men on horseback from all over the District meet at the pub. Mr. Edwards becomes their leader. "Men, let's break into smaller groups and cover as much territory as possible. John says the children originally headed for the closest heath. So, why don't you five men from Spring Hill head off in that direction." After each group has been assigned, he says, "Let's meet up back here this afternoon if nobody has had any luck. They can't have gone far. If anyone finds them, fire off a shot and hurry them back here." He turns to Duff. "We'll find your young ones, John. And they'll be fine."

Harriman takes Edwards aside. "What do you know about these kids? Can they manage in the bush alone?"

As they go out to join the others, Edwards says, "Isaac is around nine so he can probably handle himself all right. Jane is younger but she's a bright little thing. It's the other boy I worry about. Frank is only three or four."

The search begins. At first the tracks are easy to follow. But it doesn't take long to realize that the children didn't go toward the closest heath as originally thought. Instead, they went toward one more distant. This widens the search area considerably. Smaller groups travel in all directions in hope of finding at least something. Not one group finds anything through the rest of that day. The optimism that began the search is now a challenge. The men all resolve to do whatever necessary to find those kids. The day ends with no more information than it had at the start.

The entire next day becomes more of the same. Search after search in every direction yields bitter disappointment. When the main group stops for a rest, Edwards wipes the sweat from his forehead and his leather hatband. "Men, we're doing something wrong. We should have found these children by now. I blame myself as much as anyone. I'm going to order everyone back to the pub. We have to talk about this." A few hours later, when it is clear that no one has had any success, each group heads back to the pub.

It is dusk when the last group arrives. Most of the men inside the pub look distraught. They aren't speaking, just looking into the distance or into their pints. They all think they could have done more . . . or should have done more. But what more could they have done? No one could articulate that, but the sense of failure is palpable.

Many are already, privately, thinking that the rescue attempt has reached a futile stage. After two full days with no clue, no one knows where to turn. And no one wants to be the one who says the words out loud: Those children may be lost forever.

Mr. Edwards is as despondent as the others, but he has taken on the role of leader and now must be the leader. "I reckon I speak for everyone when I say how disappointed we all are. I thought we'd ride out there yesterday morning and come back an hour later with three happy youngsters. You probably did too. And now, after two full days, we are back where we started. That is disappointing and I won't deny it. But I will tell you this. Each man here can make up his own mind on this and no one will criticize. But for me, I am going back out there tomorrow morning and I am going to keep looking. I don't care how long it takes, how many days . . . or weeks . . . I am going to see those children again. I am going home now and try to get some rest. Those of you who want to meet me back here in the morning; I would like to get moving soon after sunup."

Everyone is there the next morning. They discuss their plans in the saddle on the way into the bush. The circle will need to get even wider. There will be more distance between each of the groups so messages will have to be sent on horseback. They now travel with the same motivation, but no expectation. They say their farewells and go their separate ways.

Incredibly, two more unsuccessful days are about to pass when late the fourth day, Bill, the leader of one of the groups, finds a hair ribbon. It is dirty and twisted, but the colour is vibrant and unfaded. It couldn't have been here in the bush for more than a day or two. One of the others in that group rides up to Bill. "You reckon that's Jane's?" "I reckon it is. Maybe it come off when a branch caught on it and she didn't notice. Don't look like it's been out here long either." Up ahead, another man starts yelling back to Bill, "Hey, Bill, I think these might be fresh tracks. Come and have a look." Bill goes to see what definitely seem to be fresh tracks. "Listen, Charlie. You ride back and tell Edwards what we found. We'll camp here for the night and get an early start."

Next morning, as Bill's group is breaking camp, Edwards' group rides in. They only stay long enough for a quick cup of tea. Now, they spread out into a wide rank, each man shouting distance from the next. The excitement starts to rebuild. Expectations start to rebuild. An hour passes. Then two. Then three. It isn't long before the black cloud of disappointment begins to descend once more. And it continues into the next day as well.

Later that day, as darkness engulfs them, they decide to camp where they are and start fresh in the morning. How could those children have come this far and survived, or if they didn't survive, where are their bodies? By now, the searchers have traveled nearly thirty miles.

During the night, a torrential rain thunders down on them, a deluge. It dumps down relentlessly for more than an hour. When dawn breaks, and they go to pick up the tracks, everything has been completely washed away. No one can see anything that is the slightest hint of a track. The men are heartbroken. Once again, they're back where they started. Late that afternoon, they go back to the pub. Some honest, unsentimental decisions need to be made. The kids have been missing for eight days.

Back at the pub, Edwards reluctantly takes the floor. "Men, we're all thinking the same thing. But I don't want to be the one to tell John Duff we're quitting. At least not tonight. So, let's all get some rest and come back tomorrow morning and hash this out."

Edwards is exhausted when he arrives back at Pine Hills. He knows he won't really rest, but at least he'll be with his family. He climbs out of the saddle and is leading the horse toward the stable.

Mullagh comes out to take the horse from him. "I'll take care of Thunder, Mr. Edwards. You go get yourself some rest."

"Thank you, Johnny, I'll do that." Edwards starts toward the homestead when Mullagh calls to him, "Mr. Edwards?"

Edwards turns back. "Yes, Johnny"

"You find those kids yet?"'

"No. It's looking pretty hopeless. We found a hair ribbon the other day, but the rain washed away all the tracks. I don't know what we're going to tell poor Duff."

Mullagh throws caution to the winds. "I got an idea, Mr. Edwards," he says.

"You've got an idea about what, the children?"

"Yep."

Edwards takes a moment to let this settle in. "Well, I suppose at this point, I'm open to anything. What is it?"

"Well, there's a couple of Black fellas I know that are pretty good trackers. They're over at Mt. Elgin Station."

Edwards scratches his head. No one had thought of this, incredible as it may seem. But as Edwards considers it, it's as though a lifeline has been thrown to him. "You reckon you can get over there to Mt. Elgin and bring them back?"

"You mean now?"

"Well, yes. As soon as possible. We don't have any time to lose. It might be too late already."

"It'll take me a while to get there, but I can start now if you want," Mullagh says.

"You won't have to walk. Take Thunder. He'll get you there in a hurry. I'll have the Missus put together some tucker for you too."

Mullagh laughs. "There's plenty of tucker on the way if I need it, Mr. Edwards."

"Well, let me give you a note for the manager and tell him what this is about." There is visible relief on Edwards' face, a new reason to hope. He hands Mullagh the note. "Good luck, Johnny. And thanks."

"No need for luck. These fellas are the best. If those young ones are out there, they'll find them."

* * * * *

Mullagh arrives at Mt. Elgin Station in the middle of the night. No lamps are burning at the homestead. Rather than approach at this hour and risk frightening everyone, he unrolls his swag and stretches out under a tree a short distance away. At break of dawn, he walks quietly toward the workers' quarters. The only thing he hears are snores. One of the doors opens and an Aboriginal man comes out.

"Yanggendyinanyuk!" Mullagh calls out softly.

The man turns, startled. Then he sees Mullagh. "Unaarrimin. What are you doing here?"

"Looking for you," he says. "And Brinbunyah."

"He's just getting up. I'll get him," Yanggendyinanyuk says. He goes to the door and calls out, "Hey, Redcap, guess who's here?"

"Redcap?"

"You know what white fellas are like with our names. They call me Dicky Dick now."

Mullagh laughs. "They call me Johnny Mullagh."

"Unaarrimin? Is that you?" Redcap slaps Mullagh on the arm, then hugs his shoulders.

"I am Johnny Mullagh now . . . Redcap." All three laugh.

They make their way to the homestead, where Mullagh shows the manager the letter Mr. Edwards gave him. The manager wastes no time in sending the Black fellas on their way to track the Duff children. "You boys want some something to eat before you go?" he asks.

Dicky Dick smiles. "Oh, I reckon we'll find something along the way, Boss."

* * * * *

The three friends waste no time making their way back toward the pub.

At the pub, the men wait anxiously. A few want to get started without the Aboriginals. Bill says, "We've been tracking for eight days and ain't found a thing. How in the hell are them darkies gonna find anything? I say we head out." Several agree with him.

"Let's give it a little more time," Edwards pleads. "Another hour won't make a difference now"

Harriman takes Edwards aside. "What if these Black fellas go walkabout on us?"

Edwards gives him a stern look. "I trust my boys. And I trust Johnny Mullagh above all of them. They'll show up."

Twenty minutes later, a man who has been waiting and watching from outside the pub rushes in. "Here they come,"

Everyone spills out of the pub onto the street. Some go for their horses.

As they dismount, Johnny Mullagh shoots a quick smile at Yanggendyinanyuk, then turns to Mr. Edwards and says, "This is Dicky Dick. And this here's Redcap."

"I have to say, you fellas are a welcome sight," Edwards says. "Do you need anything before we head out? Are you hungry?"

Dicky Dick speaks up. "I wouldn't say no to a bottle of whiskey. Maybe two." Everyone stops breathing. The silence is deafening. Edwards shoots a quick, not very friendly glance at Mullagh. Then, Dicky Dick laughs and turns on a big smile. "Oh, I was just making a joke. I don't drink alcohol. But some water would do me."

After he's had his water, Dicky Dick asks Mr. Edwards where the trail ended. "We'll show you," Edwards says. They mount up and start traveling with purpose. Having these two experienced trackers reinvigorates most of the searchers. Their pessimism, at least for the moment, has been replaced by a flicker of hope.

Before too long, they're back at the place where the rain washed away the tracks. Bill speaks up. "We camped around here someplace. We found some fresh tracks but it was getting too dark to see, so, like I said, we decided to camp right around here for the night. Then that storm hit and by the time daylight came; you couldn't see anything that looked like a track. We looked for an hour. More. All of us. Couldn't find a thing, not one bloody thing. And I don't reckon you will either."

Dicky Dick and Redcap are now on foot, looking over the terrain. They talk in language to each other, pointing in one direction, then another. They talk a little longer then return to the group. Dicky Dick says, "Yep. They were here all right. We found a few tracks just over there."

Bill looks at the others. He wants to see these tracks for himself, but thinks better of it. The others are silent. "We want to travel on foot now," Redcap says. "You fellas can just sort of follow behind us. We'll go as fast as we can, but these tracks are hard to follow. We gotta pay attention." It is evident that Redcap enjoys telling these white fellas what to do. Dicky Dick smiles to himself.

They start off. The Indigenous trackers lead the group in a new direction, carefully examining all the signs along the way, sure of themselves. They examine every rock and shrub. Nothing escapes their scrutiny. The others follow. It is a painstaking process. Several times, they follow their signs to a dead end and have to re-trace their steps to see where they went wrong. It is late afternoon and they still have no idea where the children could be.

Mr. Edwards decides this is a good place to camp for the night and tells the others to start preparing a fire and getting some tucker ready. They want to get an early start again tomorrow morning.

By the time dawn breaks and the others are rising, Dicky Dick and Redcap have already headed out. They leave broken twigs on the path as signs for the others to follow. They can barely read the track. The hours keep piling up. By mid-afternoon, even Dicky Dick and Redcap are beginning to feel frustration. They were sure they were onto something. Now, not so sure. Sunset comes. They're losing light when Dicky Dick calls out to Redcap. "Come. Look here. They made a little shelter under this bush."

Redcap examines it closer. "Looks pretty new too," By the time the others catch up, it is getting darker and the tracks will be impossible to follow.

"What did you find?" Edwards asks.

"Looks to me like the kids are still alive. At least two of 'em," Redcap says.

"What do you mean . . . two?"

Dicky Dick says, "Don't worry, Boss. They're still all together. We found a shelter they made under a bush up there. And the tracks say that there are only two walking now. But one set of footprints is heavier. That probably means one of them is carrying the little one. It's getting too dark to go on now, though. "

"All right men," Edwards announces, "we'll camp here for the night."

Dicky Dick looks at Edwards with a big smile. "I'll bet you a shilling we'll find those kids tomorrow."

Edwards gives him a hard look, then says, "Let's find those children first. Then we can talk about a shilling."

The next morning, Dicky Dick and Redcap again steal away before the others wake up. Now, they actually crawl along the ground, keeping their eyes peeled for any clue as the sun slowly rises. After another hour of this microscopic searching, they come to an open area. "Look," Dicky Dick points. In the shelter of a great rock are three sleeping children. They are all huddled together. Jane has taken off her dress and wrapped it around little Frank to keep him warm. The trackers smile at one another.

"Looks like them kids are all right," Redcap says. "Bet they're hungry."

"Probably thirsty too," Dicky Dick says. "You go on back and tell the others. I'll go over and give them some water and a bit of tucker."

* * * * *

John Duff bursts into the pub. "Where are those boys? I want to shake their hands." He spots Dicky Dick and Redcap and rushes over to them. "You fellas saved my family. You could say you saved my life too." He grabs them both and wraps his arms around them in one giant hug.

Dicky Dick and Redcap exchange a look that says, *Is this white fella actually hugging us?*

"You fellas are heroes. I'll never forget you," Duff says as he releases them.

"How are the kids, John," Edwards asks

"They're all fed and washed up and in their beds, sleepin' like angels."

"A happy ending," Harriman says.

"Sure is," Duff says.

"Listen, John, come over here with me for a minute. I want to talk to you."

"Sure thing, Mr. Edwards."

Edwards and Duff go to a corner of the pub. "We took up a little collection for the trackers. I thought it'd be nice if you gave it to them."

"I was gonna give 'em something too," Duff says.

"No need, John. There's fifteen quid in this bag. That's plenty. These fellas never saw that much money, I don't reckon."

Duff hides the bag behind his back as they return to the bar where the trackers are surrounded by the other searchers. He wants to get his words right, so he pauses for a moment. Then he says, "Fellas, we want you to have this little reward for finding my kids. It ain't much, but it's better than nothin'. What you done, you didn't have to do. You done it out o' your hearts. So, here." He hands the bag to Dicky Dick.

Dicky Dick takes the bag and peeks into it. "This looks like money to me." He sniffs it. "It smells like money too. It must be money. Look here, Redcap."

Redcap looks into the bag. "Sure looks like money to me too."

Dicky Dick addresses the room. "Are there any more lost kids out there?"

It gets a huge laugh. But there is another sense in the pub. One that is unfamiliar to most, if not all of them. This is first opportunity they have had to dare think of each other as people. Without being able to articulate it, they suddenly understand the nature of prejudice. When you don't know one of them, it's easy to generalize about the whole group. But once they have names and personalities, that stereotype is vulnerable.

One of the searchers calls out, "Let's give them a hip, hip, hooray." They all join in.
HIP, HIP, HOORAY! HIP, HIP, HOORAY! HIP, HIP, HOORAY!

Bill has been quiet up until now, but even he finally acknowledges their incredible feat. "I think we should call Dicky Dick Sir Richard from now on."

Bill leads the rest of the pub in shouting, "LONG LIVE SIR RICHARD AND . . . REDCAP TOO!"

In the midst of this, Harriman wanders over to Dicky Dick and Redcap. "Congratulations, boys. You did a great job. And you earned every penny." Then, as though it just occurred to him, he adds, "Say, I was wondering, do you boys happen to play cricket?"

Chapter Four – The First Eleven

Putting together an all Aboriginal team has become a passion for Harriman, bordering on obsession. He has been planning ahead since the idea first came to him. He needs money to buy equipment so he enlists two of the District's wealthier land holders in the scheme by making them partners. Now that the episode with the Duff children is behind them, he wastes no time travelling to several stations in the District to scout for talent. He already has the nucleus of a team from his station, Pine Hills and Mt. Elgin. But some of the station managers aren't convinced that this is a worthwhile use of their Indigenous workers. When he runs into this kind of resistance, he gets in touch with Mr. Edwards and Edwards gets to work, cajoling, pleading and using any means necessary to convince his fellow station managers that this would be a good thing for the entire Western District.

"You're all playing cricket anyway," he'd say. *"What can it hurt to put a team of Black fellas together and play against them?"* *"Do you realize what a great opportunity this is for the Western District? There isn't another all Aboriginal team the whole rest of Australia."* *"Everyone else is cooperat-*

ing and it's not a hardship for them." "One or two of your Black fellas. That's all."

After a few weeks, Harriman has his team. In addition to King Cole, Two Penny, Tiger and Johnny Mullagh from Pine Hills, he has Johnny Cuzens and Bullocky from his own station, Dicky Dick and Redcap from Mt. Elgin and has added Sugar, Jellicoe, Tarpot, Sundown, Neddy and Peter from other stations. Now he has to turn them into a cricket team.

Harriman decided in advance that he will manage the team. He has called for them all to come to his station for their first session. It would have been clear to anyone who paid attention that this is going to be a challenge. The Black fellas have all known each other since childhood. There has also been enough history with white people to make them all very cautious. On the other hand, Harriman believes he is giving these darkies a great honour, giving them an opportunity to play cricket. He expects them to act sufficiently grateful for what he's doing for them. Hence, the challenge.

The Indigenous men are all gathered in the empty shearing shed. Harriman is on his way. While they wait, they use the time to discuss what this means and who will benefit from it. The consensus they arrive at is that whatever happens, they will be the ones that will have to bear the weight of it; the white Boss will take the credit and it will be a miracle if anyone bothers to say, "Thanks."

Harriman walks into the shed. No one is paying any attention to him. He might as well be invisible. He stands behind a little table that's been set up and waits for quiet. He decides to begin his remarks with the expectation that they'll quiet down and listen. The first words out of his mouth are, "Boys, before we start our first practice, we have to establish some rules." He is barely heard above the chatter and laughter. Harriman doesn't have Edwards' skill in commanding attention by his mere presence. The din continues while he tries to decide what to do. This is not what he planned. His frustration builds and builds, eventually erupting into anger. He is not accustomed to this level of disrespect from anyone, let alone a bunch of darkies. He slams his hand down on the table and shouts, "GODDAM IT, I'M TALKING TO YOU!" This gets their attention.

"Yes, Boss," Dicky Dick replies sweetly. "And we're listening to you." He does a quick survey of the others. They quiet down.

"That's better," Harriman continues. "As I was saying, we have to have some rules. Let's start with this one. There is to be no consumption of alcohol. Cricket is a gentleman's game and you'll be expected to try to act like gentlemen. That means you can't be disorderly and I will not tolerate drunkenness. Next, I expect you to learn the game the way I tell you. We're not going to play some kind of rag-tag version of cricket the way most stations do. We're going to play proper English cricket. With pride and dignity and decorum. Next, when we practice, I expect every one of you to give it 100%. I want my team to be legendary. I want my team to be known all over Victoria. When someone makes reference to an Aboriginal cricket team, I want somebody to say they must be talking about are Harriman's boys."

Johnny Cuzens speaks up. "Mr. Harriman?"

"What is it, Johnny?"

"What do all them big words mean?" He has struck a chord. The others nod.

"What do they mean? They mean we are here to play cricket. That's what they mean."

"Oh," Cuzens says, "Why aren't we playing then?" Again, the others nod.

Harriman is growing visibly hot again. While he tries to regain his composure, Johnny Mullagh, who is sitting at the back of the group, says in language, "Everybody, just listen now. We'll talk about all this later."

"What did you just say," Harriman snaps.

"I just told them that you're the boss and they should be respectful," Mullagh answers.

Harriman seems pleased with Mullagh's response. He continues to hold forth. As he drones on, the Black fellas feign interest, but most are still wondering what this all means. Is cricket going to be their job now? Is Harriman just another arrogant white man who thinks he can order them around? Are they allowed to have an opinion about anything? Why didn't anyone ask them if they wanted to play this white man's game?

"All right, boys," Harriman finally concludes, "that'll do for now. Cuzens, Bullocky, why don't you go ahead and fetch the equipment from the little shed and take it out to the paddock. I have to take care of a few things in my office, then we can have our first practice session." He leaves for the homestead.

Mullagh immediately moves to where Harriman was. "Let's talk about this," he says. It goes without saying that he would be their leader. Since childhood, they have all bowed to him when it comes to athletics. But they have also recognized his leadership qualities, his calm, careful demeanor and the way he weighs everything before expressing his opinion.

Dicky Dick is the first to speak. "We also have to have some rules. Are we going to have to do our work back at the stations? I think we should say something about that."

Tarpot quickly adds, "Nobody asked me if I wanted to play this cricket. I've got a wife and kids back at the station. I want to stay on my country." There is a general hum of agreement. The argument swings in the direction of refusal.

King Cole says, "Wait a minute, brothers. There is more to this. This isn't just about playing cricket, this is much bigger. It is a chance to do something . . ."

Johnny Cuzens jumps in, "I agree with King Cole. Think about this. All us Black fellas playing cricket against all those white fellas. If we beat 'em, no one can do anything about it. It's their game. It's their rules."

Redcap stands up. "I agree. You should have seen them when I told them what to do when we were tracking those little kids. They hated it. Imagine how much they'll hate it if we beat them at cricket."

The argument swings back.

Bullocky, who rarely has anything to say, speaks up, "I can't wait to knock the hide off that ball." He looks around the shed and as if he just can't hold it in any longer, these pent up words burst out of him, "And I want to drink a beer once in a while!"

There is no clear cut answer. There's only on the one hand and on the other hand. They are leaning toward an agreement that it may be all right to play cricket. But nothing is definitive. That's because one voice has been silent during the discussion. Sugar speaks up. "Unaarrimin, what do you think?"

He looks at them all for a moment, let's out a breath and says, "Here's what I think. I think we should get so good at this game of cricket that they'll forget anyone ever played it before we did. And I know we can do it. What's the difference if it's a cricket ball or a boomerang. We throw it. It does what we want it to do. The cricket bat is like a stick we used to hit rocks with. It's like many of the games we played as kids, only a little different. All we need to do is be fast, strong and smart. If we can do that – and I know we can -- they won't have any choice but to respect us. We didn't ask to play cricket. The white fellas told us to play. Like Johnny Cuzens said, it's their game. It's their rules." He pauses for a moment. "You want to know what I think? Here's what I think. I think we should play this game like warriors."

That seals it. The First Eleven are born.

* * * * *

Their first two contests are with a group of white players from Edenhope on consecutive days. The Aboriginal team loses the first, but wins the second handsomely. Several of the regional newspapers cover the event. Almost immediately, it is picked up by Melbourne papers. There is the beginning of a buzz about this team of darkies playing cricket.

Harriman is a mediocre manager, but he knows fundamentals and that's what he is able to teach his players. Their ability takes it from there. Bullocky, Johnny Cuzens and Johnny Mullagh are all natural batsmen. Cuzens and Mullagh have a flair for bowling. When Harriman sees this, he takes the two of them aside one day.

"I have a cousin visiting from England. He's a cricketer, and he tells me that they are using a new technique for bowling there. It's called round arm bowling. He says it gives the bowler an added advantage. I want you boys to learn how it's done. I'll have him show you next time we have a practice." Mullagh and Cuzens look at each other. Cuzens says, "Boomerang." Mullagh nods.

They play a few more matches with station teams and it is clear that the Aboriginals are picking up the finer points of the game. Harriman's confidence grows with each match. He moves to the next step in his plan and challenges the Hamilton Cricket Club on their ground. This is not a station team, but one made up of some of the best players in the region. It's a big step, but Harriman likes his odds.

A larger crowd than usual is in attendance for the Hamilton match. People from all around the District have heard about this phenomenon of Black fellas playing cricket and want to see it for themselves. Among them are some familiar faces. John Duff has brought Isaac, Jane and little Frank. As they find a place to sit, Jane looks up at her father, "Dad, will you take me to see Dicky Dick and Redcap after the match so I can say g'day?"

"Sure thing, doll. That'd be nice," Duff answers.

"I want to say g'day, too," Isaac says. "They didn't just save you, Janey."

Little Frank looks from his brother to his sister and pleads, "I want to say g'day. Why can't I say g'day?"

Duff looks at his kids and smiles, "Maybe we shoulda left all of ya out there. Yeah, we'll find 'em after the match and all say g'day."

Mr. and Mrs. Edwards arrive, along with Nell, Jake and Timmy. Timmy has been in awe of Mullagh since he taught the boy how to throw a boomerang. "You think he'll do good, Pappy?" Timmy asks Edwards.

"Yes, lad, I think he'll do very good."

"He taught me how to throw a boomerang," Timmy announces.

"We know, son," Jake says.

Nell says, "You've told us about a thousand times now. How could we forget?"

"You have to throw from your shoulder," Timmy repeats for the thousand-and-first time.

Mrs. Buckingham doesn't have much interest in any kind of sport. But as Alice began demanding that she wanted to be here, and Mrs. Buckingham exhausted all her useless arguments to prevent it, she had to give in.

"Just don't act a fool, Alice. You're a proper young lady now and you need to act like one. There will be other people here and I don't want you embarrassing me in front of them," Mrs. Buckingham tells her daughter.

Alice has a triumphant expression on her face as she says, "Yes, Mother. Whatever you say."

There is a special atmosphere on this day that goes beyond an ordinary cricket match. The day looms before all the spectators as a blank page. No one knows whether this will be a cricket match or an embarrassment, a celebration or a circus.

The Hamilton team comes out in their blue and white colours. Many, but not all of the spectators, cheer. The players look up into the stands and nod and wave. They are confidence itself. They have made sure that the team they field is made up of the very best of the best. There is a smugness about them, an arrogance that makes them appear invincible.

The First Eleven come out wearing white trousers, a red sash across their chests and a red hat bands. They feel odd in these outfits but Harriman had insisted they wear uniforms. The only concession he made was one he couldn't have prevented anyway. All the Aboriginal players are barefoot. As they casually stroll out, they also look into the crowd, laughing at private jokes with a demeanor that says we're going to have some fun. As soon as they come into view, five excited fans leap to their feet and cheer: Jane, Frank and Isaac Duff, Alice Buckingham and little Timmy. Others applaud politely.

Mullagh brings up the rear as the Aboriginal team enters. He tries to appear indifferent to his surroundings, as if nothing out of the ordinary was about to take place. But he is also discreetly scanning the crowd in search of anyone from Mullagh Station. When Alice sees him, she jumps to her feet, waves her arms and starts laughing with delight. His head snaps in the direction of that sound and he sees her smiling and waving. His eyes also catch Mrs. Buckingham's undisguised scowl at the same moment. Mullagh merely nods in their direction but inside he is thrilled.

The match begins and it's soon obvious that both teams are a little tentative, like two prize fighters feeling each other out. Neither the batsmen nor the fielders seem to be completely comfortable. After the Hamilton team has taken their second wicket, Jellico is the first to break through the stalemate. He stays at the crease long enough to build a decent run total. When Johnny Cuzens joins him, they put on a spectacular batting display. Each time a run is scored, their teammates cheer and laugh. They even applaud when someone on the Hamilton team makes an especially good fielding play. But before the Indigenous side is bowled out, they have a put a respectable number of runs on the board. This won't be the pushover the Hamilton team expected.

The Hamilton team comes to the crease. They are stunned by the round arm bowling of Johnny Cuzens and Johnny Mullagh. They take nine wickets between them. Their teammates play brilliantly in the field. It isn't long before the smugness quickly fades from the Hamilton team. The arrogance is gone. Not only are they losing, their opponents are playing as if they don't care one way or another. They're just having fun. When Johnny Cuzens takes the final wicket, the Hamilton squad is 51 runs short. The people watching have been won over as well. By the time the match is finished, almost everyone is supporting the Black fellas, cheering them on and calling out many by name. This turn of events isn't lost on them. They nod confidently to each other as they leave the pitch after the match. They know what they have done.

Harriman spots a reporter from the *Hamilton Spectator*. "Well, what did you think of my boys?" he asks.

"I'd say they're either the luckiest mob of Black fellas I've ever seen, or they're bloody good at cricket," the reporter answers.

"Will you be writing that in your column?"

"Trade secret, Mr. Harriman. Let's just put it this way, I don't think you'll be disappointed with what's written."

"That's good enough for me," Harriman says. "Do you reckon the Melbourne papers will pick it up?"

"I suppose there's no harm in telling you this. We've already had some inquiries from both *The Age* and *The Argus*. I surely hope you're not trying to keep this team a secret. Because if you are, the cat's out of the bag."

Harriman shakes the reporter's hand and strolls toward the stands to bask in his success. Mr. Edwards is the first to congratulate him. "Gus, old man, you've done it. These lads played a whale of a match. Congratulations."

"Not too late to make a little investment, my friend. This is going to be a money-maker or my name isn't Augustus Harriman."

"No thanks, Gus. I'm just happy that you've done it."

"Well, thanks. But this is just the beginning. You watch. I am going to take these boys to Melbourne and play against the Melbourne Cricket Club. Mark my words."

"I'll come to the match." They shake hands and part.

Harriman is walking on air. His plan is unfolding perfectly. In his mind, it would be impossible for the Melbourne Cricket Club to refuse this unique opportunity. Now, his only task is to convince them.

Chapter Five – A White Man's Game

The city of Melbourne is a thriving metropolis, located north of the Yarra River. The Melbourne Cricket Club has been a fixture for a number of years. Its members are the city's movers and shakers: bankers, businessmen, journalists, all the important people and decision makers, men who regard themselves as indispensable to the cultural and civic life of this colony.

But the Melbourne Cricket Club has fallen on hard times. Attendance at cricket matches has dwindled. Unless the opposing team has some cachet, very few spectators are interested in the game these days, or perhaps more in particular, the Melbourne Cricket Club's games. It causes some alarm. At their monthly meeting at the Parade Hotel, members of the club's Match Committee have gathered. Roland Newton, the club's pavilion keeper, is speaking. "Gentlemen, I have been approached by a station manager in the Western District. I don't know if you have seen the papers or not, but there is a team of all darkies over there that has been attracting a considerable amount of attention . . ."

"Just stop right there, Rolly," Gerald Sampson interrupts. He is a banker with very strong views about how things should be done and who should do them. "If you are going to suggest that The Melbourne Cricket Club should dignify these animals by putting them on the same cricket pitch with our team, I am here to tell you it will be over my dead body. Cricket is a white man's game. It is a gentlemen's game. I absolutely refuse to allow you to even contemplate a match between those savages and our members. Am I understood?"

"Now wait a minute. Don't jump to conclusions, Gerry." Andrew Johnson chairs these meetings. He is always the voice of reason when things get a little testy. "Let's give Rolly a chance to say what he has to say. Is that what you were going to propose, Rolly?"

"Gentlemen, I am not here to rile anybody up or insult our game . . . or dignify anyone," Newton answers. "I am only thinking about our purse strings. We are in a bad way financially and we still don't have a match scheduled for Boxing Day. The Brits have turned us down and the fans are sick and tired of seeing New South Wales. So yes, I want us to consider bringing those Black fellas to Melbourne for a match."

"Then let's be clear. You can do it without me. I am not staying to listen to this," Sampson says. "If you are foolish enough to bring it to a vote, Andrew has my proxy. I am voting no." He storms out of the pub.

Johnson says, "As you know, Gerry can get a bit excited when it comes to the Blacks. I am not suggesting that he's wrong. It's just that he loses all control when the subject comes up. But I would like to hear what you have to say, Rolly."

"As I was saying, these darkies are getting a lot of attention over in the Western District. The papers are full of praise, but more importantly, they are attracting crowds. People are curious to see how these fellas play cricket."

One of the other members speaks up. "I read somewhere that they even have round arm bowlers. Our boys don't do that yet, but I know it's big in England."

Another adds, "I've heard the same thing. I have a cousin who saw them at Hamilton. He says it's really something to see. I have to admit, I wouldn't mind seeing it myself."

Johnson is thoughtful for a moment. "I must say the novelty of it could attract a crowd if we promote it properly. What exactly do you have in mind, Rolly?"

"Here's what I have in mind. First of all, I agree that we have to proceed cautiously. So, what if we start out by sending Tom Wills over there to see if he thinks those boys are good enough to draw a crowd here. We don't have to make a commitment until after he reports back to us. Then, if he thinks they are good enough, I would like to propose a match for Boxing Day and the 27th and 28th. We can advertise it for the novelty it is and if we do this right, we can fill the coffers, gentlemen."

"Let us assume you have put that in the form of a motion and let us vote on it. All in favour of sending Tom Wills to the Western District to evaluate the Aboriginal cricket team, say *Aye*. All those opposed, say *Nay*."

There is a chorus of *Ayes*. Not one *Nay*. Johnson says, "I would say it was unanimous except I suppose I have to register Gerry's vote. So, it is unanimous less one. Rolly, we'll leave it to you to talk to Tom Wills. And that takes care of our new business. We are adjourned, gentlemen. Let's have a beer."

* * * * *

Tom Wills is thought by most to be Australia's greatest cricketer. From a young age, he had outstanding athletic ability. As he grew, his ability grew with him. His family became prosperous despite the fact that they originally came to Australia as convicts. They had gained their respectability as pastoralists. Wills spent much of his youth on a sheep station in what would eventually become the new state of Victoria. He mingled easily with various Aboriginal peoples, learning their songs and customs and eventually speaking their language fluently. In an ironic twist of fate, when his family went to Queensland to work on one of their properties there, one of the largest massacres by Aboriginals in Australian history took the life of his father and eighteen of his father's workers. Wills survived but was understandably traumatized by event. However, to his credit, he understands that the tribe of Aboriginals who killed his parent are not the ones he has befriended in Victoria. He is one of the few people of that era who doesn't paint all Indigenous people with the same brush.   Therefore, in many ways, he is the ideal person to train this Black cricket team, assuming he finds them competent.

Harriman is waiting for Wills at the coach station. Since he contacted the Melbourne Cricket Club, he has been on pins and needles wondering how they will react to his suggestion of a match between "his boys" and the Melbourne Cricket Club. And since he learned that they were sending Tom Wills to look the team over and, if he likes what he sees, train them, Harriman has hardly slept.

Wills' coach finally arrives in the late afternoon. It has been a long journey from Melbourne, first by ship and then by carriage. Harriman greets him with too much enthusiasm. As Wills gets down from the coach, Harriman rushes over to him and extends his hand. "I'm Augustus Harriman. I certainly do hope your journey was a pleasant one, Mr. Wills. Not too taxing."

Wills immediately corrects Harriman. "The name is Tom. *Mister* Wills was my father. And my grandfather. And for your information, Augustus, the journey was long and dusty. So, I wouldn't say no to something that might cut through that dust in my throat. Can we get a beer anywhere around here? There must be a pub in town. We are still in Australia, aren't we?"

Harriman doesn't like being spoken to so familiarly, but he only says, "Well, I was hoping to go directly to the station so you could meet my darkies."

"Your darkies?"

"The team. I meant to say the Aboriginal team."

"Oh, well, there's plenty of time for that. First things first. We'll go after I've had a glass of beer."

Harriman has his schedule in mind and this isn't part of it, but it is Tom Wills, after all, and Wills is the key to going to Melbourne. "Well, yes, of course, Mr. . . . I mean, Tom. Let's pop into the pub for a quick one and then we can be on our way."

Wills takes five huge gulps and returns the half-empty glass to the bar with a satisfying "Ahhh".

Harriman doesn't like drinking alcohol at this time of day, so he merely sips from his glass before putting it down.

"So, Augustus, how does it happen that you have put together an Indigenous cricket team? Are you a player?"

"Oh, heaven forbid," Harriman says, "I am merely an enthusiast. I have the utmost respect for the finer practitioners of the sport, such as yourself. We play a fair bit of cricket here in the Western District --- you know, station against station – and some of the stations have darkies playing for them. Actually, I have a couple of boys that know their way around a pitch. And one day, it occurred to me that it might be worth a laugh to have a team of darkies for the stations to play against . . ."

Will listens to Harriman's monologue with half-interest. He is more interested in Harriman's demeanor. He seems a bit haughty, a bit superior. Wills is still trying to decide if he likes this bloke when he polishes off the remainder of beer in his glass and sets it on the bar.

In mid-speech, Harriman interrupts himself and starts to rise from his stool when Wills says, "We've got time for another, don't we, Augustus?" And without waiting for a response, says, "Barkeep, let's have another, mate. Now, what were you saying?"

The only words Wills hears from then on are "darkies this and black boys that" and nothing that draws his attention. When he finishes his second beer and sets the glass down, he looks at Harriman. Harriman would like to jump off his stool and get going but instead he looks back into Wills' face noncommittally.

"Well, what are we waiting for, Augustus? Let's go meet the team."

The Aboriginal players are assembled in the shearing shed when Harriman's buggy pulls up. They have a wait-and-see attitude about this new person they've been told will make them great cricketers. Harriman has been a little too lavish with his praise and a little too excited about this meeting. They have learned to accept much of what he says with caution, if not a grain of salt. They watch Wills and Harriman carefully as they enter the shed.

Harriman is beaming as he says, "Boys, this is Tom Wills. If I may say so, this man is a cricket legend. He knows the game inside out and he's come all this way to see if you boys are good enough to play in Melbourne at the MCG. Naturally, I think you are more than qualified. But, let me just say that Mr. . . . I mean, Tom here has forgotten more about cricket than most people know. Why, he even makes me look like an amateur."

Harriman laughs at his attempt at a self-deprecating joke. No one else does.

Dicky Dick says, in language, "That wouldn't take much. All of us make you look like an amateur." This gets the big laugh Harriman was seeking.

Tom Wills looks out into their faces, smiles and says, in language, "Why don't you speak English so Mr. Harriman can have a laugh too?"

The Black fellas all look at each other in disbelief. *Who is this blue-eyed bloke? Did he just speak to us in language?* Then it all sinks in and they have a huge laugh. He might not be a bad bloke after all. Harriman is equally taken aback and doesn't know how to react.

Wills says, "Excuse me, Augustus, but I'm going to say a few words to these men in their language, if you don't mind. I want to make sure there is no misunderstanding about what I have to say."

Harriman has no choice but to say yes.

Wills continues, in language. "Just so you know, I am going to be the captain of this team and I am going to take you scruffy wombats and make you into one of the best cricket sides in Victoria. All you will have to do is pay attention and learn. If you do, we will play at the Melbourne Cricket Ground against a team of white fellas that will, in all probability, want to kill you. Any questions?"

The Indigenous players are all smiles. Wills has won them over. Their initial caution has been replaced by a desire to live up to his lofty expectations.

* * * * *

As they go through their practice sessions, Wills gets a comprehensive idea about who is good at what. His overall impression is that Johnny Cuzens and Bullocky are premier batsmen. Jellico, Sundown. Sugar and Redcap are outstanding fielders with strong arms. King Cole is steady. But the one whom Wills recognizes as the stand-out of them all is Johnny Mullagh. He can do everything. Wills sees in this man a potential that he has never seen in all his years on a cricket pitch. Mullagh is fluid whether batting or bowling. While Wills may be able to teach the others to be better, all he ever has to do with Mullagh is make a slight suggestion that results in the tiniest tweak and Mullagh picks it up like a sponge. He understands at a totally different level.

After only a few days, Wills makes his report back to Newton. In it, Wills writes, "I give them six hours a day of good hard work. They are learning quickly. Their fielding is outstanding and Johnny Mullagh is one of the best cricketers I have ever seen. A true all rounder. It is my opinion that these Black fellas and I will be ready on Boxing Day. Signed: T. Wills, Esq."

Newton immediately informs the others on the match committee of Wills' appraisal. The majority agrees that the Boxing Day test is a go. They can hear the coins clanging into the till already. Now the promotion begins in earnest. Newspaper advertisements are placed in all the Melbourne papers proclaiming a must-see event at the MCG on Boxing Day. *The Australian News for Home Readers* publishes portraits of the Aboriginal players on the front page with an accompanying article that suggests that this is compensation for those Victorians who love the "good old English game."

Huge placards advertising the match are placed all around town and in shop windows, often accompanied by framed photos of the Aboriginal team. The racial aspect of all this is understood, if not stated. A reporter for *The Age* intercepts the Aboriginal team in Ballarat and proclaims them, "a fine body of men . . . and according to the way in which they handled bat and ball this afternoon, the eleven in Melbourne will meet with foemen worthy of their steel." The overall tone is obvious: This is a once in a lifetime opportunity; see if these darkies can play our game. The hype is epic.

Wills' team practices with intensity for two weeks. Their first test is at Lake Wallace. No one, including Wills, has any idea what to really expect. All he can do is hope. It turns out that he needn't have been concerned. The local team manages only 34 runs. Wills' team scores 170. Further evidence of Wills accurate assessment is that Mullagh takes 6 wickets and scores 81 runs. A few days later, the Aboriginals have a return match at Lake Wallace. This time the Lake Wallace side holds the Aboriginal team to 85 runs. But, once again, Mullagh shines. He takes 8 wickets while the Lake Wallace team is held to 47 runs. Two wins notched up.

They play a third match at Lake Wallace. By now, the word is out. People flock to the cricket ground. Among them is a smartly dressed and prosperous looking gentleman. Before the match begins, he looks everywhere for Tom Wills. When he finally spots him, he makes a bee line for him. "Well, Tom Wills. As I live and breathe. I was hoping I would get a chance to speak to you today. I'm Brougham Gurnett."

"Sorry, mate, I'm a little busy right now." Wills starts walking away.

Gurnett follows him. "Of course. Of course. And I wouldn't dream of detaining you for long. I was just wondering if we could have a chat after the match. There is a business proposal I would like to consult with you about . . ."

"If it has anything to do with this Aboriginal team, you can save your breath, mate. They aren't for sale."

"You cut me to the quick, Mr. Wills. I have the highest of intentions regarding your team," Burnett oozes.

Wills sees him for what he is, a slick talking hustler with a polished exterior. Instead of responding, he turns away abruptly and goes into the change room where Gurnett can't follow him.

This third match gets underway. Mullagh had injured his hand and is also affected by the heat. His performance is, by his standard, subpar. Nevertheless, the Indigenous team ends up sweeping Lake Wallace, this time outscoring them by 164 to 95.

The stage is set for Boxing Day when tragedy strikes the Indigenous team. Sugar, one of their favourites, with no apparent cause and with no prior health problems, suddenly dies. This sends a shock wave through the entire team. These are all young, vigorous men. Elders die, not their contemporaries. It casts a pall over all of them. It also dulls their desire to play cricket. It all seems so unimportant now.

Wills understands this and wants to show compassion, but he also has cricket on his mind. After commiserating with them and observing their shock and grieving with them, he does his best to use it as motivation. "We all miss Sugar," he says, "but I think the best way to honour him is to do what he and all of us set out to do. Let's play and win on Boxing Day for Sugar," he pleads. In truth, whether they do it for Sugar or not is irrelevant. Boxing Day is coming and will soon to arrive no matter what.

* * * * *

Gerald Sampson did not become a successful banker by ignoring details. Nothing was too insignificant for his microscopic scrutiny. Most of his employees cower when he approaches them in anticipation of his wrath over some act of carelessness on their part. Therefore, it shouldn't be surprising to find him in a pub on Collins Street having a clandestine meeting a few days before the Boxing Day match. He is with two men he hasn't met before.

"Gentlemen, let me introduced myself. I'm Gerry Sampson and I'm on the Match Committee of the Melbourne Cricket Club. Which of you is Mr. James?"

James nods.

"That means you must be Mr. Horan, correct?" Horan nods.

"Good. Let's get right down to business. Oh, forgive me. Would you like to have a drink?"

James says, "A beer would be nice."

Sampson asks, "And for you?"

Horan says. "I'll take a beer too, thanks."

Sampson hails the bartender and orders three pints. "Now, we can get down to business. I have a proposal for you gentlemen that I hope you'll see fit to agree to."

James is one of the best, if not the best bowler in Victorian cricket. Horan is his equal as a batsman. "I would like to make you two temporary members of the Melbourne Cricket Club for this upcoming match with those darkies who are coming to town on Boxing Day. I have every intention of making it worth your while."

James looks to Horan and says, "We're listening." Horan nods.

"To be frank," Sampson continues, "I was against this match from the beginning but they've gone ahead with it and I want to make damn sure we don't lose. Cricket is and always has been a white man's game. It is unthinkable that we could lose to those . . . " He searches for the right word. " . . . savages. Unthinkable."

The two cricketers are silent for a moment while this sinks in. "Are you sure there won't be any problem with the other members of the MCC, Gerry?" James asks.

"There won't be a problem. That I guarantee you. No one will even know about it until you take the field that day. By then it will be too late to do anything about it."

"Well, as long as we're talking business, Gerry, when you say worth your while, how much are we talking about?" Horan asks.

"Gentlemen, this is not a bargaining session," Sampson replies. "Name your price."

With that, James and Horan are made temporary members of the Melbourne Cricket Club and put on the roster.

Boxing Day finally arrives. The weather is warm but the potential of a storm looms as a crowd of 10,000 spectators fills the MCG. At last year's Boxing Day event against New South Wales, fewer than half that many people attended. Even in their wildest dreams, the Match Committee wouldn't have even hoped for this many people. But before a ball has been bowled, they are in the black.

There is an air of excitement all around the MCG as the spectators flock in. Many are there purely out of curiosity. The Match Committee guessed right. The novelty of seeing Black fellas play a white man's game is irresistible. But the biggest surprise, as the crowd fills the venue, is how many of those people have come to support the Aboriginals. There would naturally be a number of people who, on principle, would support them as underdogs. But added to that, and with the most beautiful of Australian twists, an article in *The Age* has brought in even more . . . to mock the Melbourne Cricket Club team. A reporter from *The Age* had gotten wind of Sampson's clandestine meeting with James and Horan and wrote a satirical article ridiculing them. The article essentially said that even with 400 members to choose from, the Melbourne Cricket Club felt it was necessary to recruit two more players who just happened to be the best bowler and batsman in the colony to go up against a team of 14 Aboriginals who only just learned to play cricket.

* * * * *

The mood in the change rooms is pregnant with apprehension. The team now consists of Bullocky, Cuzens, Dicky Dick, Jellico, Mullagh, Officer, Paddy, Peter, Sundown, King Cole and Tarpot. They are naturally apprehensive about playing against such a seasoned team. But it is even more so because of the venue. All their matches so far have been at country venues where at most a thousand people may attend . . . at most. The MCG intimidates them beyond imagination. This is the atmosphere Wills walks into.

He immediately reads the room and is glad he asked Harriman not to come in before the match. "What's the matter?" he asks. "Is this about Sugar?"

They all start talking at once.

"Why are they making so much noise?" Jellico asks.

"You were telling us the truth when you said they wanted to kill us, weren't you?" Tarpot adds.

Sundown says, "I never wanted to come here. I wanted to stay on my country. All these people scare me."

Mullagh is sitting quietly in a corner on his own doing his pre-match routine, keeping himself still.

Wills tries to calm them. "There's nothing to be afraid of. This is just big city cricket. There are always big crowds for these matches. These people love the game and they are excited about seeing us play. Most of them are supporting our team. They think the MCC blokes are a bunch of stuffed shirts." When he gets no reaction, he realizes he has to keep talking. "This MCG is no different than playing at Hamilton or Lake Wallace. There are just a few more people."

"A few more," King Cole mutters to himself. Even he is on edge.

"How many are out there?" Bullocky asks.

"About a million," King Cole says.

"A few thousand," Wills says. "But we have to stay focused. This is a chance to show these people what we can do. One thing that Harriman was right about is that they are going to watch how we conduct ourselves while we are here. They want to see us play cricket like the white fellas, like gentlemen. If we are afraid, they will see that."

"How does a gentleman play cricket?" Johnny Cuzens asks.

Jellico picks up a bat and pantomimes a delicate, effeminate swing. "Like this."

Dicky Dick sees a chance to help break the ice. He fashions a monocle out of a large coin and prances around the room. "By Jove. Tut-tut. Look at me. I'm a gentleman."

Mullagh looks up. "I said warriors, not women."

Jellico says, "We're not women. We're stuffed shirts."

"What do white fellas stuff their shirts with?" Sundown asks.

Dicky Dick takes the coin from his eye and holds it up. "Money," he says.

This gets a laugh. The atmosphere is immediately lighter. They all feel it. Wills breathes a sigh of relief. "I have one question. Am I the only one on our team that's going to wear shoes?"

In a chorus, they all respond, "Yes."

"Then we're ready. Let's go play some cricket."

* * * * *

When the Aboriginal team takes the field dressed in white shirt and trousers with red trim, a red belt and a straw hat with a blue band, the spectators roar. Immediately, the team is more relaxed. The crowd is no longer intimidating, a lot of it is on their side.

Wills loses the coin toss and the MCC has no hesitation about sending the Aboriginals to bat first. The first two batsmen at the crease are Johnny Cuzens and Bullocky, two of their best. James opens the bowling for the MCC. Johnny Cuzens is at the crease. The first ball comes in. Johnny Cuzens clips it. It flies directly to third man for an out. James takes a clean wicket on the first ball. This sets the tone for the match.

Harriman is watching the match from the stands. He is sitting with members of the Match Committee and feeling very important. In his mind, he has done it. He has put together an all Aboriginal team and they are now playing the Melbourne Cricket Club at the MCG. Thanks to him alone.

While he is basking in his own glory, he is approached by a smartly dressed, prosperous looking gentleman. The man stops next to Harriman.

"Well, as I live and breathe, you are Augustus Harriman, are you not?"

Harriman looks up, pleased that someone knows who he is. "Why, yes I am, sir. And who do I have the pleasure of addressing?"

"The name's Brougham Gurnett, sir. Happy to see you again."

"Again?" Harriman asks. "I'm sorry. Have we met before?"

"Why, yes. At Lake Wallace. Briefly, of course."

"Mr. Gurnett, I'm terribly sorry not to have recognized you," Harriman quickly apologizes. The truth is they didn't meet at Lake Wallace, but Harriman doesn't want to insult this impressive gentleman and the impressive gentleman prefers to keep it that way.

"Yes," Gurnett continues, "I had read about your boys in the papers and just had to see for myself. They certainly did handle themselves well at Lake Wallace."

Harriman would blush if he was capable. "Well, thank you, Mr. Gurnett. Yes, they did do well there. I was very proud of them."

"As well you should have been," Gurnett says. "I must say, you have also done an excellent job getting the word out on your team."

"Well, I can't really take credit for that. The boys are their own best advertisement," Harriman says, trying to sound modest.

"Now, don't hide your light under a bushel, Augustus . . . you don't mind if I call you Augustus, I hope."

"No, not in the least."

"You deserve all the credit due you. Don't be ashamed taking a little."

Harriman is speechless.

Gurnett moves a little closer to establish some intimacy. "I'm afraid we might be disturbing some of these folks. Why don't we take a little walk. It's fortuitous that I've run into you like this. I am a business man, a promoter, you might say, and I think we have something to talk about regarding this team of yours."

The hook is set. Harriman immediately gets up from his seat and the two of them walk off toward one of the concession stands.

* * * * *

Back in the change rooms, after the match, Wills is trying to paint a rosier picture than the one that actually exists. "We didn't do that badly for our first test match. Bullocky and Johnny Mullagh scored 30 of our 39 runs. Johnny Cuzens took six wickets."

Dicky Dick says, "And they scored 100 runs and made us look like we never played cricket before."

"We fielded well," Wills says, as if that would compensate for their loss.

King Cole says, "We got a lot of practice at fielding today."

"I've never seen such hitting," Sundown says. "Those blokes were too good."

"Maybe so," Wills finally concedes. "So, we may not have played that well, but look at how the crowd responded to us. They were on our side through the whole match."

"They also laughed at us when it was finished," Redcap says. "It felt to me like they were making fun of us."

King Cole says, "They were. They yelled at me to go back to the bush."

Just then, Harriman enters the change rooms with a big smile on his face. "You boys were excellent out there today. I couldn't have been prouder."

"We lost," Redcap says. "Are you proud of us losing?"

"Now, now. Every cloud has a silver lining. I can tell you that you played well enough for someone to offer to take you on a tour. First to New South Wales, then to England."

Wills asks, "Is that true?"

"Indeed it is. I made an agreement with a very well connected promoter who said it would be ever so easy to do," Harriman says. "We shook on it."

The players look at each other as if waiting for the other shoe to drop. Wills isn't satisfied that Harriman is telling the truth. "What do you mean?" he asks.

"I mean what I said. I've made an agreement with a gentleman who has connections in New South Wales and England to take our team on a tour. It is confirmed," Harriman says proudly.

Wills is still suspicious but doesn't want to say anything more in front of the team. "Why don't you fellas get dressed and go to the hotel. We have another match tomorrow and we want to be ready for that."

Harriman says, "Yes, you boys rest up for tomorrow," as if it isn't official unless he says so.

The team change out of their uniforms and leave the MCG in small groups, heading for the hotel where they are staying.

Once they have left, Wills turns to Harriman. "Now, what's this about a tour? Who is this man with the connections?"

"You wouldn't know him. He happened to see me purely by accident. Here's his card."

Wills looks at the card. "Gurnett? Gurnett? That rings a bell. Where have I heard about his man?" Then he twigs. "Oh, that's the bastard who approached me at Lake Wallace. He wanted to talk to me about some business involving the team. Is this swindler the one you've made an agreement with?"

"I'll have you know, Mr. Gurnett is an upstanding businessman. He has promoted cricket matches all around the country."

"Who told you that? Gurnett?"

"I think you would be well advised to keep your opinions to yourself. Your job is to coach the cricket team, not to stick your nose into my business."

"I'm telling you this man is a fraud. I smelled him a mile away."

"I think otherwise and I don't care what you think you've smelled. You can either go with us on tour or I'll get someone else. But I'm not seeking your advice on this. The decision is made."

* * * * *

The second day, the Aboriginal team does a little better, scoring 87 runs. Mullagh is the high scorer with 33. Wills scores 25. But once again, the MCC quickly make up the 27 run deficit and come away with the victory long before the day ends. The crowd isn't as large, but still respectable, numbering between three and four thousand.

The Match Committee had planned a three-day test. But with the match officially over on the second day, they hastily put together a game between Australian-born players, black and white, and players from elsewhere. They dub it Natives against the World. In the end, this match is declared a draw.

But the verdict for the three days is this, according to *The Australasian*: "Of all the cricket matches hitherto played in this colony, none probably has excited more curiosity and interest than that between an Aboriginal eleven and eleven of the Melbourne club. The Indigenous players had attracted a large crowd, their play was universally admired, especially the batting of Mullagh and the bowling of Cuzens . . ."

Further evidence of the respect the Melbourne Cricket Club has for its opponents is when they present new cricket bats to Johnny Cuzens and Johnny Mullagh.

* * * * *

It is clear that Melbourne hasn't yet gotten enough of the Aboriginal cricketers. Two days later the Amateur Athletic Sports Committee holds a meet for both cricket teams and the best amateur athletes in the colony. The program consists of ten quite diverse events, including a backwards hundred yard dash, a standing high jump, throwing a cricket ball, a 150 yard race that featured the cricket teams only and what was termed "vaulting with a pole." Johnny Mullagh is entered in nine of the ten events; Johnny Cuzens and Tarpot are each entered in eight. Despite the fact that they are amateur events, prize money is awarded to the winners. Four thousand spectators come to the MCG for this one. They roar their approval when Johnny Mullagh ties for the standing high jump, and again when Bullocky wins the cricket ball throw, and yet again when Johnny Cuzens wins the 150 yard race. In all, the Aboriginals win five outright victories and share the spoils for two more, out of a total of ten events.

A letter to the editor in *The Age* sums up public reaction to their experience in Melbourne. It said, "Mr. Wills has no doubt discovered their forte – cricket." Then in a swipe at the Christian missionaries, it went on, "Would it not be quite as well to expend funds in teaching them to play cricket? It must be admitted on all sides that it is better to be a good cricketer than a bad Christian."

Chapter Six – The Tour

Gurnett and Harriman meet in Melbourne to make specific plans for the tour. Gurnett wastes no time laying it out. "First of all, Augustus, I want you to know that I will take care of all expenses. I intend to pay the wages of the players and those who we decide should travel with the team. I will also take care of buying new uniforms. The ones you have are quaint, but we need something more professional looking if we are going to show this team off in its best light. Also, I want this to be a twelve-month tour which will include a return match at the MCG with the Melbourne club, then on to Sydney for a series of matches there and finally to England. When we return from England, there will be a bonus for the players of fifty pounds each with a little more for Wills. You and I will share the profits equally after you have paid your investors their share. Does this sound reasonable to you?"

"That sounds quite reasonable, Brougham. Will you draw up a contract or shall I?"

"What?" Gurnett is astonished that such a thing can even enter Harriman's mind. "Sir, I gave you my word when we met. We shook hands. My word and that handshake are my bond. Nothing on paper can alter that."

"I don't mean to question your integrity, Brougham. Anything but. It only seems like good business practice to have it lodged officially in writing with a barrister. It may have something to do with the way we do business in the Western District, but . . ."

"I don't know what your business practices are over there in the bush, but where I come from, a man's word is his bond. Perhaps I misjudged you, Augustus. I thought you were such a man, yourself."

"I am. I am. If it were up to me, that handshake is all we need. But I have investors that I must answer to . . ."

"Are you saying that your investors don't trust you?"

"No. On the contrary. They trust me implicitly."

"Well then, what is the problem? Do you not trust me?"

Harriman is completely cowed. If he continues to push for a written contract, Gurnett may pull the plug on him. Then, where will he be? He is silent for a moment. "Brougham, I do trust you, believe me. Perhaps I have been a little too cautious. Forgive me. The handshake and your word are sufficient for us to go forward."

Gurnett is satisfied. "I would hate for you to miss this opportunity, Augustus, after all you've put into it. My only goal is to help you realize it and, if we should be successful, make it worth both our whiles."

* * * * *

In the meantime, the Indigenous players return to their stations. Wills still schedules the occasional match to keep them sharp but, otherwise, their lives settle back into a routine less frantic. At Pine Hills, Mullagh, King Cole, Two Penny and Tiger are welcomed back as heroes. The local newspapers have also been full of praise for the Black cricketers. Mullagh, in particular, is looked at through new eyes – especially by a young boy at Pine Hills Station.

One afternoon, while Mullagh is taking a brush to one of the horses, little Timmy strolls in. Learning to throw the boomerang was already reason enough for the boy to be in awe of Johnny Mullagh. Now, he looks at his idol as a cricket giant as well.

"G'day, Mr. Mullagh." Timmy is carrying one of King Cole's boats. "Look what King Cole gave me. He just made it."

"That's a nice one, Timmy," Mullagh says. "He didn't have much time to carve boats when we were in Melbourne."

"That's what he said, too. He carved this one last night. I think it's the best one yet."

Mullagh takes up the pitchfork and tosses some hay into the stall. Timmy watches his every movement, in his mind mimicking him. When Timmy is by himself, he often pretends to be Johnny Mullagh at the crease. Every ball is hit for a four. "Mr. Mullagh?"

"Yes, Timmy."

"Mr. Mullagh, do you think you might be able to teach me to bat? My dad and Pappy say you're the best batsman in all of Australia. I'd like to play cricket when I grow up and if you could teach me, maybe I'll be as good as you are some day."

"I reckon one day, when I don't have too much work, I can show you what I know. But only if it's all right with your dad. By the time you grow up, though, I'm sure you'll be a lot better than I am."

Timmy's face explodes into a huge smile. Thanks, Mr. Mullagh. See ya later." He skips out into the daylight floating his boat on an imaginary ocean as he runs toward the homestead.

"Mum. Mum. Guess what?"

* * * * *

Gurnett wastes no time putting his tour on track. First, he goes to the Melbourne Cricket Club to arrange a return match for the Aboriginals. His expectation is that with this money, he can finance the trip to Sydney. The Match Committee agrees and a date is set for early February. With that in his pocket, he is off to Sydney.

In Sydney, he meets with Charles Lawrence. Charles Lawrence is a noted cricketer, originally from England, now captain and coach of the New South Wales eleven. Since settling in Australia, he has become a publican in Sydney. His hotel, The Pier Hotel in Manly, is where Gurnett finds him.

Lawrence is standing behind the reception desk when this elegant looking gentleman enters the front door. He looks up from his newspaper when he hears his name.

"Why, Charles Lawrence, as I live and breathe, I was hoping you would be in today." Gurnett strides up to the reception desk with his hand extended. "Allow me to introduce myself. I am Brougham Gurnett. Here is my card."

Lawrence takes the card and offers his hand. "Nice to meet you, Brougham. Are you looking for a room?"

"No. Well not immediately," Gurnett answers.

"Well then, what brings you to Manly?"

"As I said, I was hoping to find you here. I am here to secure your help in a very exciting enterprise," Gurnett says.

Lawrence takes a step back, figuratively. Experience has taught him that someone displaying this kind of raw confidence usually wants to sell him something. "Go on," he says. cautiously.

"I am bringing the all Aboriginal cricket team to Sydney for a series of matches before heading off to England. You have no doubt heard of their matches at the MCG in Melbourne."

Lawrence relaxes. "Why, yes I have. Tom Wills has been coaching them, has he not?"

"Indeed, he has. And he will continue to when we come to Sydney."

"Well, in that case, what is it you think I can help you with? I have great respect for Wills."

"As do we all," Gurnett replies and repeats, "As do we all. What I am hoping is that, since you have such strong connections with the cricket community here, you could help us arrange some matches in the area before we head off to England."

Lawrence's attitude whips around 180 degrees. "Oh, I would be happy to do that! I am very keen to see those boys play, myself. Might even set up a match between them and my team."

Gurnett says, "My goodness. I never dreamed we would be able to play against your excellent squad. That would be a treat for the spectators, to be sure." And then, as if he just thought of it, Gurnett says, "It occurs to me that we will need accommodations while we are here. Perhaps you could find room for us at your fine establishment. This could be our base of operations, so to speak. Naturally, we expect to pay your top rate, assuming you can find room for us."

"I don't know why not, Brougham. But I'll give you my group rate. That will save you a little money. You just let me know when you need rooms and I will make sure they are available. And as to arranging matches, leave that to me."

Gurnett extends his hand. "Let's shake on that, Charles. You don't mind that I call you Charles, do you?"

Lawrence takes his hand. "Not at all, Brougham. I look forward to greeting you and your team when you come."

* * * * *

Back at Pine Hills Station, Johnny Mullagh is talking with Jake. "Listen, Boss, I'm wondering if I can take a couple of hours off today."

"Are you crook?" Jake asks.

"I am a little tired, but I can work if you want me to," Mullagh says. "I've got things pretty much sorted with the animals and I'd like to take care of some business. It has to do with cricket."

The glow of Mullagh's heroics hasn't faded at Pine Hills and he knows it. "In that case, Johnny, go ahead. We'll be all right without you here for a few hours."

"Thanks, Jake." Mullagh doesn't like it that he has lied to Jake about what he wants to do, but he doesn't dare tell the truth. As soon as he is off the property, he heads for Mullagh Station. The urge to see Alice is beyond his capacity to resist.

He treks through the familiar country. It is like visiting an old friend. Stopping for a drink from the stream feels like a necessity, almost like a talisman on the journey. The distance seems shorter now because of the familiar landmarks he passes. Before long he is in the identical place where he concealed himself on his previous visit. From this brush, he has a clear view of the homestead.

He sees a worker walking around, doing chores. Mullagh remains quiet and watches. He waits for several minutes which then become half-an-hour and then nearly an hour. Disheartened, he is about to steal away, when Alice comes out of the house and onto the veranda with a ball of yarn and knitting needles. Mullagh smiles as he watches her sit down and begin to knit. *He remembers a day when they were young when she tried to teach him how to hold the knitting needles properly.* "No, Unaarrimin, hold them lighter -- lighter. Do you know what lighter means? You're holding them like you're going to beat someone with them." "My hands aren't meant for this work," he insists. "What are they meant for then?" "Throwing a boomerang," he answers. "Well, then, go throw a boomerang and let me knit," she laughs.

Mullagh makes a birdcall, hoping Alice will recognize it as their special rendezvous signal. If she hears it, she shows no sign of recognition. The worker looks up, however. He scans 360 degrees, all around the sky for a few moments until he shakes his head and goes back to his chores. Mullagh doesn't move a muscle. He looks around to make sure he is well hidden and tries the birdcall again, this time a little louder. It is the worker who looks up again. He knows he heard what sounded like a bird. He isn't certain what kind of bird it is, just that it sounds like a bird. But, again, he sees nothing. He continues staring into the sky for a few more moments, then he shrugs his shoulders and goes into a shed. Again, Alice is busy knitting, oblivious to any other sound than the clicking of her needles. Mullagh is torn between stepping into the open and shouting at her and trying the birdcall once more even louder. He compromises. He steps into the clear and makes the birdcall. This time, Alice looks up and in the direction of the call. When she sees Mullagh standing in the open, she drops her knitting, looks around and then rushes toward him.

"Unaarrimin!" She throws her arms around his neck and hugs him. "Or do I have to call you Johnny Mullagh now?" she laughs.

"You can call me Emu if you want. How are you? I've missed you," he says, trying not to make it sound too desperate.

"Come, let's hide in this brush. You aren't supposed to be here. If anyone sees you, we'll both be in trouble." They go into Mullagh's hiding place. "Let me look at you now that you are an important cricketer. When did you learn to play cricket?" she asks.

"At Pine Hills Station. That's where I am working now . . . between cricket matches," he laughs.

"I read all about you in the papers. I had to hide it from my mother, but I read everything I could find," she says.

"We are going to play in Sydney," he tells her. "And then, we are going to play in England."

"No. I don't believe it. You're going to play cricket in England?"

"Yep."

"I want to come with you. Do you think you can hide me in your suitcase?"

"Hm. You might be a little chubby for that," he laughs.

She punches him on the shoulder. "I am not chubby. I am a station woman. We need our strength," she laughs too.

Mullagh's happiness is beyond calculation. Being here – or anywhere, for that matter – with Alice is like a dream. He never wants it to end.

But at that moment, the front door opens and Mrs. Buckingham steps onto the veranda, looking for Alice. She notices the knitting needles and yarn on the deck of the veranda and looks around. She shouts, "Alice!" She pauses, listening. "Alice? Where are you, child?" She steps off the veranda and continues looking.

Alice and Mullagh are frozen in place. She whispers to him, "You had better go. If Mum sees you, she'll go get the shotgun."

Mullagh can't help himself. "When can I see you again?" he whispers. This time there is some desperation in it.

It doesn't register with Alice. Instead, she says, "I'll try to lose some weight so I can fit in your suitcase." She leans up and gives him a sisterly kiss him on the cheek. "Go." She steps into the clear. "I'm here, Mum."

Mullagh feels like a thief as he steals away. When he gets far enough away to relax, he pulls Alice's handkerchief from his pocket and holds it to his cheek where she kissed him.

* * * * *

The return match at the MCG was fraught from the beginning. Gurnett was guaranteed the use of the MCG but the Melbourne Cricket Club wasn't obliged to furnish a team to play against. Also the enthusiastic 10,000 spectators that greeted the Aboriginal team on Boxing Day were, at best, a few hundred on this occasion. The MCC had used all its resources to promote the Boxing Day event. They were indifferent to this match's success. They made their money on hiring out the ground. Gurnett lived under the illusion that the mere presence of the Aboriginal team would ensure a crowd. Plus, he didn't have the money to do any significant promotion anyway. His hope always was that the money he took in at the MCG would provide the resources to go on to Sydney. And that the money from Sydney would finance the trip to England, and so on.

In the end, a scratch match is arranged featuring a disparate group of players that Gurnett named the County of Bourke. The Aboriginal team wins easily but not enough people are there to care one way or another. The only people who care are the ones Gurnett owes money to. His cheques either bounced or were discredited by various banks. His creditors come after him in no uncertain terms.

They even take out a writ to make sure he can't leave Victoria.

Through all this, Harriman is powerless. He watches as all the good work he did to create the team dissipates. He tries to confront Gurnett when they meet at a Melbourne pub. "Brougham, what has happened? I had such confidence in you."

"Now, Augustus, don't be alarmed. It looks much worse than it actually is. These vultures are trying to discredit me and it is foul of them . . . foul."

"But you owe them money, don't you?"

"You have no real grasp of how these things are done, do you? These are merely negotiations. They are saying what they have to in order to create the false notion that they won't be paid and their only reason for that is to bargain with me. I have every intension of paying them. I am just not paying them the exorbitant sums they expect. It's just business writ large, Augustus. You are not expected to understand all the ins and outs. That is my job."

Harriman wants to be satisfied with Gurnett's explanation. If he isn't, he has to start once again from scratch and seek his dream all over again. That task seems too daunting. After he ponders this for a few moments, he says, "Brougham, you're correct. I do not entirely understand how these things are done. If you give me your word that we are still moving forward with this plan, it will be good enough for me."

"Augustus, you already have my word. But if it will give you any satisfaction, I pledge on a gentleman's honour that this is a business transaction which I am fully capable of handling. Everything is fine. Here is my hand on it."

They shake hands and re-seal their commitment to the tour.

Once Harriman is reassured, Gurnett goes to each of his creditors to see what they'll settle for. He finally reaches an agreement with them, pays them and he is allowed to leave the Colony.

* * * * *

The Aborigines Protection Board has convened a special meeting to deal with what some of the members believe to be a vital emergency.

"Gentlemen," Secretary Morgan begins, "the rumours we have been hearing are true. This Mr. Gurnett is making plans to take the Aboriginal cricket team out of the Colony without our permission. He plans to take them to Sydney and then after that on to England. We cannot allow this to happen. These unfortunate natives are under our care and it appears obvious that they are being exploited for someone's personal gain. We would be remiss if we allowed this to go forward without doing our best to prevent it and protect them."

"I agree with the Secretary," Mr. Dunphy says. "Our darkies are our responsibility. They are simply not capable of making these kinds of important life decisions without some guidance . . . our guidance."

"Clearly we must do something, but what is legally possible?" asks Mr. Owens. "If the information we have is correct, they are planning to leave in two days' time."

Even the most liberal and empathetic of these Board members has, at his foundation, a paternalistic view of Indigenous Australians. It is not only the scientists who agree that these people cannot survive, most Victorians believe it too. Most Australians, in fact. It is, therefore, understand-able how these men see their roles. To them, it's like caring for old people or the infirm.

Morgan says, "I have given it a good deal of thought. So, with your approval, gentlemen, I would like to approach the government directly and demand that some action be taken. At the very least, this situation needs to be studied carefully before any decisions of this magnitude are agreed to."

"Can't we just order this Mr. Gurnett to postpone the tour? We are, after all, the men responsible for the natives. Our refusal to allow it should certainly carry some weight. What if we threaten this Gurnett with legal action, whether we have the authority or not? That should, at least, make him pause, shouldn't it?" Dunphy asks.

The only actual legal authority in the room is Mr. Blankenship. He has been silent, just listening. But now he stands. "I believe we have to tread very lightly on this issue, gentlemen, very lightly. I have also studied the law and it doesn't appear that the governor or the government or anyone else, for that matter, has a leg to stand on. There is nothing in the law that prohibits any persons from taking these natives out of the country. In this case, to England. So, until and unless the law is changed, Mr. Gurnett is free to do what he wishes."

Everyone jumps when Morgan violently slams his hand down on the table. He looks each of them directly in the eye and says, "Then I say we change the law!"

* * * * *

With his troubles seemingly behind him, Gurnett leaves the team at Charles Lawrence's Pier Hotel in Manly. Lawrence has saved his best rooms for them, except for Gurnett, who has his own accommodations in Sydney.

Lawrence greets his newest lodgers with great warmth. "Happy to meet you, Mr. Harriman. Welcome to my hotel."

Harriman takes his hand and motions to Tom Wills. "Likewise, Mr. Lawrence. And this is Tom Wills."

Wills and Lawrence shake hands the way athletes who have great mutual respect greet each other.

"I've been looking forward to seeing you again, Tom," Lawrence says.

"You gentlemen know each other?" Harriman asks.

"Oh, yes. We go back a way," Wills says. "We played against each other in Ireland."

"Mr. Wills here was a mere snippet of a man," Lawrence says, good-naturedly. "But he still managed to take ten wickets against my Phoenix club. You don't forget a man like that."

"I've lost a little speed since then," Wills says with a smile. "You seem to have done all right for yourself since then."

"Oh, I've gotten around a little." To both, Lawrence says, "I assume Mr. Gurnett has told you about your first match here."

"Mr. Gurnett," Wills nearly chokes on the words, "said he has business to attend to in Sydney. All he did was point us in your direction and then disappear."

"Well, then, you should know that I've arranged a match with the Albert Club. It's the club I coach and, without boasting, I believe it's the best cricket club in New South Wales."

"Actually, Mr. Gurnett did tell me about it," Harriman says as he shoots a quick glare in Wills' direction.

"I've heard about your club," Wills says, ignoring Harriman. "It should be an interesting match."

"I certainly hope so. Are your boys ready?" Lawrence asks.

"Ask them," Wills says. He turns to them. They are sprawled around the lobby, looking extremely relaxed.

"Are you boys ready to play some cricket?" Lawrence calls out to them

Dicky Dick says, "Cricket? I thought we were here on holiday." It gets the desired laugh from the others.

"Are you Johnny Mullagh?" Lawrence asks.
Dicky Dick laughs. "No. He couldn't make the trip. We got rid of him. Held us back."

Lawrence looks to Wills. Wills is also laughing. "Johnny, come over here and meet Charles Lawrence. He played cricket for the English side when they came to the MCG a couple of years back. You two will be rivals when we get to the pitch so it's polite to shake his hand before you try to take his head off."

Mullagh comes over to Lawrence with a smile on his face. He extends his hand and says, "I won't take your head off unless I have to."

Lawrence looks into Mullagh's face with the same respect he showed Wills. "Are you boys ready?" Lawrence asks again.

Wills speaks for them all, "As ready as we'll ever be. When do we play?"

"Day after tomorrow."

"All right, fellas, let's get you into your rooms for a rest before we have a practice," Wills says.

In no rush, the Aboriginal players pick up their kit and go to their assigned rooms.

* * * * *

The Albert Cricket Ground is only a few years old when Tom Wills takes his team there to challenge Lawrence's eleven. It is a vast improvement over what was used before in Sydney. Before 1864, the cricketers had to play among grazing animals and random passers-by. There were no fences or any other barriers, natural or man-made, to identify the grounds. Now, they have a facility that has a grandstand around three-quarters of the ground and a row of trees to complete its enclosure. The players and the spectators all enjoy the most modern facilities of the day.

Harriman is with the team. He would sit with Gurnett in the pavilion but no one has seen him since they arrived. Harriman assumes he is taking care of some business and gives it no more thought.

In the change rooms before the match, Wills is giving his usual pep talk. "This team is so much better than any we've faced before that it's like the difference between the team we played at Lake Wallace and the Melbourne Cricket Club. And we have to be ready for them."

King Cole says, "Why don't we just go home then? No use playing here."

"They are good," Wills repeats, "but we are just as good." In language he says, "They are just a bunch of white fellas. Nothing to be afraid of." Hearing this in language relaxes them.

An attendant comes to the door and announces that it is time to go onto the pitch. As they leave the change rooms, in language, Mullagh says, "Remember, we are warriors!"

There are 8,000 spectators for today's match. It is a perfect, cloudless, summer day in Sydney. The same novelty that drew crowds in Melbourne is what brings the people from New South Wales here. The only difference being that in Melbourne, the Indigenous players were an unknown quantity. No one knew if Black fellas could play the white man's game. Here, they have been written about and praised in the newspapers and their talent for cricket is established. It promises to be an interesting day.

On the pitch, Lawrence and Wills shake hands all around as they meet at stumps with the umpires. A coin toss determines who bats first and who is in the field. The umpire shows the coin to both Wills and Lawrence and asks Lawrence to call it. Lawrence calls "heads." The umpire flips it. The umpire calls out, "Heads." Lawrence chooses to go into the field first. They return to their respective teams. Everyone, players and spectators alike, are set for a game of cricket.

Wills' team is gathers around him. "We are batting first. Don't rush. Don't be fooled. And don't be intimidated." In language, he says, "We can beat these whities. "

Cuzens and Bullocky pick up their bats and go out onto the pitch. The match is about to begin, but before any real action can take place, there is a commotion in the stands. Someone is pushing his way through the aisles and down toward the pitch. It is Gurnett storming through the crowd followed by a police officer.

"There they both are," he points to where the Aboriginal team is sitting. The policeman walks down the steps of the pavilion and onto the pitch. Gurnett is now following him. The umpires have no idea what to make of this intrusion and, seeing a police officer, have no choice but to stop play.

When they reach the team, Gurnett first points to Harriman. "This is Augustus Harriman. He is the one who embezzled the money from me. And this one is Tom Wills, his accomplice."

Both Wills and Harriman are astonished at this accusation, but before they can react, the officer says, "You'll have to come along with me. Mr. Gurnett, here, has made some serious charges against you two and until we get to the bottom of it, you are under arrest."

"Under arrest?!?" Harriman is outraged. "That is impossible. I am the one who started this team. How can I be under arrest?"

"Don't make it any more difficult than it is, sir," the policeman says. "You will have to come along with me. And you too, Mr. Wills."

Wills looks at Gurnett and then looks at Harriman. "I told you this man was a snake."

The Indigenous players are completely befuddled and secretly, amused. This is obviously some kind of white man's business that they are glad not to be a part of. They just look at one another and suppress smiles.

Gurnett is uncharacteristically silent. He is content to have put this all in motion and has the good sense to let it play out between the law and his adversaries.

Wills says, "Well, officer, you will have to drag me out of here. Neither I nor Mr. Harriman have done anything illegal. This man you are protecting is the criminal."

"How dare you?" Gurnett explodes. And to the policeman, says, "I'll have you know, officer, I am a reputable businessman and I will not tolerate this libel from the likes of this cricket player. The charges I have made are true, my word of honour."

"Word of honour? Mate, you're word is . . . " Will starts to say something colourful, but catches himself.

By now, Charles Lawrence has come over to see what is going on. "Officer, I am Charles Lawrence. I manage the Albert Club team. What is the problem?"

The police officer turns to Lawrence with a sense of relief. "Mr. Lawrence, these two men are accused of embezzling money from Mr. Gurnett here. He has filed a charge against them and I have to sort it out. Can you shed any light on all this?"

"Only this much. I am quite certain that Mr. Wills has not had an opportunity to embezzle anything from anyone. He has only been in Sydney for two days and in my company all that time. When is this embezzlement meant to have happened?"

"According to Mr. Gurnett's complaint, it was yesterday. He claims that Harriman and Wills withdrew all the money from an account they all had access to. We went to the bank with him today to verify it and the money was indeed withdrawn."

"That snake is the embezzler as sure as a wallaby can hop," Wills says.

Harriman says, "And I was with the team the entire time we have been in Manly. You can ask any of them."

"Well," the policeman says, "I'm not sure we can take the word of a Black fella. They might say anything to protect their boss."

"Then ask Mr. Wills. He knows."

"Is that true, Mr. Wills?" the policeman asks.

"Absolutely, one hundred per cent true, officer. You've come after the wrong men. Ask Gurnett where he was all day yesterday and the day before."

Gurnett is indignant. "Are you going to take their word over mine? What is your name, officer? I may have to have a chat to your superiors."

"This is too complicated for me to try to sort out," the officer says. "I'll just have to turn this over to higher authorities and let them find the truth. In the meantime, Mr. Gurnett, I think it best that we hold off on the arrests. But Mr. Harriman, you and

Mr. Wills had better stay in New South Wales for the time being."

"They will be staying at my hotel, The Pier in Manly," Lawrence offers. "I'll make sure they stay put until you sort this out, officer. My word of honour."

Gurnett looks from one to the other and says, in a huff, "I am not going to stand here and be insulted by these rascals. I have far more important things to attend to." He storms away.

The policeman watches him go off. "Gentlemen, I'm sorry for this interruption, but I am just doing my job. We'll get this sorted out immediately. Sorry. You can go back to your cricket."

Even though the crowd has no idea what is actually taking place in front of them, the mood is altered. The passion for cricket has faded. In the end, no one really cares that the Albert Club won the match, including the players.

And after the match, in the midst of all this indifference, the team returns to The Pier Hotel. Wills hasn't stopped rubbing Harriman's nose in it. "You vouched for that snake, Augustus. Important businessman, you said. If he's an important business man, I'm a platypus."

Harriman doesn't like being spoken to in this way, but makes no excuse and makes no attempt to defend himself. He knows he has been snookered. "I may have been a little hasty," he finally says

The two of them have fallen silent, but look up when Lawrence returns to the hotel. "Gents, I'm afraid I have some bad news for you . . . on top of what you're already received. The money from today's takings is also gone. Gurnett talked his way onto the counting room and convinced the boys that he was picking up the team's share for everyone. And they gave it to him. I went to the police to see if they could be of any help and they told me they can't find Gurnett. He has disappeared."

* * * * *

Harriman, Wills and Lawrence are sitting at the bar of the hotel. It is later that evening. The team has retired to their rooms. "That no account bastard," Wills says. "How I would love to run into him tonight."

"I cannot believe how gullible I was, " Harriman laments. "The signs were all there. The man had charlatan written all over his face."

"Now, gents, we were all fooled. This man is a practiced thief. You can be sure this was not the first time someone has fallen under his spell. What we need to concentrate on is what we do next," Lawrence says.

"What we need to do next is find him and have him arrested," Harriman says.

"No," Lawrence says. "I mean what are *we* to do next? He has taken all the money and he has left me with a hotel full of cricketers who can't pay for their rooms. I'm not faulting you for this and I don't expect you have the money handy to do anything about it. But I've turned away business and I really cannot afford to do that."

Wills suggests, "Maybe we can get the boys to triple up in their rooms. That will, at least, give you more rooms to hire out."

"I will write to my sponsors," Harriman says. "They won't be very happy with me and what has transpired, but they are my neighbours, so they may be forgiving. And perhaps they'll advance us the money we need to go back home."

"In the meantime," Lawrence says, "I'll try to arrange a few matches around New South Wales. We might be able to make some money that way. These Indigenous boys are a big draw card."

Harriman has a thought. "They are a draw card, especially when they can show off their other skills. Maybe we can also stage some contests after the cricket matches like they did at the MCG, where they can throw a boomerang and high jump and that sort of thing."

"That's an excellent idea," Lawrence quickly agrees. "There must be some other things like that they can do that will please the crowd."

Wills says, "That's probably our only choice. I'll go up and talk to them and tell them what the situation is."

Most of the players are congregated in Mullagh's room. They are still speculating about what this means. Johnny Cuzens says, "That Gurnett is a slick one. He fooled all those smart white fellas."

"He's slick all right," Dicky Dick says. "Like Wills said, he is slick like a snake. Poor Boss Harriman. It's like he threw a boomerang and then looked in the wrong direction and it hit him in the head."

"Redcap asks, "Do you think we'll be able to go home now? "

"It doesn't look like we're going to England. We might as well go back home," King Cole says.

"I wanted to bat in England," Bullocky says. Sundown quickly adds, "And try some of the local beer." They all laugh.

"And maybe that too," Bullocky agrees, with a smile which features his missing tooth.

There's a knock at the door. "Come in," yells Dicky Dick." Wills enters and finds a place to sit. Mullagh looks at him. "What is going to happen now?" he asks.

"It's a mess. It's even worse than you know. Gurnett got all the money from the Albert Club too. They knew he was with us, so when he told them he was picking it up, they gave it to him. Then he disappeared. Lawrence went to the coppers and they don't know where he is. Nobody can find him," Wills explains.

"Redcap and I can find him," Dicky Dick says, expecting a laugh which doesn't materialize.

Wills goes on, "That means Harriman has no money to pay Lawrence for these rooms, no money to pay me and no money to take us back to Victoria. We are stuck here."

Mullagh thinks for a moment. "Can't we play some matches here and make money that way?"

"Lawrence is trying to organize that now. And Harriman has another idea. You remember how after the matches at the MCG we had those athletic contests?"

They all nod.

"Well, Harriman wants to do that sort of thing after the matches here . . . "

"You mean the running backwards and jumping?" Cuzens asks.

"That kind of thing. Yes. But with more tribal things, like throwing the boomerang and spears . . "

Dicky Dick says, "Maybe we can get hold of a woomera and really show them how to throw a spear."

"Maybe we can skin a possum for them," Redcap says.

"Or gut a kangaroo," Jellico adds.

"That's the idea," Wills says. "Not gutting a kangaroo but the other things. Keep thinking about it while I go down and tell Harriman and Lawrence that we're on board with this."

* * * * *

Matches are played at Maitland and Newcastle; then at Parramatta and back at the Albert Club. The Aboriginal tribal shows are of much more interest to the small crowds than the cricket. But they still do not generate enough money to pay for more than room and board. It is getting toward the end of the season and things are no better. But two things have come out of this. First, Lawrence has become an active member of the team. He and Wills share the coaching responsibilities. And second, the tribal displays after the cricket add entertainment value to the experience for audiences.

Harriman, Lawrence, Wills and the team are back in Manly. The team are upstairs in their rooms. Harriman tells Lawrence and Wills, "I have heard from my sponsors. They are unable to come up with the funds to get us back home."

"The season is ending anyway," Lawrence adds.

"So, I am going to have to reach into my savings and take these boys home. I don't see any other choice," Harriman says.

"Can you afford to do that?" Lawrence asks.

"No, but there's no other choice. We can't stay up here forever. These boys want to go home and, to be perfectly honest, so do I."

Wills says, "I know I've been pretty hard on you at times, Augustus, but under the circumstances, you can consider your debt to me cancelled. You don't owe me anything."

"That's very decent of you, Tom, but no, I intend to pay all my debts."

"No. I insist," Wills says. "You and I are square."

Lawrence says, "I'll knock off what you owe me, too, Augustus. We'll share this loss. It's only fair."

Harriman is speechless for a moment. Then, "Gentlemen, I am profoundly moved. Thank you."

Chapter Seven – Lawrence to the Rescue

The First Eleven arrive back in Melbourne but the trip to their various stations is still to be arranged and paid for. All of Victoria knows of the hardships and unfortunate events in New South Wales. The public is indignant that any Victorian, white or black, is treated so shabbily by their northern rival. Many of them are also disappointed that their Black fellas were unable to go on to England and show the Brits a thing or two about cricket. But the boys are back home safe and sound, if desolate and destitute, and that counts for something.

A repeat of the post Boxing Day athletics competition is arranged at the MCG, giving Victorians an opportunity to show their support for their Indigenous cricketers in a tangible way. The contests and displays are better in theory than they are in fact. They throw spears which are of such poor quality that no one is sure where they might land. The same with the boomerangs. On their previous tribal exhibition, both Mullagh and Dicky Dick excelled at throwing boomerangs. The ones they have this time might as well be made of paper. There are also complaints that a number of the spectators have climbed over a fence to keep from having to pay. Yet, in spite of this, the event raises a sufficient amount of money to return them all to the Western District.

But while most are pleased that all has ended relatively well, the Aborigines Protection Board wants to discuss where things stand now and where things should go in the future.

"Gentlemen," Secretary Morgan begins, "Everything we feared could happen has happened with our darkies up in New South Wales. They were stranded in a hostile environment and deprived of opportunity to return to their country. It is appalling. Appalling!"

"It is unfortunate," Blankenship says, calmly.

"Unfortunate!?!" Morgan thunders. "It is a tragedy! Not to mention how it reflects on us. We are charged with looking after these boys and we have failed."

Owens says, "I don't think we can be held responsible for the chicanery of that Burnett fellow."

"I agree," Dunphy adds. "That was entirely out of our control."

"Out of our control?" Morgan says. "Protecting those unfortunates is our only function. How can allowing them to leave the colony be out of our control?"

"It couldn't be avoided, Morgan," Blankenship insists.

"Perhaps not, gentlemen, but it should be a caution for us," Morgan says. "We must re-double our efforts to have the law changed so it cannot happen again. Are we all agreed to that?"

They nod, except for Blankenship.

* * * * *

Back at their stations, the lives of the Indigenous players return to normal, becoming routine. It is nearly as if cricket never existed. Burnett and Lawrence and New South Wales and the MCG fade from memory and the reality of working their mundane jobs replaces any nostalgia they may have dared to feel about those days.

Then winter sets in. The weather in the Western District is especially harsh. Severe frosts bring a penetrating cold that affects both people and animals. Indigenous people in particular are vulnerable to winter diseases. Whereas they had their own medicines and thousands of years of history to help them through these times in the past, now many of them develop serious illnesses. The Indigenous cricketers are no exception.

King Cole and Mullagh are huddled in the stable with some of the horses, sharing what little warmth they emit. Two Penny finds them. "I have been looking all over for you."

King Cole asks, "Why?"

"Jellico is gone," he says.

"Where did he go?" King Cole asks.

"He has passed on. He has joined our ancestors." Two Penny struggles to hold back tears.

"How did you find this out?" Mullagh asks.

"Mr. Edwards was in town. One of the other station managers told him."

King Cole asks, "What happened to him?"

"White man's disease." Two Penny says.

"First one, now two," Mullagh says. Tears fill his eyes.

"These white fella sicknesses will kill us all, eventually," King Cole says, shaking his head slowly. "We want to die in our own ways." Mullagh nods.

* * * * *

Harriman has returned to the Western District with his tail between his legs. His grandiose plans are in tatters. He has managed to appease his investors, but just barely. Were it not for the press coverage of Gurnett's shenanigans, they may not have been so understanding. But they all forgive him with no hard feelings. The only person he talks freely about it with is his neighbour and friend at Pine Hills.

He is having a cup of tea with Mr. Edwards in the lounge room at Pine Hills. "Now, now, Gus, you couldn't have known that Gurnett was such a rascal," Edwards tries to assure his friend.

"To be sure, the fault was mine. I should never have allowed myself to be so vulnerable, so gullible. I gave up control of my own idea to a scoundrel," Harriman says. "If I ever have a chance to . . . Oh, what's the use? The idea is dead and I don't know how to revive it. I'm not even sure I would want to."

"And a good idea it was, Gus. You can be proud of that and what you were able to accomplish in such a short time."

"Even Wills has given up on me," Harriman laments. "Can't say I blame him."

"Experience teaches us that we should never give up on our dreams, Gus. You never know what might happen."

"Thank you, my friend. It is never a waste of time to be in your hopeful company. I'm going to head out now. Please thank Felicity for lunch for me."

"That I will, Gus." Edwards accompanies him onto the veranda and shouts toward the stables, "Johnny, could you bring Mr. Harriman's horse around?"

Mullagh comes out of the stable leading a handsome, black stallion. He leads the animal to Edwards' veranda. "G'day, Mr. Harriman. Nice animal you have here," Mullagh says.

"Nice to see you, Johnny. They say he has some Arabian in him," Harriman says while he mounts. Then, in an effort to save face, he says, "I hope you're keeping your eyes sharp. You never know when we might need you at the crease."

"Oh, I'll be ready, Boss, don't you worry," Mullagh replies.

"Thanks again," Harriman says to Edwards as he trots off.

"You're quite welcome, Gus," Edwards replies. To Mullagh, he says, "Poor chap. He had his heart set on taking you Black fellas to England."

Mullagh makes no response, merely nods and strolls back to the stable.

The truth is that Mullagh has been doing his best to keep sharp. In his down time, he can nearly always be seen with his cricket bat in hand, striking imaginary balls, or perfecting his foot work or throwing a cricket ball at targets he has put up in the paddock. In spite of himself, Mullagh takes great pleasure in being an elite athlete. In his mind, his cricketing days are not over yet.

* * * * *

Charles Lawrence has an interesting history. Before coming to Australia to play for England in 1861, he was an acclaimed cricketer in England, Ireland and Scotland. Even as a youth, he showed such outstanding potential that he was selected to play in key matches against sides with huge reputations throughout Great Britain. His cricket prowess was undeniable. However, his business acumen left much to be desired. Despite his natural optimism, he had failure after failure when he tried to make a quid away from cricket. Once he stepped off a pitch, his luck and life turned sour.

It was no different with The Pier Hotel in Manly. Soon after the Aboriginal team left, his poor management results in loss of his livelihood. Compounding his business failure, his personal life receives an unimaginable jolt: his wife dies in child birth and a few days later, so does the child. He is heartbroken, as any man would be in those circumstances. But for his faith, he may have considered giving it all up.

But after several months of grieving and soul searching, he starts to find his balance once again. He realizes that cricket has been the only thing he ever succeeded at. He has made important contacts in that world throughout his playing and coaching days, both in Australia and Great Britain. At that time in British history, when the Empire was so newly diverse and all roads led to London, it was not uncommon to bring indigenous people from all around the world there to display their cultures in one form or another. Dance programs complete with traditional costumes and instruments were extremely popular, as were demonstrations of traditional skills and artifacts. Anything that was different or exotic would always find a receptive audience in all parts of England. Lawrence knows this and sees it as an opportunity to make up for all his bad business decisions of the past. He recognizes Australia's Indigenous cricketers as his ticket to fame and fortune and begins corresponding with the people he knows in England, floating the idea of bringing an Australian Aboriginal cricket team there on tour.

His first step is to set up a meeting with a Sydney financier named William Smart at his offices in central Sydney. Smart only knows Lawrence as a man who knows his cricket.

"I'm happy to meet you, Charles," Smart says, as they shake hands. "Can I have my secretary fetch you a cup of tea?"

Lawrence is doing everything he can to remain calm. He is nervous, excited and miles out of his comfort zone. "Oh, no," he says. "I'm fine."

"Well then, what is it you want to talk with me about?" Smart asks. "It can't be cricket. I haven't played since I was a lad in school," he says with a smile.

"Well, actually, it is about cricket," Lawrence says.

Smart raises an eyebrow.

Lawrence goes on, "I don't know if you follow the game or not, but a few months ago, an all Aboriginal team from Victoria came up here for some matches. You may have heard about it."

"Yes, I heard something about that." In fact, Smart has no interest in cricket unless there is a financial angle he can exploit.

Lawrence goes on, "They were supposed to go on the England and play there. But it fell through because of a shifty character named Gurnett. I've been in contact with some people I know in Great Britain and they believe the time is right to do just that."

"Take the darkies to England?" Smart asks. He wonders if there's some money to be made and his interest level begins to improve.

"Exactly," Lawrence says. "I have it all worked out. These boys have some decent cricketers on their team, but that's not the draw card. They have also been putting on displays of their athletic and tribal skills that have gone over very well with the public, both here and in Victoria. That, combined with cricket, can be a fortune waiting to be collected."

Smart is now all ears.

Lawrence has overcome his reticence and has a full head of steam as he continues, "These kinds of entertainments are all the rage in England these days. I even have some ideas about costumes for these darkies that will add to it. I am sure I can reach an agreement with Mr. Harriman who has managed the team up until now. That was his entire reason for bringing this Gurnett into it in the first place, to take them to England. I'll keep him on as the team's manager and a partner in this enterprise."

"Interesting," Smart says. "And you came to me for what reason?" He knows he is being coy but now that it's time to talk seriously about a business proposition, he puts on his bargaining hat.

"To become an investor, of course," Lawrence says. "To finance the trip."

"Ah, I see," Smart says. "And I suppose you have already contacted this Harriman in Victoria."

"No, not yet," Lawrence admits. "I didn't want to build his hopes up until I had something more tangible to present."

"Hmm. Of course, I will have to consult with my partner about this. I believe you are asking for a substantial investment and we don't enter into those kinds of things on a whim, There is a lot of risk involved in something with this many moving parts," Smart says. "We'll have to do our due diligence."

"I fully understand," Lawrence says. "I didn't expect to walk out of here today with a bag of money," he jokes.

"Would it be possible for you to come back into town and meet both my business partner and me, say, a week from today? We will have had time to think about this and talk it over," Smart says.

"Yes, indeed, I can." Lawrence stands and extends his hand. "I will see you in a week's time, sir."

Smart also stands and takes Lawrence's hand in both of this. "I want you to leave here with some confidence, Charles. I like it. In my opinion this could be very profitable for us. I will see you in one week."

Once Lawrence is away from Smart's office, he dances a little jig on the footpath. When he notices the passersby looking at him, he smiles and announces sheepishly, "Just had some good news." They smile back at him.

* * * * *

Lawrence and William Smart hire a carriage when their ship arrives in Geelong for the long trip to Harriman's station in the Western District. Smart and his business partner have become the principle investors in Lawrence's scheme. Now they feel they have to get Harriman's blessing in order to move forward. According to Smart, if Harriman isn't a part of it, he could cause problems. It is better business if he has a piece of the enterprise. That would keep him inside the tent. But to Lawrence, there was never any question about Harriman's involvement. This was his idea from the beginning. It is only fair that he participate. So, for entirely different reasons, they agree, which is why they have made the journey.

They are tired and dusty when they arrive at Harriman's homestead. Johnny Cuzens spots Lawrence and rushes up to him. "Good to see you, Mr. Lawrence. You come here all the way from Manly?"

"G'day, Johnny. Yep. We're here to see Mr. Harriman. We want to take you boys to England. Is he here?" Lawrence answers.

"I'll get him for you," Cuzens says, with a happy smile on his face. In a few minutes, Harriman comes out of the house and greets Lawrence. "Charles, it's so good to see you. You look like you've been on the road a while. Come, let's sit on the veranda where you can relax. I'll have the Missus bring us some tea and a bit of lunch."

They shake hands firmly, smiling broadly. "And this is William Smart. He's from Sydney."

"Always glad to meet a friend of Charles', sir. Welcome to our humble abode." They shake hands.

As Lawrence and Smart find chairs on the veranda, Harriman goes inside to tell his wife they have guests for lunch. When he returns, he pulls up a chair next to theirs. "Now, then. To what do I owe this pleasant surprise?" he asks.

"If I may," Smart takes charge. "We are here to bring you into an enterprise that I am told has been close to your heart for some time, Mr. Harriman, taking the all Aboriginal cricket team to tour England."

Harriman is speechless. It's as if his life has been whipped around 180 degrees. The idea of reviving his dream makes his head spin. He is trying to get some perspective. "Please, call me Augustus." As he calms himself, he carefully continues, "It's true. I have been eager to take my boys on tour to England, but how do I fit into your enterprise?" Harriman pulls his chair closer.

"By becoming a partner and managing the team on this tour," Smart says.

Harriman is completely unprepared for such a straight forward offer. In his wildest dreams, he has never thought of anything this simple. He looks from Lawrence to Smart before venturing a response. His mind flashes on his first encounter with Gurnett. While he is excited beyond imagining, he calmly says, "I must say, that is an interesting proposal, but you'll forgive me if I ask a question. Do you intend to draw up a contract for this venture?"

Smart reaches into his bag. "Oh, yes indeed. I had a contract drawn up before we left Sydney. Here's a copy for you. Essentially, it lays out our responsibilities. Mine is to handle the finances. Lawrence's is to coach the team and yours it to manage the entire tour. In the event -- which is devoutly to be wished for – that we turn a profit, those per centages are also laid out. I think you'll find them fair."

Harriman looks at it for a few moments. "You'll forgive me for being so cautious but I'm sure Charles has told you about my previous experience."

Smart nods.

"Of course, I'll have to have my own solicitor look it over."

Smart nods again. "Of course," he says.

Lawrence says, "It's all legal and binding, Augustus. We're going to take the team to England, you and I. I've made a lot of contacts there and they are all eager to have us. I wouldn't even consider doing it without you."

At a moment like this, most men would be humbled. Harriman is not most men. In his mind, this is redemption, exoneration. What he always believed to be a money-making plan is finally going to be realized and he will play a central role. It is fitting.

Meanwhile, Johnny Cuzens finds Bullocky and tells him what Lawrence said about taking the team to England. Bullocky shows his one-tooth-missing smile and keeps grinning while Cuzens explains. "We have to tell everybody," Bullocky says. And in whatever mystical way it happens, the word spreads from station to station among the Indigenous players that touring England is back on.

At Pine Hills, King Cole is the first to hear. He immediately goes to Johnny Mullagh in the stable. "Get your cricket bat out, Unaarrimin. We are going to England." He tells Mullagh all that he knows, then goes on to tell Two Penny and Tiger.

At Mt. Elgin, Dicky Dick and Redcap have been trying to keep in top physical condition since they got back. When they get the news about England, they just nod at each other. They knew it all along. And they are ready.

As soon as possible, all the team members are assembled at Lake Wallace. Lawrence doesn't have the natural ease with them that Wills had, but he has the cricket skills and a soft approach. The combination wins them over.

"Lads, I do not pretend to be Tom Wills. I cannot speak to you in your own tongue but I can tell you, as God is my witness, that we will become a great cricket team before we reach England. But it will take hard work on all our parts. Mr. Harriman will continue managing your affairs and the tour. I'll be your captain. And there's one more thing that we need to do to guarantee success in Great Britain. I want you to work on your tribal skills. We want to impress the British public with your ability to use your own weapons and tools. They have no idea what Australian Aboriginal warriors are capable of. We want to show them. They need to see you as the proud men you are." He has said the right words. The team is willing to give him the benefit of the doubt.

Because he has the best idea of what the British public might want, Lawrence supervises the design of their new cricket uniforms and tribal costumes. He instructs the tailors on the cut of the trousers and colour of the shirts. He decides to have a different colour cap for each man. Each cap has an emblem of a silver boomerang and a cricket bat on it. Long before they make it to England, they will have traded caps several times just for fun. Later, each player chooses a sash of whatever colour he wants so the fans can identify them.

For the tribal displays, his instructions are even more specific. Here is where Lawrence becomes his most creative. He practically stands over the shoulders of the seamstresses to make absolutely certain that his bizarre instructions are carried out to the letter. After they have been completed, he swears all the workers to secrecy. He doesn't even want the Aboriginals to know what they consist of for fear they may rebel. The only thing he leaves to their discretion is footwear, for obvious reasons.

* * * * *

The Secretary of the Aborigines Protection Board has gotten wind of Lawrence's plan to take this reconstituted Indigenous team to Sydney. He has no idea of the England part. In a special meeting, Secretary Morgan informs the other members of the Board.

"We have it from a very reliable source that this English cricketer wants to take the darkies' team back up to New South Wales. I needn't remind you that more members of that team have passed on since they came back to Victoria, likely it was a result of their trauma when they were isolated up there."

Blankenship interrupts. "I believe it was actually the result of the harsh winter in the Western District. Pneumonia, if I'm not mistaken."

Morgan glares at him. "Perhaps. But nevertheless, we must prevent anything like that from happening again."

Dunphy says, "I've also heard something about this tour. Mr. Harriman, who managed the team from the beginning, remains in that capacity. He is a highly respected Victorian station manager. I doubt he would do anything that would put these boys in jeopardy."

Morgan glares at him too. "Gentlemen, we can find all sorts of exceptions and reasons not to protect these darkies, but that is not our mandate." Morgan knows he doesn't have the support to accomplish a complete ban on travel for the team, which he really wants, so he changes tack. "All I'm suggesting is that we keep an eye on these proceedings so that if anything does go amiss, we can step in and take some action. Can we at least agree to that?"

The others nod their approval, except for Blankenship.

* * * * *

Spring comes to the Western District. The harsh winter is a memory. A sense of promise and renewal permeate Harriman's soul. He now has the responsibility of getting this first leg of their journey underway. He needs to prove that he is capable of at least participating in the realization of what was once only a dream. The first leg begins with a trip to Geelong. They will stop along the way to play local teams and thus keep themselves fit. Now that someone else is financing the trip, Harriman is free to provide the best vehicles and accommodations possible. Up until now, most carriage travel in this part of Australia had been drawn by teams of bullocks. But the latest innovation is the horse drawn Conestoga wagon. It had earned its reputation for dependability and durability in America where it took pioneers across the Great Plains and into the West. This is the wagon Harriman decides will best characterize the uniqueness of the journey. To transport his Aboriginal cricket team in this iconic American wagon says it all. A second vehicle, a baggage cart, carries all their gear. The entourage consists of Harriman, Lawrence, a cook, a coachman and the twelve Indigenous players.

Their first stop is to be Warrnambool. Everyone is excited to start the journey to England. For the Aboriginals, it is like a party. They often walk alongside the wagon and have impromptu races or toss a cricket ball back and forth, always laughing and having fun.

The Conestoga wagon is bouncing along the track on a lovely Spring day. Birds are chirping. Insects are buzzing. And all of a sudden the tranquility is shattered when Bush rangers appear out of nowhere and shout, "Stand and deliver!" Four armed men have their weapons raised. The team of horses is pulled up to a halt. Lawrence and Harriman are taken by surprise and have no opportunity to draw their weapons. Harriman is distraught. All he can think is how inauspicious their start is. Lawrence is cooler. His eyes find Mullagh, who had been playing catch with Sundown. They exchange a look and read each others' thoughts.

"Gentlemen," Lawrence shouts to the robbers, "we are but a team of cricketers on our way to play a match in Warrnambool. Surely there is nothing we have that is of any value to you, just some cricket equipment, some balls and bats and a bit of tucker for while we travel." He keeps talking to draw their focus and, hopefully, identify their leader. "We are more than happy to share what little food we have with you, but as for anything of commercial value,"

"Shut your bloody mouth." It turns out that the smallest man among them is their leader. "You don't fool me," he says. "You've got to have something we want or you wouldn't talk so bloody much. Let's have a look, shall we?"

Before he can move and while everyone's attention is focused on the head outlaw, Lawrence makes the slightest nod toward Mullagh. In an instant, Mullagh rifles the cricket ball he is holding directly onto the forehead of the leader with a force that nearly knocks him off his horse. Lawrence immediately draws his weapon and fires it into the air. The startled bush rangers quickly scatter in all directions and disappear into the bush.

The team gathers around Mullagh afterwards, slapping him on the back and laughing.

"Looks like you took a wicket with that one, Unaarrimin," King Cole chuckles. "He never saw it coming."

Lawrence dismounts and joins them. "Well done, Johnny. Well done, lad, well done."

Mullagh smiles, "I read your mind, Boss."

Harriman has also dismounted but instead of joining the others, he wanders off the track and into the bush. At first, Lawrence thinks Harriman must be relieving himself, but when he doesn't come out, Lawrence grows concerned. He starts to follow where Harriman went when he hears Harriman call out, "Dicky Dick, can you come in here and help me find the cricket ball Johnny Mullagh threw? It came over this way somewhere. It's brand new. We don't want to lose it. These things cost money."

Dicky Dick walks into the bush where Harriman is and in thirty seconds walks out again with a big smile on his face and the cricket ball in his hand. In language he says, "It was real hard to spot this red ball against the green leaves."

But, Spring doesn't just bring a sense of renewal. It also brings thunderstorms. Late the next day, toward evening, the skies open up and a deluge follows. The road, which is questionable to begin with, becomes a quagmire. In practically no time, the wagon gets bogged.

Harriman is perplexed once again and begins to wonder to himself if the whole operation has been cursed. "What are we going to do now?" he cries out.

Lawrence looks at the situation. "We're pretty well bogged here. We might be able to get out of it but I think it's too late to try. It will be dark soon. And we would also have to unload the wagon first. Hmm." He strokes his chin and thinks about it.

As Lawrence is pondering the situation, King Cole motions to the other teammates to join him. The rain is pouring down. In language, he says, "Let's build a hut. If we wait for these white fellas to figure things out, we will all be drowned."

Without asking permission or any hesitation, some get busy finding material lying around in the bush that can be used to build an adequate shelter. Others find a place to build a fire and get that started. Another one or two go searching for bush tucker.

Harriman and Lawrence stand and watch as a shelter large enough to accommodate everyone begins to take shape. Dicky Dick goes over to them. "We can unpack the wagon in the morning and get it going then. In the meantime, we'll have a dry place to eat and have a sleep . . . if that's all right with you gents," he smiles.

Before long, the shelter is complete and the fire is roaring. Bullocky has fetched his didgeridoo from the luggage cart and after everyone has had a feed, he begins blowing it, emitting its hauntingly plaintive baritone twang and wow. Mullagh has found some wood he can use as clap sticks and soon a mini-corroboree is underway. The Aboriginal men are having the time of their lives. The white fellas look on with wonder as the team entertains them with a little spontaneous bush culture. Outside, the cold rain continues to pour down on their makeshift refuge.

Next morning, they carefully unload the wagon. The rain has stopped but the ground is wet. It takes an hour or so, but eventually they are able to muscle the wagon out of the mud, some pulling, some pushing and some tugging on the horses. Once it's clear, they re-pack the wagon and continue on their way.

Lawrence is gaining a new respect for his Black teammates. The speech he made at their first meeting about them being Aboriginal warriors and proud men was made mostly for effect. Now that he has had a chance to see them functioning in their natural environment, he realizes that his language was not hyperbole or flattering. It was fact.

* * * * *

After one more minor mishap, when Johnny Cuzens decided he wanted to see if he could drive the wagon and ended up being thrown from it onto his head, the entourage arrives in Warrnambool. During their almost two-week stay, they play one match with a group of local cricketers. The rest of the time they relax and recuperate from the journey. The local newspaper, like all the others before it, lavishes praise on the Indigenous players and the way they conduct themselves on and off the pitch. It describes them as being like a happy little family.

As the self-appointed father of this happy little family, coupled with his newfound "respect" for his teammates, Lawrence does what many people in his situation do. He decides to introduce them to a better way of thinking and being and believing; one that takes the myths and superstitions that they and all their ancestors have lived with for millennia, and replaces them with this own myths and superstitions.

Christianity is one of the constant themes among Europeans, as regards the Indigenous people. It is generally agreed among Christians that the Aboriginals must become acquainted with Jesus and his teachings for their own good, not to mention for their salvation. Anyone who doesn't know the principles provided by the Gospels cannot possibly survive contemporary life. It should be said that this has been the modus operandi of the religion throughout its history. Lawrence is himself a devout Christian and often sprinkles his talk with references to God, in general, and Christ, in particular.

One day, when they are just lazing around, Lawrence begins talking about his faith. Dicky Dick and Johnny Cuzens are especially intrigued by Lawrence's simple interpretation of some of Jesus' parables. On the following Sunday, he invites these two to join him for church services. They agree. It is a way to kill some time and could be interesting. Just as the white fellas are becoming better acquainted with the ways of their traveling companions, the Black fellas are doing the same thing.

Afterwards, back at their lodgings, they discuss the church experience. Dicky Dick is particularly interested in the collection plate. "Who gets all that money?" he asks.

"Who do you reckon?" Lawrence asks in return.

"I reckon it's that preacher bloke," Dicky Dick answers.

"And what do you think he does with it?"

"Puts it in his pocket." Johnny Cuzens nods agreement.

"That's where you are wrong, my friends," Lawrence says. "He gives that money to poor people for food or clothing or medicine or whatever they need. It is what Jesus teaches us, that we have a responsibility to those less fortunate than we are. We must show them God's generosity and love."

Dicky Dick and Johnny Cuzens stare at Lawrence, then at each other. They are incredulous.

Lawrence is pleased that his teachings seem to have been sown in fertile ground. "I'm happy you lads came with me this morning. And I hope you will consider coming with me again. I'm off now. See you at practice," he says as he leaves their room.

Now that they are alone, Dicky Dick and Johnny Cuzens discuss it further. "I am not sure about this Jesus bloke," Dicky Dick says. "Our people know that we are all sons and daughters of Nature. We are natural people, not more than Nature and not less. We are a part of Nature. If this Jesus bloke is preaching that Nature and God are the same thing, I agree with him. But if he thinks God is separate from Nature . . . "

"Tell me something," Cuzens says. "If that preacher bloke gives that money to poor people for food and medicine and clothes, how come they come here to our country and take all those things away from us?"

Dicky Dick thinks about it a moment. "I don't think we should go back to church with Mr. Lawrence. What do you think?"

"I think you are right." They shake hands on it.

The relaxation time is over and it's time to move on. Their travel routine is quickly re-established, with the exception that only the coachman will drive the wagon. Harriman does not want a repeat of Johnny Cuzens' accident. The team is thin enough already, in his opinion.

Once again, the players continue to play their made up games along the trail. But this time, with an eye out for unexpected visitors. Several of them are now carrying cricket balls in their hands and Lawrence makes sure his weapon is easily accessible. But there is no sign of bush rangers anywhere between Warrnambool and their next stop 30 miles away, Mortlake.

Here they are planning to play a match with some of the locals when the weather intervenes. The pitch becomes so sodden that any ball that isn't caught plops down into the mud without a bounce. No one cares that the Aboriginal team is ahead when the match is called off. They just want to get dry.

Their next destination is Geelong. The match scheduled here has extra special significance for the team. Tom Wills has come up to captain their opponents. In the change rooms before the game, Wills and his former teammates are in high spirits as they banter and laugh together.

"Do you remember what you told Mr. Lawrence in Sydney about getting his head taken off?" Mullagh says as he smiles at Wills.

"Oh, yes. I remember it very well," Wills answers and adds in language, "You better look out for your own head. I'll be bowling for my team." They both have a good laugh.

Dicky Dick says, "Wait until you see the show we put on after the match. We have added a few new tricks."

"I just hope the weather holds up so we can have some fun," Wills says.

On the pitch, the match is like a huge party. One thousand people show up to watch two teams have so much fun that the outcome of the contest is almost irrelevant. Just as at every venue before, the Geelong spectators are here to see how well the Black fellas can play cricket. They soon find out. The Aboriginals easily outclass Wills' side and spend the entire match rubbing it in. All in good fun.

After the cricket, Wills watches with keen interest as Dicky Dick puts on his part of the show. When they were brainstorming ideas that could have appeal with their white audiences, Dicky Dick suggested what has now become a staple in the show: A few men from among the spectators are given cricket balls. They surround Dicky Dick and from a designated distance, throw the balls at him with all their might. Wills counts sixty balls that Dicky Dick dodges successfully. He is untouched. The crowd loves it.

For a laugh, Mullagh urges Wills to pick up a ball and walk out toward Dicky Dick to see what he will do. Wills loves the idea. He walks out onto the pitch and into Dicky Dick's field of vision tossing a cricket ball up and catching it. Ever the showman, Dicky Dick seizes the moment and runs toward Wills wagging his finger back and forth and shaking his head, yelling, "Oh, no. Not this bloke." The crowd explodes with laughter.

After the match, several of the players have congregated in Mullagh's room. It is a time to bask in the glow of their victory and let off a bit of steam. They are engrossed in a discussion about who they should go to in order to ensure they get the most reliable boomerangs and spears for their tribal performances.

All of a sudden, Dicky Dick shushes them. He has heard something. He creeps to the door, peers through the keyhole and sees the owner of this establishment slowly making his way toward their door. He stops and puts his ear to it, where he can eavesdrop on their talk.

Dicky Dick indicates that they should continue talking. As they begin to chatter once again, he raises his voice above theirs and interrupts, "I am very angry at the man who owns this pub. The food he gives us is rotten and these beds are filled with bugs. I think we should skin him like a possum and set fire to this building."

Dicky Dick watches through the keyhole as the man hurries away from the door and down the hall. The publican pounds on Lawrence's door and continues pounding until he hears Lawrence's sleepy voice say, "Just a minute."

When Lawrence opens the door, the publican is shaking with fear. Through his panic, he makes it clear what the darkies have said. Lawrence asks him to wait until he can pull on some trousers and they walk down the hallway to Mullagh's room.

Lawrence taps on the door and opens it. "Lads, our host is a bit concerned," Lawrence says. "He believes you mean to do him harm."

Dicky Dick says, "Oh, do you mean about skinning him and burning down the building?"

The publican recognizes the voice. "That's him," he says. "He's the one who threatened me."

Mullagh speaks up. "Dicky Dick heard him at the door listening to us talk and decided to have a little fun. It's just a joke."

"You were listening at their door?" Lawrence asks the publican.

The man is exposed and embarrassed. By now the Aboriginals are all having a good laugh. He softens and joins them. "You got me," he says. "Sorry, gents."

Lawrence says, "No harm done. All right, lads, time to get some sleep. We've got an early start tomorrow."

* * * * *

When they learn that the Indigenous team is in Warrnambool and intending to go on to Geelong, Ballarat and, Bendigo, The Aborigines Protection Board calls a special meeting. Chairman Morgan has the bit in his teeth about Lawrence and Harriman taking the team to Sydney. Despite the fact that there are no legal grounds, Morgan is undeterred in trying to prevent this trip.

"Gentlemen," he begins, "we have an opportunity to stop those men from taking our charges out of the colony. And I believe we must seize it before we regret taking no action at all."

"We have been all through this before," Blankenship says, not trying to conceal his impatience with Morgan's fixation.

"I do not give a damn," Morgan shouts. "Have you no compassion, sir? These unfortunate natives are being exploited. Think of them."

"I do think of them. But I also think of the law and the law says we cannot intervene. It has nothing to do with compassion," Blankenship replies.

Owens tries to find middle ground. "I suggested before that we might – how can I put this – assume . . . no, maybe pretend is a better word. Why can't we pretend that we have the authority to step in and protect these darkies? Just use our position as guardians to try to stop their departure from our jurisdiction. That might work."

Dunphy asks, "You mean bluff them?"

"I do not like the word, but, yes, bluff them," Owens replies.

Morgan is pleased with the direction of the conversation. "Gentlemen, I think you are onto something. My suggestion is that we get to Geelong as soon as possible, before they have a chance to go on to Ballarat. The sooner we intercept them, the better. I will happily lead."

Blankenship shakes his head slowly. "I do not wish to be any part of this illegal action," he says.

"So noted," Morgan responds. "May I assume, then, that we have reached a consensus?"

All but Blankenship express their approval.

"Then it is settled. We will intercept them in Geelong before they set out for Ballarat."

* * * * *

Lawrence and Harriman are sitting at a table in the hotel's pub. Harriman is concerned. He has heard some things. "I am almost certain that the Aborigines Protection Board is going to try to keep us from leaving Victoria."

"Didn't you get permission from the government?" Lawrence asks.

"I did and I have it with me. But a friend in Melbourne sent me a letter that I received yesterday," Harriman replies. "He said one of the board members told him directly. If they have any idea that we are actually taking the team to England, they could try to thwart all our plans."

Lawrence nods. He loses himself in thought for few moments. Then he has an idea. "What if we change our plans? What if we say we are going on to Ballarat and Bendigo, but instead, we go to New South Wales? Once we are out of the colony, we will be safe."

Now it's Harriman's turn to think. Finally, he says, "If you can get us a few matches in Sydney, they will make up for the matches we miss in Victoria. That would keep the boys fit. I'll make the arrangements. We can get a ship from here in Geelong."

Lawrence thinks a moment. "Wait. Get a ship from Queenscliff. That way we can leave here and they may not catch up with us." Harriman agrees and starts for his room to pack. Lawrence continues. "I will tell the lads to pack their gear. The sooner we get moving, the better." Lawrence says.

A few hours later, all their gear is packed and they are ready to head off to Queenscliff. As luck would have it, Secretary Morgan and his delegation arrive just as they are coming out of their lodgings. "Who is in charge here?" Morgan thunders. Harriman answers, "Mr. Lawrence and I are. May I ask who you are, sir?"

"Morgan is the name. I am the secretary of the Aborigines Protection Board. These are my associates, Mr. Dunphy and Mr. Owens. Tell me, sir, do you intend to take these darkies out of Victoria?"

Harriman is indignant. "I have written permission from the government to take this team to New South Wales."

"Consider that permission revoked," Morgan answers with a great air of authority. "We have spoken with the government and they have reconsidered."

"I have not been made aware of any changes," Harriman says. He is beginning to lose his composure.

Lawrence decides to step in. "Mr. Secretary, perhaps I can clear things up. We were planning to take the boys to New South Wales. That is true. But they are fatigued and in need of some rest and relaxation. I intended to tell Mr. Harriman just before you arrived. We hadn't had a chance to discuss it. Mr. Harriman is unaware of this decision. He has been busy with other things."

Harriman shoots a glance at Lawrence. He wonders what Lawrence is leading up to but can't ask.

Morgan is not swayed. "And where do you intend to go with all this gear?"

"I was going to suggest that Mr. Harriman go ahead of us and get accommodations in Queenscliff so we can give the boys a little fishing holiday before we return to the Western District. Obviously, we have to take all our equipment with us for the journey home."

Harriman catches on. "I wish you had told me that before, Charles. But I suppose you didn't really have an opportunity since I've been so busy. This changes everything. I'm sorry, Mr. Morgan, if I seemed abrupt with you. Please accept my apology.

And with your permission, I'd like to leave for Queenscliff and see to these details."

"Just a minute," Morgan says. "Are you not planning to play matches in Ballarat and Bendigo?"

"No, sir. The lads are exhausted. We're going straight home after the fishing," Lawrence says. As if on cue, all the players begin looking tired and worn out.

Morgan looks from Lawrence to Harriman. "I sincerely trust you are not trying to hoodwink us. We will not tolerate any chicanery."

"We are going to Queenscliff. I can assure you, Mr. Secretary," Lawrence says in his most convincing voice.

Morgan knows he cannot now execute his plan to forbid the Aboriginals from leaving for New South Wales. But he needs to save face in front of his colleagues and these cricket people. "Let me advise you in no uncertain terms that we shall pursue this to the extent of the law if you dare violate my, er, um, our orders. The full extent."

"There will be no need of that, sir," Harriman says. "Now, I must be off to make arrangements for these poor, fatigued darkies." He leaves to find transportation for himself to Queenscliff.

Lawrence says, "Gentlemen, you must be a bit parched from your journey here. Will you give me the pleasure of shouting you a bite to eat and some refreshments? I believe my lads could also use a feed before we go. Is that right, lads?" He hears no descent.

Neither Dunphy nor Owens needs to be asked twice. They are on their way inside the pub. Morgan has no choice but to follow them. Harriman looks at Lawrence to get his attention. When he does, his eyes say, *Nice job*.

Lawrence smiles.

As soon as his lunch guests have left, Lawrence gets the team mobilized. "Come on, lads, we have to make tracks before those Protection blokes change their minds.

Dicky Dick says, "I thought we were too exhausted, Boss."

Lawrence says, "Not now, please. We are in a race with time. Now, hop to."

Mullagh looks over his teammates and says, in language, "This is our chance to go to England. We can always have a laugh in Sydney." He doesn't have to say anything else. Immediately, the Indigenous players get onboard or take their places alongside the wagon. They are soon on their way.

* * * * *

Secretary Morgan is troubled as he and his colleagues head back to Melbourne. Something tells him that the managers of the cricket team are up to something. It's only an instinct. He is torn between taking the time to explain to his colleagues why they should turn around and just ordering the driver to do so and be done with it. He doesn't like having to force his will on them, but whatever this feeling is continues to nag at him. Before long, it becomes too much and he has to take action. "Driver," he shouts out the window. "Stop the coach."

Dunphy and Owens brace themselves as the driver applies his brake. "What is it, Morgan?" Dunphy asks.

"We have to go back. Those two are up to something," he says with conviction.

Neither of his colleagues would challenge anything Morgan says. They always leave that to Blankenship. Owens asks, "What did you notice? Why do you think that?"

"I just know it. They are up to something. We have to . . . Driver, turn around and let us head back . . . We have to intercept that wagon . . . We have to find out what they are up to. Are you gentlemen agreed?" he asks.

Both Dunphy and Owens nod their heads and brace themselves once more as the coach swings around 180 degrees.

* * * * *

Lawrence is sitting up next to the driver. "You know, mate, I have a bad feeling about those Protection blokes."

The driver says, "Funny you should say that. I was thinking the same thing when we were back there. What do you reckon?"

"I reckon we ought to get a move on. It can't hurt to arrive as soon as possible." He calls out to the players, "We're going to try to make some better time, lads. You will either have to jump onboard or you might have to trot to keep up. As you wish."

The driver cracks the reins and the horses pick up their pace. Most of the players who have been trotting alongside the wagon hop onboard. Mullagh and Johnny Cuzens continue to run with the horses. But soon they look at each other and nod. They jump onto the baggage cart.

* * * * *

Morgan and the Board have arrived back in Geelong. Morgan asks at the hotel keeper how long ago the Indigenous team left. The publican has no intention to giving these stuffed shirts any useful information. He answers, "Well, sir, I know it was after you people went toward Melbourne. I must have lost track of time. And for the life of me, I cannot remember exactly how long. I just cannot say for sure. I wish I could be more help to you, sir."

Morgan is erupting with anger on the inside. But he merely smiles and says, "Thank you for your help, sir." He goes back to the coach and demands that the driver get some fresh horses. He says, "And make it snappy. We need to catch that wagon and there's no time to lose."

* * * * *

The Conestoga wagon is traveling at a brisk pace, with Mullagh and Cuzens having to hang on to whatever they can for fear of falling off the baggage cart. Lawrence is feeling anxious. He turns to the coachman and asks, "How much longer to you reckon we will be? How far away are we?"

The coachman replies with confidence, "I reckon another five minutes or so. We might have gotten there sooner but the horses are starting to slow down a bit. They are getting tired and I don't want to force them."

* * * * *

The landscape flies by. Dunphy and Owens are holding on for dear life as the carriage sways and bounces along at top speed. They are terrified. Morgan is on the edge of his seat looking out the window at the road ahead. If he could, he would get out and push the horses even faster. Huge clouds of dust swirl in their wake.

* * * * *

"Isn't that Mr. Harriman up there?" the coachman asks. Harriman is waiting at the pier. His sense of relief on seeing the wagon come into view is palpable. "Thank God," he mutters to himself. As the wagon is pulling up to the dock, even before it comes to a complete stop, he calls out, "All right, boys, let's get everything unloaded and onto this boat. It will take us out to that bigger one out there." He points out to the small ship that will take them to Sydney. Everyone helps in unloading the gear with a sense of urgency.

* * * * *

The fresh horses are now all lathered up from galloping at top speed for such a long time. The driver is concerned but says nothing. Morgan has already paid him handsomely in advance. It is hard to hear anything above the coach's squeaks and clatter. Morgan has to shout at the top of his lungs, "How much longer?" The driver looks back toward the coach and holds his hand wide, showing five fingers which he wiggles for Morgan to see. Dunphy and Owens are pale as sheets. Morgan has his jaw set. "Five more minutes and I've got them," he says to himself.

* * * * *

Harriman tells the boatman to shove off as he steps onboard the craft. He is the last passenger. "We need to get to that ship as quickly as possible," he shouts. In seconds, they are untied and away from the dock, on their way toward the waiting ship. Before they are a hundred yards out from land, Harriman hears some raised voices from back on shore. He turns to see Morgan, red faced, shouting hysterically and shaking his fists.

"Charles," Harriman calls. "Come look at this." He points back at Morgan.

Lawrence joins him. He has a smile on his face as he says, "Looks like they just missed us. What a pity. I think we should wave goodbye."

So, while Morgan is screaming and jumping up and down with frustration on shore, Lawrence and Harriman are smiling and waving happily from the water.

* * * * *

Newspapers in both Victoria and New South Wales get wind of the slick coup Harriman and Lawrence pulled off. They unanimously agree that the Aborigines Protection Board deserves whatever humiliation it receives. Most people in the colony believe they over stepped their bounds, that they were more concerned with the appearances than the actual opportunity this represents for Aboriginal Australians. *The Argus* told its readers that the Black cricketers were, in an expression of the day, too many for the Board. *The Age* used different language, saying that the Board had been checkmated by the managers. *The Australasian* and *The SydneyMorning Herald* both congratulated the men they referred to as the smugglers. Yet another Sydney paper said that the Board tried to keep the team from leaving, but were outsmarted by Messrs. Harriman and Lawrence.

Secretary Morgan can hardly show his face in Melbourne. His zeal and tunnel vision have resulted in serious damage to the Aborigines Protection Board's reputation as a caretaker of Indigenous people. At their next meeting, Blankenship says not a word, but sits there with a slight smile on his face.

Chapter Eight – The Vast Beyond

The boat ride from Queenscliff to Sydney is like a victory lap. Now that they are out of the Protection Board's jurisdiction, everyone is celebrating. The other players are teasing Mullagh and Cuzens.

Dicky Dick says, "We didn't know where you two were. The last we saw you were trying to keep up with the horses. Then, you disappeared."

Mullagh laughs. "I thought poor, little Johnny here was going to fall off the baggage cart. I had to grab him a few times to hold him on."

Cuzens is laughing too. "If Mullagh hadn't grabbed me I would have been lost like Bullocky's didgeridoo."

Bullocky panics. "Did you lose my didgeridoo?"

King Cole pulls it out of the bag where the cricket bats are carried. "Does it look like this?"

Johnny Cuzens points his finger at Bullocky. "We almost got you." Everyone has a good laugh. Even Bullocky smiles his one-tooth-missing smile.

Lawrence and Harriman are discussing where they should make their home base in the Sydney area now that The Pier Hotel is under new management.

"I don't want to cause you any unnecessary woe," Harriman says. "But that former hotel of yours in

Manly was a convenient location and the boys are accustomed to it . . ."

"Don't let that concern you, Augustus. The gent who took over the license is a mate. He will be happy to welcome us back there. And I agree, Manly is a good location."

"Are you sure you can handle it?" Harriman asks sympathetically.

Lawrence nods. "As to my feelings, let me just say that I am only focused on getting our lads to England. Everything else is behind me now."

* * * * *

With the team comfortably ensconced at The Pier Hotel, Lawrence gets busy arranging some matches. The first is in Woolongong. The team is not nearly as rusty as he had feared they might be. The Aboriginals win easily against the Illawarra team they meet there. However, their performance after the match is interrupted when some fans charge onto the field and intentionally get in the way of Dicky Dick and Johnny Cuzens while they are running a backward race. This causes some distress among the players. This is a new experience. They are not accustomed to this kind of unruly behaviour. To them, it seems to have unwelcome racial overtones. They have always been conscious of maintaining a certain decorum. They expect the same from white fellas.

Next they go to East Maitland and after that to Newcastle. They dominate in those two matches as well. And the fans are better controlled. Harriman and Lawrence are pleased with the way the team conducts itself both on and off the pitch. They are also on the alert for people who might not be there just for the spectacle. So far, at least, the vast majority of spectators have been supportive of the Indigenous players. They want to keep it that way, if at all possible.

The only match they lose is against the Albert Club, at the same venue where Burnett caused his ruckus. Lawrence has conflicting loyalties for this one. It is the team he coached for so long. The Albert Club ends up eking out a victory.

In the change rooms after the match, Lawrence gets the team's attention. "Lads," he says, "I'll be leaving you for a short time when you play at Bathurst on Boxing Day. I've been contracted to go down to Melbourne for a match at the MCG."

Johnny Cuzens asks, "Who is going to run the team while you are gone?" When the others hear the question, they immediately look in Mullagh's direction.

Mullagh knows the position he occupies with the team, but decides this is not the time for him. He shakes his head and says, "I think King Cole should be our captain for Boxing Day. Anybody else think that's a good idea?"

The others understand immediately and in a chorus say, "Yes!"

Lawrence says, "That is decided then. King Cole it is."

Nothing of any consequence takes place at Bathurst and after the holidays, the team is back at The Pier Hotel relaxing. Lawrence has returned from playing in Melbourne at the MCG and Harriman has gone on ahead of everyone else to England to see to things there.

One afternoon in February, while they are lazing around, Lawrence comes bounding into Mullagh's room where most of the team is congregated. Lads," he says. "We are about to have the experience of a lifetime." He can hardly contain his excitement.

"We are going to fly to England on an eagle's back," Dicky Dick jokes.

"No. Better than that," Lawrence says. "We are going to have another match at the Albert Club."

"What's so great about that?" Johnny Cuzens asks.

"The Duke of Edinburgh will be there to see us," Lawrence says. It is clear that he is awed by the mere thought of it.

"Who is he?" Bullocky asks.

King Cole says, "He's the King of England. That's who he is."

Lawrence doesn't like this joking. To him it is disrespectful. "Now listen, lads. We will soon be on our way to England where royalty is very important indeed. The Duke of Edinburgh is Queen Victoria's second son and, therefore, a member of the royal family. Queen Victoria is the monarch of Australia. Australia is part of her Empire. Playing a game of cricket before him is a great privilege. It is almost like playing before the Queen, herself. You should feel honoured."

In language, Mullagh says, "He must be like some kind of an elder. Be nice."

The message must have gotten through. The team scores their highest first innings totals ever, 237 runs. Johnny Cuzens takes eight wickets and scores 86 runs to lead the team. The Duke of Edinburgh is present for two of the three days, despite the fact that he isn't much of a cricket enthusiast. And you'd have thought Lawrence just got knighted he is so happy.

* * * * *

A few days later, on the 8th of February 1868, against all odds of it ever happening, an all Australian Aboriginal cricket team stands at a dock in

Sydney, staring at the largest sailing ship they've ever seen, The Parramatta. Its three masts reach into the sky like gigantic gum trees. It is over two hundred feet long and almost forty feet wide. In addition to its cargo, it has accommodations for enough passengers to make up a small village. It dwarfs any other water conveyance they have seen, let alone boarded. They had been mightily impressed by the little ship that brought them to Sydney from Queenscliff. They approach The Parramatta cautiously, as if it were some kind of other worldly marvel.

They are dressed in the latest fashions as they gaze up at this behemoth. Harriman had insisted before he left for England that the team be presented at its finest from the time they board the ship until they leave England to go back home. They are dressed as gentlemen. Dicky Dick even has a top hat that he purchased at a shop in Melbourne.

"Come on, lads," Lawrence encourages them. "This is going to be your home for the next few months. Let's get onboard and get acquainted."

The Indigenous men just stand there, waiting to see who will be the first to start up the gangway. No one seems too eager. Finally, Dicky Dick doffs his hat to the ship and starts his ascent. "I believe it's this way . . . gentlemen," he says. The others laugh and then follow, reluctantly at first, but eventually realize that it is a *fait accompli*, and board with no further hesitation. Mullagh brings up the rear, not because of any fear or trepidation, but because he sees himself as their shepherd.

Once they are all onboard, they are led to a large cabin amidships which will be their ocean home. Each of them is silently pleased that they will all be together, rather than in separate cabins. They may be onboard an ocean going vessel, but that doesn't mean they are comfortable with the idea yet. Being in one cabin together makes them feel safe.

The captain of the ship, Captain Williams, is there to greet them and try to allay any fears they may have about travelling on the ocean. "Boys," he says, "this should be an easy crossing. The Parramatta is a sound, Blackwall frigate. It is made of the finest teak wood. That may not mean much to you, but what it says is that this ship was built especially to carry people and cargo from England to India or Australia and back again, safely, through any weather. In other words, you are in good hands onboard this beautiful sailing vessel. I have personally made these voyages many times and I am still here." He laughs, hoping this will loosen the Black fellas up a bit.

They are not quite ready to relax just yet, but they give him their full attention. Captain Williams continues, "We will be shoving off in a few short hours so let me suggest you get your gear stowed and make your way up on deck. You'll want to watch as we sail through this beautiful Sydney harbor. There is nothing like the thrill of watching the land recede and looking out into the vast beyond. It is not a sight you'll easily forget and you should not miss it."

Captain Williams starts toward the door and pauses. He turns back. "Mr. Lawrence, with your permission, I would like to conduct prayer meetings with these boys on a regular basis. They should know that Jesus is watching over them and protecting them from harm. And if there is any time you or any of your charges require any information or reassurance or anything whatsoever, I am at your service."

"Thank you, Captain," Lawrence replies. "I think a regular prayer service will be good for all of us."

Dicky Dick and Cuzens exchange a glance.

"All right, lads," Lawrence says, "let's give the captain a hip, hip . . ."

The team adds, "Hooray!"

For the next half-an-hour or so, they busy themselves picking places to stow their gear and making the large cabin into a space comfortable enough for their needs. It isn't long before it morphs into a satisfactory home. They have certainly had to make do with much less in the past. King Cole sums it up for everyone when he says, "It isn't the bush, but it will have to do."

Now that everything is under control in their living space, Lawrence leads them up to the top deck and toward the stern. Many of the other passengers are already there introducing themselves and chatting. Most of them are Australian, so when the Indigenous players walk in their direction, the chattering stops. A few knew they would be travelling with a cricket team, but no one told them what colour it was. The atmosphere becomes awkward.

Dicky Dick, always the diplomat and entertainer, breaks the ice. He walks directly at them. The others follow behind him. He clears his throat and at his most charming, asks, "Who would like to learn how to throw a boomerang? Would you like me to show you?"

Women and children are among the passengers. For the kids, any racial consideration takes a back seat when weighed against the option of seeing an Aboriginal man throw a boomerang and teaching them how. A loud chorus of, "Me! Me! Me!" follows.

Dicky Dick produces the boomerang he carried up with him and gathers the kids around him. He says, "Give me a little room. I don't want to hit anyone in the head, except maybe him." He points at Bullocky who flashes his one-tooth-missing smile at them. The children laugh.

Dicky Dick suddenly has a better idea. "I am a good boomerang thrower," Dicky Dick says, "but our leader, this man, Johnny Mullagh, is the champion. Johnny, come up here and show these children what to do."

Mullagh is not prepared for this, but he knows it is important to create a positive impression on their fellow passengers. He steps up. Dicky Dick hands him the boomerang.

While Mullagh is checking the wind, Dicky Dick says, "Clear out that space just there," and points to an area in front of where they are standing. The passengers make room.

"You hold it like this," Mullagh says, as he demonstrates. "And you throw from your shoulder. That is the way my father taught me and how to get the truest throw. The boomerang will do the rest."

All eyes are on him as he steps into his throw and the boomerang flies out beyond the stern. The passengers watch as the weapon swings in a wide arc and comes back, landing in the area that Dicky Dick had cleared.

They all burst into applause, men, women and children. Mullagh has already eased back out of the spotlight. But Dicky Dick is ready. He doffs his hat and makes a deep bow. The team all smile at Dicky Dick and then nod at each other. They are welcomed onboard by their fellow passengers. It promises to be a good voyage.

* * * * *

King Cole and Bullocky are standing alongside the deck rail, looking out at the ocean. It has been a week since The Parramatta set sail. The strong wind fills the great white sheets of canvas fore and aft as the ship cuts through the waves. There is nothing but water on every side, an endless view of nothing familiar. Occasionally dolphins frolic alongside the ship, but even though dolphins are not unknown to Indigenous people, they have always been near land. Seeing them out here, bounding along next to the ship, even they look foreign

For a long time they look out in silence. Then King Cole says, "I don't like having to wear all these clothes all the time. I'd like to build a fire and cook a kangaroo. Do you remember what walking on country feels like? I don't."

"I was thinking about shearing sheep before I fell asleep last night," he smiles his one-tooth-missing smile. "I miss being on the land too," Bullocky says.

Soon Johnny Cuzens joins them. As if he had been privy to their conversation, he says with a sigh, "Look at this." He points out at the rolling ocean. "This is all we will see for months."

The three of them continue to look out in silence, searching in vain for something familiar, something that will ground them, as it were.

Charles Lawrence sees them and approaches. "There you are, lads. Beautiful sight, isn't it? Smell that fresh sea breeze."

They continue to look without responding.

"All right, lads, it's time we go below and have our English lesson," Lawrence says.

Reluctantly, they follow him to the cabin. Lawrence has decided that it would be useful for the Aboriginals to learn the basics of reading and writing and has taken it upon himself to be their teacher. This is a bad idea for two reasons. First, Lawrence has no idea where to begin when it comes to teaching anything but cricket. Second, as a group, the team isn't interested in learning anything but cricket from Lawrence.

This is the second day of their lessons. They all have pencils and paper. Lawrence goes through what he believes is a proper teaching routine. He writes the letter A on the slate, first as a capital and next to it in lower case. "This is the first letter of the alphabet, remember? What is it called?"

No one responds. "Right. It is called A," Lawrence says. "Copy it down on your papers."

Each of them copies both A's. He continues this way through the rest of the alphabet, just as he did yesterday. "All right, lads, copy all these letters a few times and say them until you can do it all by heart."

They follow Lawrence's instructions by rote with no enthusiasm.

Suddenly Tarpot says, "Look. I made a wombat out of the little M." He shows it to the others. Tarpot is acknowledged as the premier artist among them.

A few minutes later, with a certain amount of artistic pride, Tiger says, "I made this one (he is pointing to a Q) into an emu.

King Cole doesn't have the artistic talent of his teammates, but he gives it a go anyway. He looks from one letter to another hoping for inspiration. Finally, he settles on the S. "Don't anybody use the S. I'm going to make it into my totem, the snake."

Lawrence is quick to seize this opportunity. "That's good, King. Snake starts with the letter S." He writes S-N-A-K-E on his slate. "See? This is how it is written."

Johnny Cuzens gets an inspiration. "Look. I can make this W into wickets." The others applaud.

Again, Lawrence writes W-I-C-K-E-T on his slate. "Wicket starts with the letter W. Well done, Johnny."

Bullocky sits staring at his page with his pencil poised, waiting for an idea. Mullagh has known how to read and write since Alice taught him when they were children together. He and Dicky Dick are the only completely literate members of the team. The others are on an English literacy scale from some to virtually none. But this is in no way a measure of each man's native intelligence or his ability to communicate. They just don't do it in English.

Mullagh moseys up to where Bullocky is. "Need some help?" he asks.

Bullocky looks up at him. "All I know is batting and shearing," he says.

"That's not true, brother," Mullagh says.

"What else?" Bullocky asks.

"What about your didgeridoo?" Mullagh says.

He stares at his alphabet for a few seconds. Then the light goes on. "I can make this one into a didgeridoo," he says, pointing to the "I." He draws two small circles and connects them with two straight lines and admires them for a moment. "If I stand it up like this, it looks like that letter."

Dicky Dick has joined them. "Still needs a little art work, don't you think?" he says.

Bullocky looks stumped for a moment while he processes Dicky Dick's suggestion. Then he smiles his one-tooth-missing smile at Mullagh and Dicky

Dick and nods. He begins copying the design of his real didgeridoo from memory onto the one he has just drawn.

Mullagh announces, "Bullocky has made the I into a didgeridoo." Again, the others applaud.

By now they are all choosing a letter and drawing something familiar on their pages. In its strange way, this variation on Lawrence's exercise engages their imaginations. It also re-attaches them to country and lifts their spirits. Lawrence is satisfied that he has taught them the alphabet and, figuratively, pats himself on the back.

* * * * *

Up until now, Captain Williams' prediction about this being an easy crossing has been correct. A few weeks have passed and it has been like a holiday cruise. Also by now, the team is fully integrated into the activities that all passengers enjoy. Some have learned to play billiards and before long they play with an expertise that belies their time at the green velvet. Some have learned to play cards. Whist is a popular card game akin to Bridge. After a few sessions at the card table, many of them have mastered its intricacies and are sought after as partners. Also, it is not unusual to see Johnny Cuzens and Tarpot at a rummy table with three or four white people, laughing and melding with the best of them. They have taken up dancing the polka and waltzing. Their natural agility and tribal dancing traditions make this an easy transition. Virtually none of the ladies onboard shows any reluctance to taking the Black men as partners.

King Cole has been able to collect a few scraps of wood from the sailors and busies himself carving little boats like the ones he made for Timmy and giving them to the children. He does his carving in the sunlight on the upper deck. As he works his knife, he is always surrounded by a group of boys. Some of the older boys have borrowed pocket knives from their fathers, wanting to copy what King Cole does. He is a patient teacher, always emphasizing safety first and attention to detail. These sessions are happy occasions both for him and for the boys.

Lawrence has given up on trying to teach his teammates how to read. Each of his sessions turned into drawing contests anyway. His latest project for them is to teach them etiquette. He has more success at this one. In the cabin, away from the others, he tells them, "Lads, when we get to England, you are going to be an oddity. I do not wish to insult you by saying this. But no one has ever seen an all Aboriginal cricket team. For that matter, they have never seen Indigenous Australians at all. But just as you have been able to become part of the activities with the passengers onboard, you will be able to do the same with the people in England. Mr. Harriman expects you to conduct yourselves like gentlemen there because you will be representing your colony and your country. You may be mingling with important people. So, it is equally important to learn correct manners. You are already in the habit of saying 'please' and 'thank you.' That is just common courtesy. But there are other situations that call for certain manners. For instance, if you are going into a building, it is correct to hold the door for a lady so she can go in first.

With a modicum of superiority, Dicky Dick says, "It is also correct to allow another gentleman to enter before you."

Lawrence says, "Yes. That is also polite. But let's go on. When you are at a dinner party – and when we are in England, this could happen – you always make sure the ladies are seated first. Or if a lady comes to your table after everyone is seated, all the gentlemen rise. And you could be required to hold a lady's chair for her."

Johnny Cuzens says, "This one I know. Tiger, come here." Tiger goes to him. Cuzens says, in an affected way, "Madam, may I help you to your seat?" and pulls a chair back slightly.

Tiger, equally affected, says, "Why thank you, kind sir," and poises himself over the chair. Everybody knows what's coming next. Predictably, as he starts to sit, Johnny Cuzens pulls the chair back and Tiger lands on his butt. Everybody laughs, including Tiger.

However, despite all the jokes and pranks, little by little, they learn how to conduct themselves in polite society. Their time on The Parramatta gives them ample opportunity to practice. These natural men from the bush are truly transitioning into the definition of proper gentlemen. Even they are aware of it as they go through Lawrence's drills and when they are with the other passengers. They take a certain amount of pride in it. Some even take it a step further.

In the dining hall, a few days later, one of the card-playing young ladies approaches the table where Tarpot and other card-playing colleagues are seated. Dicky Dick is also at this table. There is one unoccupied chair. "May I join you," she asks.

Dicky Dick is immediately on his feet and behind the empty chair. "Please," he says. "I was afraid I was going to have to talk with Tarpot all through dinner."

"My, how gallant," she says as she takes her seat.

One of the ladies says, "Nice of you to join us, Virginia. You know Tarpot, of course, but this other gentleman is called Dicky Dick."

"How do you do," Dicky Dick says. "May I call you Virginia?"

"That would be convenient," Virginia answers, "since it is my name." There is something rather coquettish about the way she speaks to Dicky Dick and it isn't lost on him.

The two of them progress in this playful cat and mouse manner all through dinner. As the dessert is being served, it is announced that for those who would like to stay in the hall after the tables are cleared, some of the sailors will be playing music for anyone who might wish to dance.

Their dinner companions have all gone to their quarters, leaving Dicky Dick and Virginia at the table by themselves. There are a number of other people still in the hall, so they are not entirely alone.

"Oh, my," Virginia says. "I do love dancing. Do you dance, Sir Richard?"

"Sir Richard?" he says. "How did you know I was called Sir Richard?"

"Tarpot told us of your heroic exploits finding those children," she says. "How ever did you do it?"

Dicky Dick feigns modesty. "Oh, tracking is one the skills you learn in the bush. You get so you are able to read the subtlest of signs."

"Really?" she says.

"Really," he answers.

"Do you mind if I call you Sir Richard? she asks. "I refuse to keep referring to you as Dicky Dick. It sounds . . . dare I say . . . it sounds a bit naughty, don't you think?"

"I never thought about it," he answers.

"Well, I prefer to call you something special, so Sir Richard it is," she says.

In his mind, Dicky Dick is trying to interpret what she is really saying. He cannot believe a white woman is being so brazen, and virtually in public. But outwardly he remains calm.

Virginia becomes even more flirtatious. "Tell me, Sir Richard, will you be in London while you are in England playing your game?" She asks this in such a way that it could be interpreted as an invitation.

"Some of the time," he says. "I know that we will be playing our game, which is called cricket, by the way" he emphasizes cricket, "at several places in England."

Virginia smiles at being corrected. "My, my, aren't we touchy about our game?"

Dicky Dick is emboldened. "Not only touchy about the game," he says. "I can be touchy in other ways as well."

"Oh my goodness," she says, as she looks down demurely.

This could be dangerous territory for Dicky Dick to venture into. But black or white, he is a man, and like many, if not all men, danger doesn't enter into a situation like this. Danger loses all its power to inform. It is not a consideration. This is about biology.

"Virginia," he says. "Are you blushing?"

She doesn't answer immediately. Instead, she keeps her eyes down a moment longer, then looks up directly into his eyes and says, "No, I am not blushing. I am excited."

* * * * *

A few more weeks have passed. The calm seas have become less predictable. Some days the weather is idyllic with beautiful blue skies dotted by a few pure white clouds. On other days, the weather is more foreboding. The skies darken and the sea becomes choppy. The ship is stable but it rocks with the waves. On the occasions when it is rocking with a bit more gusto, the Indigenous men become alarmed. There is nothing in their experience that could prepare them for this.

Late one afternoon, when the rocking is more pronounced, Captain Williams and Charles Lawrence are conducting one of their prayer meetings.

King Cole is on edge. The rocking has gotten to him and he realizes he has no place to go in order to get away from it. In a panic, he asks, "Captain Williams, are we going to die?" He is the one who asks but the others are equally interested in what the Captain has to say on the subject.

Williams looks at King Cole and the others with his kind and gentle eyes and says, "Let me tell you a story. It may be good for all of you to hear it. It comes from the Book of Matthew in the Bible." From memory and while holding the book, he says, "Jesus was on a boat with his disciples. The lake they were on was calm just as it has been on most of our journey. And Jesus fell asleep. All of a sudden an enormous storm arose, much like this one we are experiencing, perhaps even bigger. The waves were coming over the sides of the boat and filling it with water. His disciples were panicked. They shook Jesus awake and pleaded with him to save them. He looked at them and said, 'Why are you afraid? Do you have no faith?' And he stood up in the boat and told the winds to stop and the sea to calm. And they did. His disciples couldn't believe that even the winds and the sea would obey his commands. The lesson here, boys, is that

Jesus will not let anything happen to you or any of us as long as we have faith. Our belief is our protection."

Most of the Aboriginals seem to have relaxed after hearing Captain Williams' assurances. Dicky Dick and Johnny Cuzens look at each other with expressions that say, *maybe we were wrong.*

The next day, the sea has calmed down with only occasional bumps along the way when the winds get a bit excited. Mullagh is standing alone at a rail, looking out into the vastness that surrounds the ship, seemingly lost in thought.

In a few moments, Charles Lawrence approaches him. "Ah, there you are, Johnny. I've been looking for you."

"G'day, Mr. Lawrence," he says. "I'm just looking at all this. It is easy to see how a sailor might feel the same way about the ocean as we feel about country. I'm sure he can read the ocean the same way we can read the land."

"You should have a talk to Captain Williams about that. I'm sure you would have a lot in common. You can no doubt learn quite a bit from each other," Lawrence says. After a moment, he continues, "I've been wanting to talk to you away from the others, Johnny. They all look up to you. You know that, don't you?"

"Yes. I know that," Mullagh says matter-of-factly. "I am their leader."

"Exactly, and I'd like to enlist your help in making things run smoothly once we get to England."

"In what way?"

"Just generally. For instance, I have noticed that Bullocky doesn't mind a drop of alcohol now and then. Mr. Harriman would take a dim view of that kind of thing. Here, on the ship, I don't think it hurts anyone. Let the lads have a bit of fun, I say. But Harriman is another story. He has a different agenda. He sees things in a much broader way," Lawrence explains.

"Do you want me to say something to Bullocky?" Mullagh asks.

"No. Not now. Just keep an eye on him once we are in England," Lawrence replies.

"I can do that," Mullagh says and turns back out toward the sea.

"There's something else, Johnny," Lawrence says. Mullagh looks at him.

"Dicky Dick and that young lady are spending quite a lot of time together," he says. "I'm not sure that looks good to the other passengers."

"Has anyone said anything?" Mullagh asks.

"No. Nothing specific," Lawrence says. "It's just that . . . er . . . "

"What are they doing that you object to?"

"It isn't that I object," Lawrence says. "It's more how it appears."

"And how is that?"

Lawrence is beginning to feel boxed in. He doesn't want to come out with what actually bothers him because he has to spend the foreseeable future with these men as teammates. What he really wants is for Mullagh to see things from his point of view without having to detail chapter and verse. "Not everyone is comfortable with it," he finally says.

Mullagh knows where Lawrence is going with this and it brings his situation with Alice boiling to the surface of his mind. He has never even spoken of Alice with any of his teammates. That she is constantly in his thoughts is intensely personal and private. "Are you saying that white women should not be with Black men?" Mullagh asks. He is able to say that much out loud.

"Society looks down on that sort of thing," Lawrence feels forced to say. "I may say that it could be against the will of God."

Mullagh goes quiet.

Lawrence feels the awkwardness. "As a Christian," he finally says, "I believe we must obey God's will.

Mullagh looks into Lawrence's eyes. "Mr. Lawrence, Dicky Dick and I come from a people who have had their own customs and beliefs for thousands of years. Long before there was anything like Christianity. We are not Christians." He turns back toward the sea.

Lawrence stands there for a minute longer, then starts to leave. "Well, just keep an eye on Bullocky," he says, as he moves away.

Mullagh has been rocked completely off balance by this conversation. Even though Alice is always in his thoughts, subliminally, talking with Lawrence has brought her to the surface and he doesn't like it. It is the source of nothing but frustration and pain for him. He would like to have told Lawrence that he is in love with a white woman and the same society won't allow that either. He is not permitted to have such thoughts. But instead of saying anything, he has to swallow this bitter pill and keep it all to himself.

He pounds the rail with his fist and goes back to the cabin, hoping there will be some distraction there to take his mind off Alice.

* * * * *

The farther north The Parramatta gets from the equator, the rougher the seas become. The result is that fewer and fewer of the passengers are seen in the dining hall and on deck these days. Many have taken to their cabins and spend most of the day horizontal. It is much easier to ride out the movement of the ship lying down. There is no place for landlubbers to find refuge. The weather continues to worsen until only the heartiest sailors can go about any otherwise normal tasks. Soon, it becomes a monstrous storm, the likes of which few of the passengers have ever experienced. The First Eleven have *never* experienced anything like this. It makes what they were concerned about before look like a picnic. The strong howling winds make a terrifying sound and are relentless, lashing everything in their path with torrents and torrents of rain. The saturated, black clouds are impenetrable, hanging like a heavy drape all around the ship. Deafening thunder and blinding lightning crash and flash without ceasing. And have been doing it for countless hours now. The swells raise the ship to the top of the waves, then plunge it into a canyon of water, time after time. Each time the ship bangs down, most of the Indigenous men fear that the ship will break apart.

They are all huddled in their cabin, terrified at the storm that rages outside. Lawrence is with them, but even his assurances that Jesus will protect them fail to ease their mounting fear.

"Come now, lads," Lawrence says. "This storm will pass just as the others have. Captain Williams told you the story of how Jesus stopped the winds and calmed the sea. That story is true. It actually happened. Jesus gave his life for us to learn his lessons."

King Cole isn't convinced. "They were on a lake. We are on the ocean."

"Yes," Johnny Cuzens says. "They knew they were close to land. We haven't seen land in months."

"I want to go back to Australia," Tarpot says. "We know how to live when we're on country. Here, we can't do anything."

Lawrence is at a loss. He doesn't have the calming presence of Captain Williams. Nor is he a seasoned salt. Inside he is as nervous as the others about what might happen. "I think we should pray together that this storm will pass. Let's bow our heads," he says. Some of them do and some don't.

At the helm, Captain Williams is guiding the ship through this tempest with the skill of a master. When the worst of the storm seems to be passing, and he can see the clouds clearing up ahead, he tells the crew to carry on and goes below to where he is sure the Aboriginals could use a little reassurance. He enters the cabin just when Lawrence is saying, "Amen." He repeats for the others to hear, "Amen."

"The worst is behind us, boys," he says. "It will still be a bit rocky for a while but it won't last too much longer." Just as he says this, the ship crashes down from the top of a wave with a force that makes even the captain look around.

He looks from one to the other of the Black men and realizes that Mullagh is missing. He turns to Lawrence. "Where is Johnny Mullagh?" he asks. Lawrence only has a vague answer. "I thought all the lads were here in the cabin."

"My god," Williams says. "If he is on deck anywhere, it is impossible for him to survive this storm."

Dicky Dick says to the others, "Come on. We have to find him."

Captain Williams stops them. "No. You boys stay here where you are safe. I'll go. I know how to manage these things much better than you do."

He goes up on deck and begins his search. The storm has crested but is still formidable. Captain Williams has to proceed with extreme caution, holding on to whatever is available as he goes along the deck. As sure-footed as he is, he still has difficulty managing to make his way from one safe place to the next, always clutching onto anything solid and on more than one occasion nearly losing his footing. He is blinded by the virtually horizontal rain until a lightning flash allows him to see Johnny Mullagh. He has lashed himself to the railing and is facing the storm. The wind plasters his soaking wet clothing against his skin. His demeanor is calm. Williams finally makes his way to where Mullagh is and shouts above the screaming wind, "Johnny, are you all right?"

Mullagh looks in his direction and cups his palm to his ear.

"Captain Williams repeats, "Are you all right?"

Mullagh nods his head.

"Have you been here all through the storm?"

Mullagh nods again.

"Johnny, you are not accustomed to traveling on the sea. It isn't safe to be up here on deck during a powerful storm like this. I don't allow my sailors to be up here unless they have something that needs their attention."

Mullagh looks at the captain and shouts, "I am all right, Captain. I wanted to feel the storm."

Captain Williams shakes his head. "This is weather at its most ferocious. It is not a wise idea to tempt Nature like this."

Mullagh turns and looks directly into his eyes. "It's all right, Captain Williams, I am Nature."

Captain Williams looks at Mullagh for a long moment. He is sure he cannot understand this man and realizes he has no argument to make that will change him. Finally he says, "The others are worried about you. They wanted to come looking for you. Best we go below and let them see you are all right."

Mullagh looks at the captain for another moment, then un-lashes himself and follows Williams as he carefully makes his way back to the cabin. When they are safe from the storm, Captain Williams says, in a much more gentle way, "You are a unique individual, Johnny. But you have an obligation to set an example for your mates. Please help me to keep them calm and unafraid."

Mullagh nods, "I will, captain. But I had to experience the storm in my own way."

* * * * *

The remainder of the ocean journey is very much more of the same. There are other storms, but none that come anywhere near the same magnitude or intensity. All the passengers, Black and white, have well and truly developed their sea legs so that even when a storm might be more than casual, they are able to go to the dining hall, play cards, spend time on deck and remain mostly vertical. Only one incident mars what would otherwise be an exemplary voyage for the Indigenous men.

It is after dinner and most people have left the dining hall. There is no dance tonight, but by now, several are in the habit of staying and enjoying a drink . . . or two. Tiger and Bullocky are among them. They have developed a taste for Scotch whiskey and there is no short supply onboard The Parramatta. The two of them are well into their cups, especially Bullocky, when one of the other male passengers decides this is a good time to discuss racial subjects. Mr. Power, as he is known, pulls up a chair, uninvited, and joins them.

"Say. Tell me, boys, is it true that Black women are especially fond of a good fuck?"

Bullocky looks at Power to see if he is too drunk to know what he is saying or just an idiot. He decides Power is too drunk and ignores the question. Tiger takes his lead from Bullocky and also ignores him.

Undaunted, Power continues his discussion, even though he is the only one discussing anything. "I understand that African men are very well endowed. Does that hold true with you blokes too? I mean, you are all black. I am wondering if it is a colour thing."

Bullocky looks at him again, this time with a little more interest. He holds his gaze for a few seconds, then returns to his Scotch. It is clear to Tiger that Bullocky is trying to mind his own business but finds it difficult when Power won't leave him alone. Tiger is concerned what Bullocky may do. It is known that Bullocky has a short fuse. Before it can go any further, Tiger says, "Hey, Bullocky, let's go back to the cabin. It's getting late."

Power says, "You two stay where you are. I'm going to buy you another drink. I'm not finished talking to you." It isn't a request.

Tiger says, "I'm very tired, sir, I am going below. Bullocky, come on. Let's go."

Bullocky likes the idea of one more drink. In language, he says, "You go. I'm going to stay for a while."

As Tiger is leaving, he hears Power say, "What is that gibberish you talk? Is that a language?"

Tiger wastes no time getting to the cabin. He goes immediately to Mullagh. "Unaarrimin, you've got to come up to the dining hall with me."

"What is it?" Mullagh asks.

"It's Bullocky. There's a white bloke up there and he's drunk and he's asking a lot of stupid questions. Bullocky isn't ready to quit drinking yet and I'm afraid there will be trouble."

Mullagh says, "Let's go." They quickly make their way to the dining hall.

Bullocky has continued to try to ignore Power but it is an uphill climb. This insensitive Englishman still wants to discuss sexual issues with this Black fella.

As Mullagh and Tiger approach, they hear Power ask, "Tell me, mate, do all your women run around naked when they're in the bush. I've heard that. How are their bosoms? Big? Like this?" He holds his cupped hands to his chest.

Bullocky is now looking at Power directly in the eye. Any sensible person would know to back off about now. But instead, Power is pushing his finger into Bullocky's arm, ready to make a point. Mullagh is quick to get to Bullocky before any damage can be done. In language, he says, "That's enough drink for tonight. Let's go back down to the cabin. This guy is too drunk to waste any more time on." He takes Bullocky's arm.

If it were anyone else, Bullocky might show some resistance. But with Mullagh, he knows better than to try. He pushes his chair back and stands on wobbly legs. Tiger takes his other arm and they start toward the door.

Power tries to stop them. "I'm not finished talking to you Nig-Nogs. Come back here."

Mullagh turns toward him. He doesn't have to say a word. Even in his drunken state, Power perceives the danger in Mullagh's stare. He remains speechless. Mullagh and Tiger continue leading Bullocky to the cabin and the incident ends without any more fuss.

A few days later, three months after leaving Australia, The Parramatta docks at Gravesend.

Chapter Nine – The Tour (Take 2)

The First Eleven arrive in Kent, at a place called Town Malling. They are unaccompanied. Harriman is in London on business and Lawrence is meeting them here later in the day. The closest anyone in this little village has come to people of colour might have been at one of the shows that were popular at that time. Native Americans from both the United States and Canada toured England with displays of their athletic prowess. In the former, running and jumping events and in the latter, lacrosse. No one has ever seen a Black or Brown man up close and personal.

So when these fashionably dressed Black Aussies arrive, it goes without saying that they are noticed. Some people are slightly fearful of something or someone so out of the ordinary. But most are just curious. For those who are better informed, Darwin's *Origin of the Species* has brought attention to these "others". Tales from all over the Empire have made the public aware of indigenous people from far off lands. But from this vantage point it is an entirely different matter.

As they stroll the streets, looking in shop windows and taking in the strangeness of this place, and because they are all together, they are very relaxed and speak freely to anyone with the courage to come close.

Dicky Dick is especially gregarious. A man and a woman are walking together trying not to be too obvious about staring when he goes up to them, "Good afternoon," he says, as he tips his hat.

The shock of hearing this Black man address them in English, and so politely at that, sends them into a kind of social panic. They are momentarily stunned and speechless. They look at each other and mumble something incoherent and, as if they suddenly remembered another appointment, quickly turn and go in the opposite direction. All the team have a good laugh at this.

The word quickly spreads through Town Malling that the Black Aussie cricket team is in their midst. Before long, a number of people find a reason to go into the middle of town. Soon the streets are crowded. One man appears to be on a mission. As soon as he spots The First Eleven, he swoops down on them like a hungry eagle.

"There you are," Jim Gilbert says. He has his son, Billy, and his daughter, Betsy, with him. "We have been looking all around town for you." He has a big smile on his face, as do his children. It's as if they have found some old friends.

Dicky Dick says, "And we have been looking for you too." He says it with such sincerity that the Gilbert kids are taken aback.

"You are?" Betsy is incredulous.

"I think he's just joking," Jim tells his daughter. "We want to make you gents feel welcome in our little town," he announces to the players. "You are the most important people we have ever had here in Town Malling."

In language, King Cole says, "These white people are very different from the ones we know back home." The others nod.

"We would greatly be honoured if you would come to our home and share a bite to eat with us," Billy says, as if it were a prepared speech. Which it is.

The First Eleven look at one another. There is a general, *Why not?* understood among them. "Where to?" Dicky Dick says.

Jim Gilbert leads the way to his modest, frame cottage a few blocks away. And as if there were nothing unusual or unnatural about it, six-year-old Betsy takes Bullocky's hand. Bullocky looks up to Johnny Mullagh as if to ask, *Is this all right?* and Mullagh nods.

When they arrive at the Gilbert home, the table has already been set. There is also another family there, the Wests, with their three children. All of the children are under 10 years of age. Once everyone is settled, Jim Gilbert says, "Tell us your names. We probably won't remember all of them, but we would like to know who you are, what you are called. I'll start off. I'm Jim Gilbert. This is my wife, Julie, and these are our two youngsters, Billy and Betsy. These people are Orrin West and his wife, Penelope, their twins, Edward and Edwin, and their little girl, Jane. Now, tell us who you are."

The Indigenous men, each in turn, say their names. When it is his turn, for a moment, Dicky Dick considers starting with his Aboriginal name, but realizes that might be too confusing for these nice people. As, one by one, they introduce themselves, the very act of it relaxes them and what little awkwardness that may have existed evaporates. The freedom to be themselves gives them enormous confidence. It's as if these people don't see or care about their colour, just them. And they are actually experiencing it in a little village in England, an unimaginable distance from country. By the time Johnny Cuzens says who he is, it already feels like a black and white corroboree.

As the afternoon wears on, Orrin West and Jim Gilbert haul out a guitar and a banjo and all the white folks sing along with them. The Black fellas are stomping their feet with the rhythm of the music. In the midst of it, King Cole says, "It's a shame Bullocky doesn't have his didgeridoo with him."

"Next time," Julie says, with a big smile on her face as she claps in time with the music, confident that there will be a next time.

Bullocky flashes his one-tooth-missing smile.

No one alive at that time in that place could have ever dreamed of, let alone predicted, this kind of welcome for a group of native Australians more than ten thousand miles from home.

By now, everyone is so comfortable that they are lounging around in little groups carrying on individual conversations. A burst of laughter erupts from any one group at any time.

It is at one of these moments that Charles Lawrence appears at the front door. He looks around to see if this is the house where he was told he would find the Aboriginals. The laughter makes him pause before knocking. When he is satisfied this is the right place, he knocks gently at first and, after hearing nothing but laughter, knocks again much louder.

Julie Gilbert comes to the door. "Can I help you?" she asks.

"Sorry to bother you, madam, but I am looking for my Black fellas and I was told they were in your house," Lawrence answers.

"Come in," she says. Lawrence is completely nonplussed as he crosses the threshold. He stops cold when he sees his fellow cricketers relaxing around this home as if it were their own.

"You missed the music," Dicky Dick says.

"They want me to come back with my didgeridoo," Bullocky says, smiling his one-tooth-missing smile. Lawrence is speechless.

"We have some leftovers," Jim Gilbert says, "if you would like to have a bite."

King Cole says, "It's mighty good tucker. You should have some, coach."

Without waiting for an answer, Julie has prepared a plate for Lawrence and tells him to have a seat. "I hope you enjoy it," she adds.

Lawrence still hasn't said a word, but sits at the table and gets stuck into the food with a confused look on his face.

Johnny Cuzens looks at Dicky Dick and says, in language, "He forgot to thank you-know-who before he ate."

Dicky Dick tsks.

After an hour or so, despite the fun he is also having, Lawrence announces to the team that they have to check into their hotel and tomorrow begin training for cricket matches. "You lads need to lose all the fat you have put on on The Parramatta . . . and here." He gives Julie a smile and a nod.

Their grumbling is kept to a minimum as they say their thank yous and goodbyes to the Gilberts and the Wests. Jim Gilbert says, "Come back any time, gents. You are always welcome at the Gilberts." Betsy goes to Bullocky and gives him a hug. "Don't forget to bring your digger-doo-doo next time."

*****

Since arriving in London several weeks before, Augustus Harriman has been hard at work trying to build up excitement for the visiting Black fellas. Through Lawrence and his own connections, he lobbies the cricketing community throughout Great Britain. It is as though some of Gurnett's DNA has merged with his own. He has become single-minded about his goal and will say whatever he has to in order to convince his current audience of its timeliness and importance.

His standard pitch to cricketers is: "Gentlemen, these darkies have taken to our game like ducks to water. They learned over arm bowling as if it were native to them." Here, he adds a little aside, "Actually, it is very much like throwing a boomerang to them." Then he continues, "You know, of course, that Britain's great Charles Lawrence is coaching the team. He has consented to guide them for this tour." Then, as if it just occurred to him, "Come to think of it, Charles Lawrence has also been encouraging them to display some of their tribal skills after the matches, just to give the audience a little something extra, besides the amazing cricket they are capable of." He and Lawrence had already decided that the "native games," as they called them would be a major attraction given the current trends in Britain. The only place he gets any resistance is when he proposes a match at Lord's, the most famous and pre-eminent cricket venue in the world.

"Mr. Harriman," Walter Nichols says, "To be perfectly honest with you, we are reluctant to honour your request for a match here at Lord's. We are proud of our centuries' old tradition of cricket in Great Britain, as I am sure you can appreciate. The idea of allowing these savages to play on our ground will be difficult to get agreement on from our board."

"I do appreciate your position, sir," Harriman answers. "But I must tell you that these men, far from being savages, are polished gentlemen in their own way. We believe the English public will welcome their cricketing skills and be quite impressed."

"Perhaps so," Nichols says, "but you mentioned native games and boomerangs and the like. Those are hardly gentlemen's activities."

One of the most important goals of this tour, for both Harriman and Lawrence, is the imprimatur of having played at Lord's. Therefore, Harriman is quick to respond. "Sir, if that is in any way an obstacle to our playing the game of cricket at Lord's, we will dispense with those native games. I am a great supporter of our wonderful game and would not want to tarnish this great institution's reputation in any way."

"Well, then," Nichols says, "under those circumstances I will allow the board to consider a match at Lord's. Come back in a fortnight and we'll have an answer for you. Good day, sir."

When Augustus Harriman speaks to journalists, he says, "You have to remember, gentlemen, that these Australian darkies are not only a phenomenon as far as their cricketing ability is concerned, they are also a dying breed. Your scientists here in London are agreed that this may be the last generation of Indigenous people from the Antipodes that the world will ever see. This is the opportunity of a lifetime for your readers to see them in their natural state and in authentic costumes. It is our intention to have them display their tribal skills at the conclusion of each match. They will be throwing boomerangs and spears and showing other of their natural and unique athletic skills in various ways, like backward racing and standing high jumps and the like. We even have one darkie who can dodge missiles thrown at him by spectators. Believe me, your readers have never witnessed anything like this before."

He has even been able to make some penetration into the academic and scientific communities. He tailors a slightly different pitch for them. "You learned gentlemen have far more experience and expertise in these matters than I do. But I believe it is generally agreed that the Aboriginal population in Australia is living on borrowed time. This may be the last opportunity many of you will have to observe them closely, from a scientific or anthropological point of view. I have heard it said that their bone structure and general physical attributes are of immense interest to your intellectual community. I can personally assure you that you will be able to make any examinations you need to in order to get a more complete picture of this dying race."

After this meeting, the scientists and academicians have their own discussion.

"Can you imagine? This man from the colonies has read our thoughts. I would personally give my first born to examine a few of their skulls. I believe a lot can be learned from phrenology alone," one says.

"And that colonial is quite right. They will be unlikely to survive to the next generation. This could be our only opportunity for a comprehensive, scientific research project. I don't think we can pass up this moment," says another.

"We will also be able to study some of their artifacts," says another. "I have always been curious about the boomerang. How in the world could those ignorant, primitive people have constructed such an instrument? It defies logic."

"I am told they also have another tool that allows them to throw a spear great distances, far greater than by hand, and with accuracy. Where would they have learned such a skill?"

"Excuse me, gentlemen, but there is no way these savages could have made these mathematical calculations on their own. An extremely sophisticated study of aerodynamics is required to make a boomerang fly away and come back."

"How do you suppose they did it?" another asks.

"Well, my best guess is that they have undoubtedly been throwing sticks and small limbs for eons and little by little, someone accidentally found one that sort of circled back and after that they found sticks that had that sort of shape and perhaps smoothed them out or some such. What else could it be? They clearly don't have the ability to work it out otherwise. That would take a Pythagoras."

"Or a Da Vinci."

"Or a Newton, chaps."

"To be sure. Or a Newton."

"So, you are saying it had to have been a bit of a fluke."

"Of course. There could be no other explanation."

"It appears that we have a great deal to discover about these Stone Age relics," the chairman of the meeting adds as punctuation.

* * * * *

Charles Lawrence holds his first workout session on the day after the team's arrival at Town Malling. It wasn't hyperbole that they needed to lose some fat. Bullocky tops the weight gain chart with a whopping twenty pounds. Most of the others have also put on some extra weight. The only exceptions are Johnny Mullagh and Johnny Cuzens. Therefore, Lawrence is merciless in his effort to get them match fit. He starts them out with a series of calisthenics which he calls the Swedish technique. Few of the Aboriginals have any idea what Swedish means, but they feel the result as they stretch and squat, inhale and exhale, do leg lifts and push-ups. Next he has them swing heavy Indian clubs in a variety of directions and methods. After that, it's wind sprints. By the time he finishes the day's exercises, all the Black fellas are exhausted, even the ones who were in shape to begin with.

"All right, lads. That is enough of that for today. Now, let's play some cricket," Lawrence says. They look at him to see if this is a joke. It isn't. Out comes the cricket gear and those drills begin. After a break for some tucker, Lawrence says, "Now, let's finish the day with some of your tribal skills," and the boomerangs and spears come out. By the time they return to their hotel, they are spent and humourless.

"Today was very hard, lads. I know that. But I promise you, by the time we have our first match, you will be in top condition and glad we did this," Lawrence says as they drag themselves to their rooms. "We will start tomorrow at 8 am. Goodnight, lads." And the next day is more of the same. And the next. Before long, even Bullocky has to admit that this regimen is showing some results.

Lawrence reports to Harriman that the Black fellas are ready.

The Kennington Oval in South London is the site of the first match.

When they take the pitch, the team is wearing their new cricket uniforms. The trousers are white flannel. Their shirts are red and cut in a military style. They have blue belts and ties and white linen collars. At first sight of the Aboriginals, seven thousand spectators leap to their feet and applaud. Each of the players is wearing a different coloured sash to help identify him. All except for Johnny Mullagh. The fact that he is the only one without a sash identifies him. All are in their traditional cricket footwear, which is to say, barefoot.

The tone is set even before the match actually begins. The First Eleven give three cheers and a rollicking whoop. From that moment on they are on a dedicated mission of having fun. It is reminiscent of the way they played their first match back home in Hamilton. They shout to each other in language and laugh constantly. The ones who are near the boundaries banter with the crowd. And just as they had in Hamilton, they applaud their opponents whenever one of them makes a particularly good play, even if it is to their detriment. The joy they create on the pitch in Kennington is contagious. Not only are the spectators enthralled, their opponents, however reluctantly, join in the fun too.

The pace of the game is electrifying. None of the spectators has ever seen anyone dart between wickets like these Black fellas. Or run down a ball. Or throw with such consistent accuracy. In addition, they watch Johnny Mullagh wield the bat like a master. He scores 33 runs in the first innings and 73 in the second. Bullocky displays his wicket keeping talents by stumping two batsmen. After bowling for a spell, Mullagh shows what an all rounder he is when he relieves Bullocky as wicket keeper and makes what is generally regarded as the catch of the match. King Cole also has a spell at bowling since Johnny Cuzens is not able to attend the match because of a stomach ailment. The local team wins the match, but for the Aussies, it is like losing the battle but winning the war. Mullagh is carried off the pitch on the shoulders of fans and given a cash prize for his outstanding cricketing.

The newspaper reaction is mixed from the beginning. While one paper noted that there was not a third rate batsman among the Indigenous players, *The London Times* looked down its nose at the Aussies with comments like the bowling being second rate and their running between wickets was slow. But the *Times'* most insulting comment was referring to the team as "the conquered natives of a convict colony and a travesty upon cricketing." Let the critics say what they will, Harriman and Lawrence only care about attendance and the gate receipts, both of which are good news.

Back in the change rooms, after the match, the mood is pure delight. Mullagh gets everyone's attention. "You see this money?" he says, holding up the prize he received, "This isn't my money. This is our money. Whenever anyone gets a prize like this, it goes into a bag. And it will divided equally among us all."

Harriman is quick to disagree. "Johnny, that money is yours. You earned it."

Mullagh looks directly into Harriman's eyes as he repeats to his brothers, "If this money is mine, this money is ours!"

Harriman looks away and says, "As you wish."

The two days of cricket at the Kennington ground are followed by the first day of their native games. Lawrence has remained secretive about the team's "tribal" costumes he had designed. It is in the change room at Kennington that he reveals them for the first time. His fear of a revolt has been for naught.

Dicky Dick is the first to try on his gear. He laughs as he says to the others, "Imagine if we wore this in the bush? The elders would run us out of the clan."

"Is this all we are wearing? This is it?" Bullocky asks, smiling his one-tooth-missing smile.

Charles Lawrence is relieved to hear them joking about the costumes. "Lads, the British public want to see warriors. That's why you will look like what they think a warrior would look like."

King Cole says, "If we really showed them what our warriors look like, the ladies would blush and turn their heads."

Dicky Dick says, "Or maybe they wouldn't."

The costumes consist of tight leggings dyed as close to their skin colour as possible so that it looks as though they have naked legs, a fur cod piece that reveals nothing but leaves little to the imagination and the look is completed with a headdress of lyre bird feathers.

"As soon as the cricket match ends," Lawrence says, "we will hurry to our tent and put on this gear." Then he remembers something he and Harriman discussed. "And, lads, when you run onto the pitch with these costumes on, we want you to whoop and yell and wave your weapons above your heads as if you were chasing a wild animal."

Mullagh, who has been silent through all of this, says, "When we hunt, the last thing we would do is yell, coach. It would frighten the animals away."

"These people don't know that," Lawrence replies. "And this is a show for these people."

"I thought this was to show our warrior skills like the boomerang and woomera," Dicky Dick says.

Lawrence doesn't like the direction this talk is taking. "Lads, you will be displaying your warrior skills. That is why we are doing this. But we just need to embellish it a little for effect. You must trust me, the people will love it. They will love you."

And they do. For many in the stands, it is the highlight of the day. And it is the only thing the various newspapers and publications agree on.

Harriman and Lawrence have taken a calculated risk and it has paid off.

* * * * *

One of the perks for entrepreneurs like Harriman and Lawrence, when bringing the exotic to Great Britain in the Victorian Age, is not only press attention, but social exposure as well. Socialites like to have these entrepreneurs in their midst. Landing one of them for an event at the peak of their popularity or notoriety, as the case may be, is a mark of great social success and draws its own attention.

For Charles Lawrence, this is a variation on a theme, having been a successful athlete in his own right in the past and receiving a certain amount of attention as a result. But even for him, this is new territory. It brings him a different and special kind of attention and respect. For Augustus Harriman, it is recognition beyond his wildest dreams. People he regards to be "important" have noticed him and sought his company at dinner parties and soirees. His vulnerability in this regard was amply exposed by Gurnett. The only thing that blemishes it in any way now is the equal amount of curiosity that exists among these socialites for Harriman's Aboriginal charges. If the truth were told, it is only because of them that he enjoys any attention at all. He would much rather keep them in the background and talk about how fortunate the darkies are to be playing cricket in England, than to have them in the spotlight. But it is impossible. They draw the attention. They have the heat. And most frustratingly, some of them are clever and articulate besides. There is nowhere they go in public where they do not cause a sensation. It is a larger, more glitzy version of their experience in Town Malling. It is their Parramatta experience writ large.

For example, on a rare day-off early in the tour, they are invited to attend the Derby at Epsom Downs, where they charm their way through the fashionable attendees while Harriman is virtually ignored and looks on with a tolerant smile plastered on his face.

On another occasion, after they have been in England a bit longer, they are guests of honour at an elaborate soiree in a fashionable London home. The swanky surroundings leave Harriman dumbstruck, but The First Eleven take it in stride as if they were born to it, some with more poise than others, to be sure, but by now all of them are growing accustomed to the being noticed.

At this soiree, Johnny Mullagh and Johnny Cuzens are surrounded by cricket fans who hang on their every word. "Where did you learn to bat like that?" one of them asks Mullagh. He is less inclined to engage with these people and his natural reticence inhibits him.

Not so with Johnny Cuzens. "You won't believe this but Johnny Mullagh, here, has only played cricket for a year. But he has always been one of our best athletes since we were children together. So, you might say it started a long time ago."

In another part of the room, Bullocky and Tiger keep to themselves as they sample the alcohol. Their taste for Scotch whiskey hasn't diminished. Occasionally, someone approaches them politely and tries to engage them in conversation, but is quickly discouraged when the Aboriginals begin talking to each other in language.

Dicky Dick is in his element. "Ask King Cole? He's knows," Dicky Dick says.

King Cole says, "It's true, he is our best tracker. He found three children who were lost for nine days. Nobody else could, only Dicky Dick."

"And when Johnny Mullagh isn't around, I'm the best boomerang thrower too," Dicky Dick boasts. "Why, I once threw a boomerang so far that we were able to kill a kangaroo, skin it, cook it and eat it before that boomerang came back." He quickly adds, "And drink a cup of tea." Everyone around him has a good laugh.

Then he adds, "And a biscuit." They all explode at this one. King Cold just smiles and shakes his head.

"Well, if it isn't Sir Richard," a female voice says.

Dicky Dick whips around and there is Virginia, his playmate from The Parramatta. He doesn't miss a beat. "I've been thinking about you every day since we left the ship," he says, flashing a knowing smile.

"I'm sure you have," she answers, with a knowing smile of her own. She takes his arm and begins to lead him away from his audience. "Sir Richard and I are old friends from our ocean-going days," she says to them.

When they have found a relatively secluded spot, she turns to him. "I have been waiting and waiting to hear from you. Why haven't I?"

"Virginia, I am here to play cricket. It's taking all my time. We hardly have a free moment."

"Are you playing cricket here too? Or doesn't this count as a free moment?"

"Mr. Harriman insists that we attend certain functions as part of our tour. Believe me, I would much rather spend time with you."

Virginia calms herself, then coyly asks, "And when will that be?"

"As soon as possible," Dicky Dick says. "As soon as possible."

As if on cue, Harriman comes up to them. Lawrence has told him about his concerns regarding Dicky Dick and white women. "Ah, there you are, Dicky Dick. If you have a minute, I would like to have a little chat, if you will excuse us, Miss."

Dicky Dick says, "This is Virginia, Mr. Harriman. We met on the ship and she just happened to be invited to this event."

"Excuse us, Virginia. We have some cricket business to discuss. I am sure you would find it too boring for words," Harriman says, hoping he is being charming enough to break this liaison up, at least for the moment.

"Actually, I am fascinated by the game of cricket," she smiles. "Nothing could interest me more than your little game." She shoots Dicky Dick a glance to be sure he got her dig.

"When may I call on you, Virginia?" Dicky Dick says. "I want to take you up on your invitation to tea."

She is quick to catch on. She reaches into her tiny purse and pulls out a card. "My address is on this. Come whenever you want. My parents have heard so much about you. My father, in particular, wants to meet you. He is a great fan of your little game."

Harriman gives them a look. This all seems so harmless and above board suddenly. Could Lawrence have misjudged the situation? But now that Harriman has intruded, he doesn't want to lose face. "Nice meeting you, Virginia. Give your parents my regards. I am Augustus Harriman, the manager of this tour." He puts an arm around Dicky Dick's shoulder and gently leads him away.

* * * * *

True to his word, Walter Nichols has an answer for Harriman regarding Lord's. Harriman has been nervously cooling his heels in an outer room until he is summoned by Nichols. He gives nothing away when Harriman walks in.

"Mr. Harriman," he says, "thank you for coming." Harriman tries to read Nichols for the slightest sign. He finally says, "Per your request, sir. Per your request."

"Right," Nichols says. "Now then . . . Oh, forgive me, would you like a spot of tea, or perhaps something a little stronger?"

"Thank you, no, sir," Harriman replies.

"I notice that you have a couple of players who are not too bad," Nichols says, still postponing the obvious.

"Some members of the press have been very generous," Harriman answers. He's sure Nichols is smugly referring to the hatchet job *The London*

Times did on the Indigenous team, but doesn't want to give Nichols the satisfaction of acknowledging it. Nichols finally gets to the point. "Well," he says, "I suppose you are curious as to our decision."

Harriman doesn't like being toyed with by someone who has the slightest power over him and it is obvious that Nichols holds all the cards. "At your leisure, Mr. Nichols," he says as calmly as possible.

"We are prepared to invite your Aboriginal players to Lord's," he says, "but under the strictest of conditions."

Harriman is dancing inside. There are no conditions that he won't meet to get his darkies on the Lord's ground. "And they are?" he asks calmly.

"We will have none of your native games. No suggestion of them. We expect your cricketers to behave as gentlemen on and off the pitch. No exceptions. If that is clearly understood and agreed to, we can proceed. If not, thank you for your interest." Nichols has enjoyed every moment of his power play. Being able to say yes or no to this colonial wannabe is like a tonic.

Harriman ignores Nichols' lofty demeanor. He only heard the word *invite*. "I am sure we can accommodate your demand, sir, without question. What would be a satisfactory date for this historic contest?"

"We have determined that the 12th day of June would suit us, assuming you have no objections."

With the shoe marginally on the other foot now, Harriman decides it's time for him to be coy. "That should be all right, but I do have to consult with Charles Lawrence before we can agree for certain, assuming *you* have no objections."

Nichols merely grunts and looks down at his desk. The meeting is over. As Harriman reaches the door, Nichols says without looking up, "We will expect an answer as soon as you have talked with Lawrence."

This time, Harriman grunts. As soon as he leaves Nichols, he rushes to Lawrence who is sitting in a pub nearby waiting to hear the news.

"They have agreed. We are playing at Lord's," Harriman says before even pulling up a chair. "But he made me assure him that we will not do the native games."

"What? No games? That's what most people are there for," Lawrence says.

"Now, now Charles, don't excite yourself. We will assume I forgot to tell you about that. Of course we will go ahead with the native games. That's where the money is."

* * * * *

On Friday, the 12th day of June, 1868, Lawrence and his Aboriginal team find themselves in the tent that is their change rooms at the Mecca of cricket, Lord's. Harriman is with them. Harriman and Lawrence are caught up in the significance of this momentous event.

"Boys," Harriman says, "this is what we came to England for. This is the most important cricket match you will ever be a part of." Of course, he is projecting his own excitement onto them. This is the most important cricket match *he* will ever be a part of.

To the players, it doesn't have the same shine. They know it's important because Harriman and Lawrence have said it is. But, they are in the habit of doing their best and having fun wherever they are.

Harriman continues. "I expect you to give it your all when you are out on the pitch. The British public knows their cricket and I want you boys to show them what we Aussies can do." As a pep talk, it falls short, as most of Harriman's talks do. But Lawrence steps in and takes a different approach. "Lads, we are capable of outstanding play. We've proven it again and again. Today and tomorrow will be no different. I know many of the other team's players, some personally and some by reputation. They are good. Some say they are the best in all of

England. But they put their trousers on one leg at a time, the same as we all do . . . "

Dicky Dick can't resist. "Do they put their fur loin cloths on the same way we do too?" It gets the desired laugh from the others.

In language, Mullagh says, "We know what to do. These white bosses are as excited as girls. Just listen to them and agree with what they say. Then we will go out and play cricket like warriors." They all raise their arms and cheer.

Harriman would like to say something equally as motivating but can't. Lawrence doesn't even try. Instead, he says, "I agree with Johnny Mullagh. Now let's go out and play cricket."

They run onto the pitch in their uniforms with colourful sashes flying. The spectators for the most part are very fashionably dressed for both days of the match. And they have come in impressive numbers. On the first day, estimates of as many as twenty thousand people showed up. Even on the second day there are more than six thousand people there. Each day, when they see the Aboriginal team take the field, many applaud politely. But there is another contingent that leap to their feet and shout their support for the Black fellas in no uncertain terms. The team plays with their customary enthusiasm and sense of fun, laughing and applauding their opponents and chatting with the people near the boundaries.

Even the most serious cricket fans are charmed by their antics. Walter Nichols and his colleagues may not be that impressed by the Black boys' cricket skills, but they are delighted with the size of the crowd they drew. Nichols is also pleased that they are conducting themselves in a civilized manner. He could do without the fun part, but no one else in his entourage seems to mind so he keeps his opinion to himself.

After their first innings on Friday, the local eleven are 21 runs behind. The Aussies are looking good. Johnny Cuzens is back with the team and on more than one occasion bowls with such power that when the ball hits the wicket, the bails fly yards behind the wicket keeper, like a ten-pin bowling strike. Johnny Mullagh is equally effective when he bowls, taking eight wickets in the two innings. With the bat, Mullagh excels as well, scoring 87 runs over the course of the match.

In the change rooms before Saturday's continuation, Lawrence has a talk with his teammates. "Lads," he says, "after today's match, we are going to do something a little bit sneaky. The people who run Lord's have forbidden us to do our native games. But we are going to have a little surprise for them. The people want to see the boomerangs and the spears and we are here to give the people what they want." He says this as if he were a participant. It isn't lost on the others but no one says anything. "Mr. Harriman has ordered me, and therefore us, to present the native games anyway. So, here's what we do. As soon as the last wicket is taken, we run to our tent and as fast as possible change into our costumes. Then we rush onto the pitch as we always do, whooping and yelling and brandishing our weapons. Before anyone can say anything, we'll begin with the boomerang throwing and go on from there."

On the second day, the tide is turned. The locals get their game together and eke out a victory. But once again, the Black fellas have stood tall and made a good showing. This doesn't keep Nichols and his crowd from saying that the darkies are inferior cricketers and generally putting them down, but the public has taken to them. This is what matters most to Harriman and Lawrence.

No one is prepared for the quick change and when the Indigenous men come out of their tent whooping and yelling what Lawrence has decided is a war cry, the spectators, who have begun exiting the grounds, return to their seats and scream with delight. Their enthusiasm is so great that Nichols dares not utter one word of protest.

Dicky Dick and Mullagh put on a display with boomerangs that dazzles the crowd. Dicky Dick throws his into the crowd and watches while people duck and gasp. No one is in any real danger, but they couldn't have known that. This Black man threw an Aboriginal weapon at them. When it sails over their heads and makes its wide arc, landing at Dicky Dick's feet, the applause is deafening. Mullagh throws one from one of the boundaries and they all watch it fly all the way to the opposite boundary before it arcs back to him. It is a phenomenal feat. But Charlie Dumas, whose only real purpose on the team is in the native games, steals the show by throwing four boomerangs at once, all of which return perfectly.

As soon as these three finish and are on their way to the tent, Bullocky, Red Cap, King Cole, Two Penny, Sundown and Jim Crow dash onto the pitch. Bullocky, Redcap and King Cole position themselves in a grouping, approximately one yard apart about 80 yards from their teammates. Two Penny, Sundown and Jim Crow alternate throwing spears down the pitch. They throw three spears each and after each throw, the spear lands close enough to King Cole and the others that one of them could reach out and touch it. When all spears have been thrown, they make a perfect arc in front of their teammates.

Next Johnny Cuzens comes out carrying a woomera. He retrieves three of the spears and goes to a boundary. He shouts for one of the grounds keepers to walk off a distance of 100 yards and set up a bow and arrow target. When the target is set, Cuzens fits the spear into the woomera and hurls it one hundred yards. The spear lands in the target with a thud that is heard all through the venue. The crowd applauds enthusiastically. Johnny Cuzens shouts to the grounds keeper again. "Move it another twenty yards." The grounds keeper paces off another twenty yards and sets up the target again. And again, Johnny Cuzens fits the spear into the woomera and launches it. It strikes the target with an even louder thud. The crowd goes crazy. When the applause and shouting have died down, Johnny Cuzens shouts, "Move it another thirty yards." The grounds keeper moves the target so that it is now 150 yards away. Silence falls upon the crowd as once again Johnny Cuzens fits the last spear into the woomera. He milks the moment, as Dicky Dick had instructed him, pausing for a slow count to thirty as if he is preparing himself mentally before he launches the last spear. When he does, it lands closer to the center than either of the first two with a colossal thud. The spectators go mad with delight and applaud him off.

Dicky Dick and Johnny Cuzens pass each other as Dicky Dick makes his way to the center of the pitch. He is carrying a small, oblong shield in one hand and an **L** shaped club in the other. When he gets in position, four men from the crowd, who were picked at random, walk onto the pitch and position themselves in a circle around Dicky Dick, each about fifteen paces away. Each is armed with a number of cricket balls. At the signal, they begin hurling the balls at Dicky Dick. He deftly sidesteps one, knocks another away with the club, blocks another with the shield, all the time taunting the hurlers and mugging for the crowd. This goes on for a full fifteen minutes with not one ball touching him. This final display causes the spectators to erupt in a thunderous applause, all the while cheering and laughing. Dicky Dick takes deep bows in all directions with a huge smile on his face. It is reminiscent of corroboree days. Even Nichols is smiling.

Lord's has been an unmitigated success. Despite their loss on the pitch, the Aboriginal men have made an enormous impression on the British public. The pride they display performing their warrior skills; their poise and accessibility in social situations, and their sense of fun on the cricket pitch all succeed in creating an indelible impression on the public. If their stock was high before Lord's, it is cosmic now. They are 19th Century rock stars. Photos of them appear in all the papers. They are invited to more and more glamorous events. Their fame is beyond anything any other Indigenous group has ever experienced in Great Britain. The First Eleven, whether acknowledged or not, have created an aura that paints the entire colony of Australia with a golden brush. Their mere presence has changed the Empire's view of people of colour, all thanks to the Black fellas from Down Under.

* * * * *

Buggies, wagons, carts and saddled horses are parked around the homestead at Mullagh Station. It is the depth of winter. The mood is funereal, and for good reason. Mrs. Buckingham sits on a chair in the parlor, weeping as guests attempt to console her.

"Sorry for your loss," a neighbour mumbles as he passes her. She makes no acknowledgement, only sniffs into her handkerchief.

"Come, dearie, let's go into the kitchen and get some food into you," one of her lady friends says, as she takes Mrs. Buckingham by the arm and lifts her from her chair. "You can't just sit and cry forever."

Three of the nearby station managers are huddled together near the fireplace with drinks in their hands. One says, "Poor bastard didn't know what hit him, I hear."

Another says, "Yep, they say he just dropped dead out in the wool shed."

The third says, "If one of the darkies hadn't come along, he'd be out there yet."

They sip their drinks in silence for a moment. Then, the first man says, "Buckingham has a pretty good spread here. Wonder who the lucky bastard is that will get a hold of it."

The third man says, "They will have to sell it. These two women can't run it without a man around and the girl is still single."

The first says, "I heard tell that the daughter wants to give it a go anyway."

Number Two says, "You reckon?"

"That's what they say."

"Well, she has some spunk, I'll give her that, but running a station? I'm not so sure."

"I'm just saying what I heard."

"I'd like to see that," he gives a little smirk.

"So would I. Imagine a girl like that trying to run a station without a man." The three nod, smile at one another and take another sip.

"Thank you for coming, gentlemen." Alice breaks in, after overhearing the tail end of their conversation. "Dad would be happy to know that he has such good friends." She gives nothing away with this remark. They have no idea what or how much she may have heard.

"Sorry for your loss, Alice," one of them says. The other two nod. They all shuffle a little and look down at their shoes.

"Do you need refills?" she asks.

"No. We're going to have to get going. Just wanted to pay our respects," one says.

"Yep. There's a lot of work to be done, even as cold as it is . . . "

"Yep, keeps a man busy alright."

"Well, thank you again for coming," Alice says somberly. "And by the way, you needn't worry about who runs Mullagh Station. It's all under control."

The men at first are shocked at this, wondering if she did indeed overheard them. They look at her with new interest. "Oh, how's that?" one asks. Each is thinking that someone else has already sneaked in ahead of him and made a bid for the place.

Alice's eyes turn to steel as she looks from one to the other. "Yes. And in case you might be wondering *who* is going to manage the station without a man now that Dad's gone, you are looking at her. That would be me." She gives a slight smirk of her own and walks away.

Alice's announcement is more bluster than fact. It is her intention to take over the station, but she knows she has to deal with a large obstacle to her ambition: her mother. For a station woman, Mrs. Buckingham is an anomaly. Whereas most of her female neighbours are actively involved with station life, she conducts herself like a woman of leisure. She has help to do everything. Hanging the washing with Alice that one time was very much out of character. She only did it because the Aboriginal girl who would normally do it was sick and Alice was available. Mr. Buckingham indulged his wife to a fault from the time they began courting.

So, when enough time has passed, following Buckingham's death, the inevitable confrontation plays out.

"Mother, we have to have a talk," Alice announces.

"Not now, Alice. I am still far too distraught," Mrs. Buckingham answers.

"Yes, mother. Now!"

Mrs. Buckingham's eyes pop at her daughter's tone.

"We have to talk about what we are going to do with the station," Alice presses on.

"Why, we are going to sell it, of course," her mother answers.

"Why?"

"Alice, you know perfectly well that I can't run this station. I have no aptitude for it and the idea has no appeal for me."

"I'm not asking you to run it, Mother. I'm telling you that I want to. You can go on living just as you have."

"Don't be silly, Alice."

"I'm not being silly. You know very well that Dad was hoping I would find a husband and keep the place going."

Mrs. Buckingham glances around the room and says, "Well, I don't see any husbands around here, do I?"

"Nevertheless, Mother, Dad knew I *do* have the aptitude for it, as you say. That's why he said what he did."

"He said that to humour you, Alice."

"No, he didn't and you know it. I want to have a go. I'm going to have a go. With or without your consent! I'll fight for it if needs be."

Mrs. Buckingham sees a lot of her husband in Alice and knows that like him, when Alice has made up her mind about something, she will pursue it to the end. Mrs. Buckingham has never forgotten the braids incident.

"I don't like the idea of it, Alice. It is unseemly for a young woman to even think of running a station.

You'll have to deal with all the men here for one thing. How do you expect to do that?"

"I'll find a way. We have employees here who loved Dad and will do anything to help me just because they want to keep working here too." Her mother is silent. Alice thinks for a long moment. Much more subdued, she says, "All right, Mum, I don't really want to fight with you. I'll make you a proposition. Give me two years to make it work. We have enough money in the bank to last us at least that long. If it doesn't work out, we'll sell."

Against her better judgment, and because she has no stomach for trying to fight her daughter, she nods. "All right, Alice. In two years' time, we will decide. But don't expect me to help. You know I don't like station work. I can barely stand station life."

"Thanks, Mum." She goes to her mother and puts her arms around her.

Mrs. Buckingham hesitates for only a moment before embracing her daughter. "Don't make me regret this," she says.

"You won't, Mum. I promise."

* * * * *

Johnny Mullagh and Charles Lawrence are standing quietly in the visitors' area of Guy's Hospital in

London. They haven't spoken for several minutes. Each is deep in his own thoughts. King Cole has been feeling weak lately. He hasn't been able to perform very well on the cricket pitch. At first, he tried to slough it off as nothing special, but soon it became evident that he was in some kind of trouble.

Johnny Cuzens is the first to notice. He goes to Mullagh's room in the hotel. "Unaarrimin, I think King Cole is crook. He won't say anything but I heard him coughing and his breathing sounds bad."

Mullagh says, "I'll talk to him." He goes to King Cole's room and taps on the door.

King Cole starts to say, "Come in," but instead begins a nasty coughing fit.

Mullagh opens the door and enters. "What is the matter? Why are you coughing like that?"

King Cole shakes his head, tries to wave Mullagh off and continues coughing.

Johnny Mullagh goes immediately to Lawrence's room and enters without knocking. "Coach, we have to get King Cole to a hospital. Now."

Lawrence might have said something about being barged in on in this manner, but the look on Mullagh's face and the tone of his voice have communicated an urgency that does away with all formality and protocol. Lawrence leads the way out his door and they go quickly to King Cole's room.

King Cole has stopped coughing but he looks as weak as he feels. Both Lawrence and Mullagh notice for the first time how much weight he seems to have lost. He is a shell of his former self. He looks very ill. They waste no time in getting him dressed and into a carriage.

This is the second day they have been waiting at the hospital. Yesterday was taken up with examinations and tests. They have yet to be permitted to see King Cole for fear of contagion. Today they hope to talk to a doctor.

Mullagh's thoughts take him back to the conversation he had with King Cole when Jellico died.

"First one, now two." "These white fella sicknesses will kill us all, eventually. We want to die in our own ways."

The doctor approaches Lawrence and Mullagh. He has a grim expression on his face. "It is not good," he says. "We believe he has tuberculosis and it is pretty far along. He is having a great deal of trouble breathing. We will do everything we can to keep him comfortable, but we believe it is only a matter of days . . . "

Tears fill Johnny Mullagh's eyes. "He has been my biggest supporter. He got me my job at Pine Hills. It is because of him that I learned cricket." Lawrence feels the loss too, but in his own way. He is sorry that such a fine fellow is going to die, but he also knows it will take one man off a team that can ill afford to lose anyone. But wisely, he says none of this now. "Thank you, doctor. Make him as comfortable as possible. Is it all right if we see him?"

They are ushered to King Cole's ward. He is awake but unresponsive when Lawrence tries to speak to him. He can only look through half-closed lids at them. Mullagh takes his friend's hand and squeezes it lightly. He feels a slight squeeze in return. That is the extent of King Cole's ability to communicate. Mullagh strokes his friend's forehead and smoothes his hair. They remain like this for some time, observing no change in King Cole's behaviour or his ability to communicate.

Finally, Lawrence looks at Johnny Mullagh and motions toward the exit. "There's nothing we can do for him, lad. Let's leave the nurses to look after him."

Two days later, King Cole is dead. Only Lawrence is with him at the end, holding his hand as life slowly leaves him and he passes away. No one else has been permitted to see him.

Back at the hotel, all the Aboriginals are congregated in Mullagh's room waiting for Lawrence to return with some news. When he arrives, his expression says it all.

"No. Not him," Dicky Dick wails. "Not him. No."

Lawrence senses that this is not a place for him to be right now. On his way to the door, he says, "Lads, I'm going to go to see Mr. Harriman and tell him."

Once Lawrence is gone, Bullocky says, "I wish we could take him back to country."

Johnny Cuzens says, "This is no place for our brother to die."

"We are in England. We can't send him off to our ancestors from here." Tarpot says.

"We should be able to take him back to country," Sundown agrees.

The conversation continues in this vain for more than half-an-hour. Each of them brings up some thing that is absolutely necessary for a successful transition, but per custom, no one says his name. Johnny Mullagh has been listening. "I will talk to Mr. Harriman," he says. "I agree. We have to do something."

There is a tap at the door. Harriman's voice says, "I would like to come in, boys. We need to talk about King Cole and what we do from here." Without waiting for a response, he enters. Lawrence is with him. Before he says a word, Johnny Mullagh says, "Do not say the name of our departed brother."

Harriman looks at Mullagh sternly. He doesn't like being told by any darkie how to refer to the dead. But in light of what he needs from these Aboriginals, he only says, "This is a severe blow for all of us." He says this without empathy. "But we cannot lose our focus," he continues. "We are here to play cricket."

"We need to honour him," Mullagh says. "We have traditional ways. He must go to our ancestors properly. We have ceremonies. It is our way."

Harriman immediately looks to Charles Lawrence for help. Lawrence tries to soften Harriman's approach. "Lads, it is impossible for you to carry out any of your rituals here in Great Britain. You must know that. If we were in Australia, I would agree with you and we would do everything according to tradition and custom. But here, no."

"We cannot even honour our dead?" Dicky Dick asks. He is incredulous. "Who is anyone to tell us how to look after a brother who has passed? Our ways are sacred."

Harriman has the discretion not to say what is on his mind. "I will leave you with your coach, boys. I have funeral arrangements to see to."

Lawrence goes to his default position. "Lads, you know we would do everything possible, but we are in Great Britain. It is a Christian country. They have ways here too. But I will make you one solemn promise. I will personally see to it that he has a proper Christian burial. You have my word on that."

In language, Mullagh says, "May our ancestors forgive us. We will have to let these white fellas have their way. We are at their mercy here in this place. After we return to country, we will try to make amends and ask the elders what to do for our brother."

King Cole is buried in Victoria Park Cemetery in London. Lawrence goes. It is a Christian service. No one from the team attends.

* * * * *

The tour continues. They play a number of matches in the London area, in nearby towns. King Cole's absence is felt in more ways than just morale. It puts added pressure on the better players. They have virtually no time to rest. They must play match after match. They have Sundown and Jim Crow as subs, but they are markedly inferior cricketers. Sundown is yet to get into a match and Jim Crow has only played in one. The pace of the tour is grueling. The crowds are acceptable for the cricket. But when they put on their native games after each cricket match, attendance swells. This adds even more stress.

Fourteen matches are scheduled for the North of England. This schedule is even tighter. Again, the cricket draws acceptable crowds. The native games remain enormously popular. The native games are now the only things the papers mention. On the only days they might have had off, they are required to travel to the next venue, adding to their exhaustion. Only Johnny Mullagh and Johnny Cuzens remain at their peak.

At Bootle, in the far north of England, Mullagh puts on a spectacular display. He scores 51 runs in the first innings and 78 in the second, takes 12 wickets and even stumps a player out while relieving Bullocky. After this match, there is another ceremony honouring Mullagh's amazing feats, as has been the case for many of the players throughout the tour.

The president of the Bootle club addresses the spectators: "Ladies and gentlemen, we have witnessed today one of the most remarkable players in the history of our great game. He is Johnny Mullagh from Australia. Please come forward, Johnny."

Mullagh comes and stands next to the president of the club. "This man," the president continues, "has shown us how our game should be played. I do not think there is a better cricketer in all of England than Johnny Mullagh. We have decided to honour his amazing accomplishments by presenting him with a small token of our appreciation. This purse of 50 shillings is yours, Johnny."

Mullagh takes the purse and begins to speak.

"And let me just add," the president interrupts, "just three short years ago, he did not know what a cricket bat was. He knew nothing whatsoever about cricket. Please join me in giving him a hearty round of applause."

All the spectators rise to their feet and applaud and shout their approval. When Mullagh starts to speak again, the president shouts: "Hip, hip" and the entire venue responds with "Hooray!" Mullagh looks into the crowd and decides he doesn't need to say anything after all and just smiles in all directions and waves his hat.

But the tour grinds on. Matches in Southern Wales and Norwich are added, making it even more challenging. The tour was originally meant to end in Middlesbrough at the end of August. But Harriman decides to add six more matches in the Midlands and a further twelve back in the south of England. This stretches the tour into October. They will have been playing cricket virtually non-stop for six months. It is the longest cricket tour in history. The Aboriginal players are completely spent, yet Harriman is relentless in pushing them further. Their sense of fun has long since disappeared. They are now virtual robots going through the motions.

Harriman and Lawrence are alone in Harriman's hotel room.

"I had to make this extension of the tour, Charles," Harriman says. "Too many clubs around London want the boys to come back. I can't tell my investors that I ended the tour when there is still money to be made."

"The lads are losing their zest for the game, Augustus," Lawrence says.

"Yes," Harriman says, "I have noticed that too. That's why I think we have to make some adjustments."

"What kind of adjustments?" Lawrence asks.

"From now on, I think we should end the cricket matches at a prescribed time so that we can get right into the native games. Clearly, that is what most people want to see anyway," Harriman says.

"But, Augustus, what about the cricket? This is a cricket tour." Lawrence says.

"Oh, bother the cricket. No one gives a damn about the cricket," Harriman explodes. "The attendance numbers tell you everything."

Lawrence doesn't show his hurt at this insult to his profession because he knows what Harriman has said is true. Johnny Mullagh, Johnny Cuzens and Bullocky are still playing at the top of their game out of sheer competitiveness, even though there are times when Bullocky is so hung over that Mullagh has to replace him as wicket keeper. But the others, including Dicky Dick have been less effective. Lawrence is also aware of the thinness of his squad.

"There is something else I have to discuss with you, Charles," Harriman continues. "Sundown and Jim Crow have asked me to send them back to Australia and I am doing it."

"That will leave us short," Lawrence protests.

"It cannot be helped. They came to me two nights ago and cried for half-an-hour, begging me to send them back ahead of the others. It was pathetic. King Cole's death has affected them badly. And besides, they don't contribute much to the cricket or the games anyway," Harriman says without emotion.

Lawrence gazes out the window as he considers how to manage the team short one player. "I am going to have to recruit someone to fill out the team," he finally says.

"Do whatever you have to," Harriman says. "Running the team is your responsibility. I leave all of that to you."

"Where will I find another Aboriginal Australian?" Lawrence says.

"Get a white fella and paint his face with shoe polish," Harriman says. "I don't care what you do. We have to finish this tour."

The players are gathered in Mullagh's room. "I'm sorry, but Jim Crow and I decided we just can't take it any longer," Sundown says. "We never played much cricket. All we did is sit and watch. And besides, we both have families and country that we miss."

"We all have families and country that we miss," Dicky Dick says. "What makes you special?"

Jim Crow pipes up. "What makes *you* special? Your white lady friend?"

This is the first time any words of anger or insult have been spoken by any of them. It is the best indication yet that they are completely out of sorts from mental and physical exhaustion.

"You shouldn't talk like that to him," Bullocky says coming to Dicky Dick's defense.

Jim Crow isn't finished. "You shouldn't drink so much," he says. "You and Tiger have become drunks. You are a disgrace. You can't even finish a cricket match."

"I'm sick of cricket too," Tarpot says. "And I don't like having to dress up like a fool just to please a bunch of white fellas."

"So am I," Redcap adds. "We should all be able to go back to country."

Twopenny stands up. "I think we should all just stop playing. What can they do to us?"

Johnny Mullagh has heard enough. "Stop," he shouts. This is the first time they have ever heard him raise his voice. He has never had to. He pauses for a moment to still himself. "Think about this," he says. "We are here in a foreign land. *All* of us are away from country. But we can't just walk home from here, can we? If we ever want to see country again, we have to do what these white fellas say, whether we like it or not. We should be happy for Jim Crow and Sundown. They are our brothers and they are going back to country. `We cannot be at each other's throats. We cannot fight each other. We are kin. We must be proud. We must be generous. It is our way."

* * * * *

They are back in the London area. The end of the tour is in sight. Lawrence sees how exhausted his team is and wants to do something nice for them as the tour winds down. He decides to take them to a public bath so they can soak away some of their aches and pains. As soon as they arrive en masse, as always, they attract attention. People crowd around them until the footpath is impassable.

At first, Martin, the ticket clerk at the baths, is excited to have these celebrities at his facility. But among the onlookers are also a few people who are not as thrilled to have these Black men in London. One of them gets Martin's ear. "Listen, mate, these darkies aren't real. It's a bunch of white blokes with make-up on, trying to get a free bath. The Australian cricket team isn't even in London. They're up-country."

"How do you know that," Martin asks.

"It was in all the papers today. Didn't you see them?"

Martin is now in a quandary. He hasn't seen the papers. So, if these are imposters, he will be humiliated and probably lose his job. With his limited ability, Martin makes a decision to take action.

Lawrence and the players have been standing at Martin's desk patiently while the wheels of his mind slowly turn. Finally he asks, "How do I know that you blokes are the Australian cricket team like you say?"

Dicky Dick thinks this is a joke. "Where is my boomerang when I need it?" He pats his pockets and looks to the others. "Do you have my boomerang?"

Lawrence looks at Martin with a tolerant smile. "I'm the manager of the team. My name is Charles Lawrence. These men have been playing cricket all over England for the past several months. Surely you've heard of them."

Martin looks at the man who first alerted him about the fake darkies. The man slowly shakes his head.

"I can't allow you in the baths until I find out if you are really who you say you are," Martin says. "How do I know you don't have shoe polish on to make you look black?"

Dicky Dick still thinks this is funny. "Here," he says, sticking his arm out, "see if any of this comes off."

Martin thinks for a moment. "That's a good idea. Wait here," he says and goes into the baths. He comes out a minute later with soap, water and towels. "I'll see for myself." He concentrates like a watchmaker, methodically trying to wash the black off each of the players until he is positive that it is their true skin colour. It only takes four men for him to be satisfied.

This public humiliation is just another in a number of embarrassments they have endured. In other instances, they have been denied accommodation. Or the rates are suddenly doubled. On the cricket pitch, they are regaled. In encounters with the public, this is the treatment they sometimes suffer. Racism is constantly a consideration in any setting. No situation is immune from it. For some people, no amount of fame can compensate for dark skin.

Also, here in the south of England, a white player now completes the team. No one cares. He merely fills a position. When a match is finished, he goes about his business. There is no fraternization.

Lawrence has also become indifferent to coaching the team. He has no one to substitute with if a substitute is needed. He can teach them nothing. They have already learned everything they can. What they haven't learned, they have no interest in. Besides which, up to now, most matches end in a draw because the cricket has given way to the native games.

The team is in their change rooms before the next match. Lawrence has been late in arriving. When he does, he ignores any routine and gets straight to the point. "Lads, I have been contracted to play in a match this coming weekend in London. It's with one of my old clubs and it will mean a lot to me. But you needn't worry. I will have a very competent replacement here to join you. He is a mate from early cricket days too. His name is Geoff Conway and he will also be your captain and run the team."

Dicky Dick is immediately on his feet. "What do you mean he will be our captain and run the team? We have a captain!"

Johnny Cuzens is quick to add, "Johnny Mullagh is our leader. He will captain the team."

Lawrence sees the potential rebellion start to grow and knows he needs to put a stop to it right away. "Lads! Lads!" he shouts. "This isn't like it was when we needed a captain in Australia. There are certain rules we have to follow. I didn't make them up. It's the law." He knows it isn't the law but says it anyway. He has to be able to quiet them and get away. If the team rebels and Harriman finds out about it, he will not allow Lawrence to take the job in London. "I am just as disappointed as you are that Johnny Mullagh can't be captain while I am gone, but we have no choice. You have to believe me."

No one says anything. They all look at Mullagh to measure his reaction. He stares at Lawrence for a full minute without saying a word. It is not a hostile stare. But it is intense. Lawrence doesn't like holding Mullagh's gaze, but he also doesn't want to show weakness. So he stares back. Time has stopped. Finally, Mullagh says in an unemotional but firm voice, "I am sure what you say is true, Mr. Lawrence. A Black man cannot be the captain of an all Aboriginal cricket team in England. It is the way of this British world. But, as a proud, Black, Jardwadjali man from Australia, I want you to know that I am insulted."

His teammates all smile and nod.

When they take the pitch, it is with lackluster enthusiasm. There is no laughing. There is no talking in language. There are no congratulations to the other team. They simply go through the motions. When it is their turn to bat, they show an equal amount of enthusiasm. The match means nothing to them. The spectators don't know what to make of this. They came expecting a cricket match. They came to see the Australian Aboriginals do their stuff. They are not getting their money's worth. And they don't like it.

When Mullagh finally comes to the crease, it brings the crowd to life and the spectators begin to murmur with excitement. They know who this one is. In different parts of the stands, you can catch bits of conversation. "This is the bloke I was telling you about." "You want to see some batting? Here it comes." "This is Johnny Mullagh. Some say he is the best cricketer alive today." "About time we saw some real action." Figuratively, they all sit forward in their seats in anticipation of a great athletic display about to unfold.

The first ball comes at him. Mullagh draws back his bat and steps out of the way. It barely misses the wicket. The crowd responds with a collective "Oooh,"

Harriman has been watching "his darkies" play like zombies. He is not pleased. However, he is sure Mullagh will redeem the situation.

The bowler releases his second ball. It bounces above Mullagh's head. He makes a gesture as if he is going to hit it. The crowd gets excited because early in the tour, Johnny Mullagh introduced a method of batting that was never seen before. When a ball like this bounced high in front of him, he instinctively met it with a flick that sent it in a soft arc over the wicket keeper's head for a boundary. This isn't one of those occasions. He doesn't try to hit this ball.

When the next ball comes at him, it is the one Mullagh has been looking for. He steps to the side and barely clips it so that it floats harmlessly to the player at gully for an easy catch. It looks even to the most supportive fans as if he did it intentionally. The crowd begins booing and loudly shouting insults at Mullagh as he leaves the crease. He looks into the crowd as he walks slowly back to the players' section. Then to everyone's amazement, including his teammates, he smiles and waves his hat.

Harriman leaps to his feet and goes immediately to the players' section. When he reaches Mullagh, he is livid. "How dare you? How dare you? These people have paid hard earned money to watch

Johnny Mullagh, the master batsman, perform. And what do you do? You thumb your nose at them. What have you got to say for yourself?"

Mullagh fixes Harriman with his eyes and says not a word. Lawrence has joined them now. "I'm sure he's still feeling bad because of King . . . " He catches himself. "Because of the loss of his teammate, right Johnny?"

Mullagh's eyes have not left Harriman's. He makes no response. By now the other players are observing this scene carefully as well. Mullagh is the last person they would ever expect such an overt act of defiance from. They can't believe it. But at the same time, they are secretly loving it. The crowd is still booing.

Harriman is infuriated. By now, he is virtually screaming. "Who do you think you are? You are only here because of me. Without me, you wouldn't be receiving all the prize money you get. You are nothing without me!" Lawrence attempts to step between them and quiet Harriman but he is ignored. Harriman pushes him aside. "You are hereby suspended from playing cricket!" Harriman announces. "Don't look for help from your coach, either. I will tell you if and when you can return to the cricket pitch, you ungrateful, Black bastard!"

Lawrence wants to protest and claim all decision-making regarding the team for himself. But he knows it would be futile while Harriman is so enraged.

Mullagh holds his eyes on Harriman for a few more seconds, then turns away and starts unbuttoning his shirt on his way to the change area.

Lawrence pulls Harriman aside. "Augustus, you can't do this. We are short of players as it is. If you take our star player out of the line-up, the spectators won't like it. It could cause a riot. We will lose money."

Harriman is still seething. He is not to be dissuaded. "I don't give a damn. No Black bastard is going to humiliate me in public and get away with it. I've given these bastards everything. I brought them to England. They played cricket at Lord's, for god's sake. Your star player can cool his heels for a few days until he learns who is the boss around here! Let's see how he likes that."

Lawrence would love to correct a few of Harriman's statements, like who salvaged the idea of coming to England and who raised the money and who makes decisions about the team, but while he thinks Harriman is wrong, he hasn't liked Mullagh's attitude much lately either. The suspension will be carried out.

The following Saturday, Johnny Mullagh reports to the hotel kitchen early in the morning. Harriman has arranged with the hotel management that Mullagh's punishment for disobeying him is to become a scullery maid, so to speak, and scrub pots and pans. Johnny Mullagh appears to be unfazed by this punishment. He took a stand for what he regards as principle and has no regrets. He is almost cheerful as he ties on an apron. "Where do I start?" he asks one of the kitchen staff.

"These coffee urns could use a good cleaning," the man says. "And you will do a good job if you know what's good for you. We have high standards at this hotel." Mullagh nods and starts on the coffee urns. A short time later, another of the staff comes into the kitchen. He looks at Mullagh and smiles. "They said you were here. I wouldn't believe it. But by god, here you are. I'm Chester. You're Johnny Mullagh, aren't you?"

Mullagh looks up and wipes some sweat from his forehead. "Yep. That's me."

"I can't believe it," Chester repeats. "I read about you in the papers. Saw your picture and everything. I read about you getting 50 shillings up in Bootle. They say it was the best cricketing they ever saw. What in the bloody hell are you doing here? Don't you have a match today?"

"The team does, but I am helping out in the kitchen today and tomorrow. And maybe after that too. I don't know."

"Did you get sacked?" Chester is in shock. Mullagh shrugs his shoulders, as if to say, *yes*. Chester calls to the others in the kitchen. "This gentleman right here is the best cricketer in England, boys. The best! All the papers say so. He's Johnny Mullagh from Australia."

The others in the kitchen staff surround Mullagh. They have a celebrity in their midst. All work stops for the moment. "Is that true? Are you the best cricketer in England?" one asks.

Mullagh is far too self-effacing to answer such a question. But Chester is not. "I bloody well told you, didn't I? The president of the cricket club up in Bootle gave him fifty bob. That's how bloody good he is. How many of you got fifty bob for playing cricket?"

The first staff member that spoke harshly to Mullagh joins the others. "Listen, mate, you don't have to clean that bloody urn. We'll get someone else to do it."

Mullagh says, "Then give me another job. I want to do something useful as long as I'm here.

None of them can believe it. Who in his right mind would keep Johnny Mullagh off a cricket pitch? Only an idiot, they conclude. This turns out to be how Johnny Mullagh spends his two days of punishment, with men fawning over him. He can only smile to himself when he thinks how angry

Harriman was and how determined he was to demonstrate his authority.

Harriman re-instates Mullagh for the match at Reading. In the change rooms before the match, Harriman struts around like a peacock. He approaches Mullagh. "I hope you've learned your lesson, young man."

"Oh, yes, Boss. I'm here to play cricket and nothing else," Mullagh says without sarcasm.

Not entirely satisfied, Harriman needs to get the last word in. "I should certainly hope so." He leaves for his seat in the stands.

Mullagh calls for everyone's attention. In language, he says, "We only have a few more matches in this cold, ugly place. I say we go out onto the pitch and show them what we can do. We are men. We are warriors. We will make them remember us!"

Everyone cheers. Lawrence can only cheer with them. Even though he has no idea what was said, he sees the kind of spirit they had when they first arrived in England and it's good enough for him.

This match is like old times. They have fun and laugh and joke with fans and applaud the opposition. Johnny Cuzens plays his usual brilliant game both bowling and hitting. But the surprise of the day is Twopenny. He takes nine wickets. Lawrence had called on him to bowl because he had no other choice. But, from that match until they leave England, Twopenny joins Mullagh and Cuzens as one of the top bowlers on the team. Rarely does he take fewer than nine wickets per match. It is too late for Lawrence to regret not trying this sooner. Nevertheless, he does. No one is surprised when the outstanding performance of the day goes to Johnny Mullagh. He sets a team record with 94 runs in the first innings. He spends his time at the crease in absolute bliss. He sees the cricket ball as if it were a coconut. He executes his full repertoire of shots with ease, imagination and a big smile. He is in the zone. This sets the tone for the remaining matches. Pure enjoyment becomes the order of the day.

* * * *

These last days are not only enjoyed on the cricket pitch. There are perks to be obtained elsewhere. Tiger and Bullocky spend their spare time being feted at whatever local public house they happen to frequent. It is the kind of attention experienced by elite athletes the world over since time immemorial. Now the Black fellas from Australia are getting their turn. These days, it is every night. It definitely affects Bullocky's play and he frequently has to be relieved. But no one on the team cares. Everyone plays for the joy of it. If Bullocky wants to have a drink now and then, so be it.

This particular evening, they are in a pub just down the street from the hotel where they are staying. The moment they walk in, someone recognizes them and shouts the first round of drinks. Other drinks follow. Many others. The evening wears on and the two Indigenous Aussies are as happy as they can be, soaking up the attention like sponges, enjoying every minute. This kind of thing couldn't even have been imagined just six months ago. They revel in it. Before long, everyone but the barkeep is at least two-and-a-half sheets to the wind.

"You should move here, mate. You could make a fortune playing cricket here," says one of the "experts" in the pub. At this time of the evening, they are all experts at something. All you have to do is name a subject.

"I'm not joking, mate," another of the experts slurs. "I would give up me wife and kids to be able to hit a cricket ball like you, Bullocky. Honest to god, mate."

Bullocky flashes his one-tooth-missing smile at this expert. By now, Tiger can barely stay awake. His head is in his hands as he leans against the bar. Suddenly, his arm slips and he nearly falls down. In language, he says, "That's enough drink for tonight. Let's go back to the hotel."

Bullocky waves him away. In language, he says, "Go if you want. I'm having one more drink." Tiger shakily slides away from the bar and toward the door. He can barely walk, but somehow makes it out the door and down the street to the hotel.

Another of the patrons at the pub has been quiet up until now. It is time for him to reveal his area of expertise. He staggers toward Bullocky and bumps him as he stands next to him. "What's all that gibberish you were talkin', mate? Is that some kind of Nig-Nog talk?"

The barkeep moves toward the bloke. "That's enough, O'Reilly. Don't start anything." This is obviously not the first time O'Reilly has had a drink at this pub. His reputation is as well known as is his area of expertise. In fact, they are one and the same. He's a nasty drunk who is an expert at picking a fight.

"I'm not startin' anything. All I asked was if that blabber he was talkin' with that other darkie was Nig-Nog talk. What's the problem?" He turns to Bullocky. "Tell me, Sambo. Was you two talkin' Nig-Nog talk?"

Bullocky picks up his drink and moves down the bar.

"Hey! I'm talkin' to you, Sambo. Was you talkin' Nig-Nog talk or not?"

"Easy, O'Reilly," the barkeep says.

"What? I'm just havin' a friendly conversation with this Nig-Nog here," O'Reilly says. He follows

Bullocky down the bar. "Hey, Nig-Nog. Let me ask you somethin'."

Bullocky looks away. He doesn't want to cause any trouble, but this white fella is getting on his nerves.

"Don't you turn away from me, Sambo. I'm jist havin' a friendly chat with ya. Jist because you can play a bit of sport, do you think it makes you better 'n the next bloke? Jaysus, a man can't even have a friendly chat with this Nig-Nog," O'Reilly laments.

Bullocky clenches his jaw and tries to ignore his tormentor. O'Reilly sees he is getting to Bullocky and instead of easing off, as any sensible or sober person might, he would rather demonstrate his expertise. He shoves his chest into Bullocky's. "Did you want to make somethin' of it then?"

Before anyone can stop him, Bullocky folds his fingers into a huge fist and punches O'Reilly square in the nose. Blood gushes everywhere. The barkeep yells to one of the other patrons, "Go find a bobby, mate. This is about to get out of control."

O'Reilly staggers from both the drink and the blow to his nose. He catches himself before he crashes to the floor. When he steadies himself and looks up, there is murder in his eyes. But by now, Bullocky has turned squarely toward him. Both of his fists are clenched. O'Reilly reads this body language fluently and has the good sense not to move a muscle, except for pulling a handkerchief from his pocket and shoving it in his nose to stop the bleeding.

In a moment, a bobby strolls in. "And what do we have here, Donny?" he asks the barkeep.

"It's just O'Reilly up to his usual tricks," Donny answers. "He's been goading and pushing this Australian cricketer until he caught one in the snout."

"I think I'd best take care of this quietly," the bobby says. "Come along, lad," he says to Bullocky. "Let's get you back to your hotel."

Bullocky follows him without resistance. He is remarkably steady under the circumstances. The brief fight pumped enough adrenalin into him to sober him up enough to walk to the hotel without weaving.

Harriman is in his room when there is a tap at his door. "Who is it?" he calls.

"It's Officer Clarke, sir. I have one of your lads with me," he says.

Harriman quickly puts on a dressing gown and opens the door. He looks at Bullocky and can't help noticing the blood on his shirt. His expression says, *I told you this would happen.* Then he turns to the bobby. "What happened, officer?"

"Your lad here got into a bit of a blue with an Irishman down at the pub."

"I see," is all Harriman has to say.

"I didn't think it would go over well to have one of your lads arrested," Clarke says.

"Very thoughtful of you. Thank you." Harriman decides to offer the bobby tickets for the next match as thanks. "Are you a cricket fan?" Harriman asks.

"No, sir. Can't say that I am. Well, good evening to you, sir."

"Thank you again, officer. I'll be able to handle this from here." He glares at Bullocky. "You are bent on humiliating me, aren't you? Look at yourself. You are a drunken mess."

Bullocky looks at the floor.

"Thank god we are going back to Australia soon," Harriman says. "Go to your room and sober up. You disgust me."

* * * * *

The final match of the tour is against a team made up of journalists. It is more a frolic than a cricket match. By agreement, no one takes any of it seriously. Both teams just have fun. This was a ploy on Harriman's part. He is hoping that it will create enough good will so that their journalistic farewell will be a series of positive articles. *The London Times*, which has been consistently critical of the Aboriginal team, fails to send a representative to play in this match. Nevertheless, the purpose is achieved. All of the reporting shines a bright light on Harriman and Lawrence as major entrepreneurs who had the foresight to show the world what the Black Aussies can accomplish on a cricket pitch. One column summarizes the general attitude of the press. It says, ". . . the Australian Aboriginals have proven that they are capable of advancing from their natural state to a condition of respectable civilization." This is regarded as the highest compliment that can be paid. An accurate translation of the subtext would be, *They are almost white.*

At this point, it should also be said that over the past six months, the Indigenous Aussies have played 47 matches. Most were more than one day affairs. Some three days by the time native games were added in. They won 14 and they lost 14. The rest were draws. It has been the most ambitious cricket tour ever attempted in England, with a schedule that is unmatched both in length and as a test of physical stamina. Add to that the time and effort required for the native games.

And through all of this, the Aboriginal players received not one penny from their labours with the exception of awards like the ones Johnny Mullagh and others have received. Their accommodations and food were obviously expenses assumed by Harriman. But otherwise, this endless cricket tour of England results in no other payment of any kind beyond what a generous British public bestows on The First Eleven as recognition of their remarkable accomplishments.

* * * * *

The players return to Australia in two groups. Bullocky, Tiger, Peter and Twopenny leave from Gravesend ahead of the others on *The Dunbar Castle*, a ship built only four years ago. The three month sea voyage would seem formidable were it not for the fact that each day brings them closer to home, closer to country. The rest of the team, along with Harriman, will leave from Plymouth in a few days. This latter group spends their free time resting or exploring or shopping for trinkets to take back to Australia. Their time is their own until it is time to board the ship.

Dicky Dick uses this time to have a final rendezvous with Virginia. Their trysts have continued throughout the six months of the tour, whenever they can be together. She has come to Plymouth with one last hope. It is a mild October day when they meet in a park. Virginia is looking radiant. Dicky Dick looks quite comfortable in his fashionable clothes, complete with his top hat. They sit on a park bench together, looking into each other's eyes. Virginia is holding tight to Dicky Dick's hand. It is a sweet scene.

"I have never felt this way about any man in all my life," Virginia says. "I don't know what it is about you that I find so desirable, but whatever it is, it is too strong for me to resist."

"I am very fond of you too, Virginia," Dicky Dick says, guardedly.

"No, Richard, I mean something more than just fondness. This may be my last chance to say this. I am in love with you. I want to be with you. Forever."

"But I am leaving for Australia. That is my home, my country. My life is there."

"Why can't you make England your home? Make a life here. A man of your qualities can certainly find something to do here. You could be an actor or play cricket or any number of things. I know this. I believe in you."

"You see me through different eyes than most people, Virginia. Most people see a Black man and that's all."

"I don't care what most people see. I see you. I see your soul. I see your heart. I don't want to ever lose you. You belong to me."

Dicky Dick doesn't know how to respond. Their time together has been lovely and he has obviously enjoyed it, but it has always been a temporary thing for him. He knows where he is from and who he is. He doesn't want to be cruel to this lovely young woman, but his choices are narrowing.

"I want you to stay in England. Marry me. My family has some money. We can live a beautiful life here together."

"Marry you?" Dicky Dick has always known that she is more committed to him than he is to her, but marriage? This is far beyond anything he would ever consider. "I'm afraid that is impossible, Virginia."

"Why?" She tries to imagine what possible obstacles there could be, aside from the obvious one, one that means nothing to her. She knows he doesn't have a wife. Or at least so he said. After another moment of deep thought, her tone changes. She asks pointedly, "Do you have someone back in Australia?

She is asking too many questions that he can't answer. So he says, "No. Not exactly."

"What does not exactly mean?" Virginia's colour rises. Her cheeks are flushed. This is not the kind of rendezvous she was hoping for.

Dicky Dick realizes he has to follow through with this, even though it was said more as a diversionary tactic than a statement of fact. "I know some women back in Australia," he says enigmatically.

"And?"

"And," he is usually quicker on his feet than this but he is caught unprepared. "And . . . some of them expect certain things from me," he says in an ambiguous way. He knows this is nonsense but it's the best he can come up with under the circumstances.

She looks at him for a long minute. She is shocked. "So, you are saying that you are not in love with me? You don't love me?"

Dicky Dick remains speechless and watches while Virginia processes his silence. Slowly and pathetically, her eyes fill with tears.

But the tears aren't sad tears. They are defiant tears. She wipes the tears away with the back of her hand, and with great dignity stands and stares down at him. She may be a rejected lover, but she is also very British. She holds his gaze for a long moment, wipes the tears away again and with total control says, "Well . . . Right, then . . . . Ta-ta." She turns and walks away without looking back, head held high and arms swinging.

Dicky Dick sits there for a few moments longer. He wishes he could be heartbroken. He wishes he could feel guilty. But his only feeling, when he thinks about it seriously, is relief. He smiles to himself and returns to the hotel, where he will wait to board the ship with Johnny Mullagh, Johnny Cuzens and the others for the long journey back to Australia.

* * * * *

Harriman and Lawrence are sitting together at the hotel bar.

Charles Lawrence raises his glass. "Here's to a successful adventure, Augustus."

Harriman says, "Well, Charles, we did it. God only knows how we got through it all, the drink, the death, the stubbornness of these Black fellas, all of it. But somehow we did. To be honest, there were times I would like to have given it all up. And if we hadn't made a commitment to our investors, I might well have."

"I don't believe that is true for a minute, Augustus. This is something you have wanted to accomplish for a long time, investors or no. We are alike in that way. We are both helpless devotees to the game of cricket. Neither of us would have missed an opportunity like this in a million years," Lawrence replies.

"Well, perhaps you're right," Harriman says. "I suppose it has been its own reward. However, I also hope it proves to be a financial success too. It shouldn't take long to get the accounting in order.

We likely won't make enough to retire on, but we will be able to shout a round of drinks and maybe a little extra," he smiles.

"Whatever it is will be most welcome, Augustus," Lawrence says. "But more to the point, we have done something that Australian sporting history will always remember us for."

"I'll drink to that," Harriman says, as he offers his glass to Lawrence.

They clink glasses and smile a contented smile at one another.

Chapter Ten - Back to the Real World

The Australia that The First Eleven left is not the Australia they return to. During the year that they were away, the wheels of bureaucracy slowly altered things. Secretary Morgan and the Aborigines Protection Board decided that, for their own good, of course, Indigenous people in the colony of Victoria needed the Board's protection and guidance more than ever.

"I am happy to announce, gentlemen," Morgan says as he opens their first meeting since the decision, "we have been able to get legislation passed by the Victorian government that will give us absolute control over our natives."

The members all applaud the good news.

"They will no longer be able to wander around the bush like savages," Morgan continues. "With the help of the Church, we will re-locate them into missions where they will learn to be proper Australians for as long as they survive. And to further protect them from the kind of exploitation the cricketers have been subjected to, no Aboriginal person will be allowed to leave the colony unless it is approved by a government minister."

Blankenship asks, "Will these missions be on land familiar to the various cultural groups?"

"What exactly do you mean by that, Blankenship?" Morgan asks in return.

"It is well established that these people have a special connection to their land, or country, as they call it," Blankenship replies. "Is that being taken into account?"

"Why do you insist on making trouble, Blankenship?" Dunphy says. "Don't you want to see these darkies integrated into society?"

Blankenship says, "What I want is for us to look after them, as is our mandate, to protect them. We have had countless examples of these people being disoriented when they are forced away from where they have lived traditionally. I am merely trying to take everything into account. How would you like to be uprooted from your home and arbitrarily placed somewhere else?"

Morgan is losing his patience. "Look here, Blankenship," he says, "if you are implying that these darkies are like us, you disappoint me. If it weren't for our care and protection, they would have all perished by now. At least we are giving those who remain an opportunity to integrate into white society. It starts with giving them living quarters on government land where they can learn to dress properly and speak English and eat proper food and learn domestic skills that will serve them in the future. And with the aid of the Church, they can learn to accept Christ as their saviour and follow Christian ethics and values and morality. Surely you don't begrudge them that."

Blankenship is subdued. "Perhaps you are right. I just have a soft spot for them. They seem like such innocent children," he says.

Owens, who has been listening without taking sides, says, "Yes they are. Look what has happened to one of the Black cricketers. We couldn't stop them from going to England and the poor lad died there. These missions may not be a perfect solution but we must do something and this is a step in the right direction."

"Well said," Morgan adds. "This is an act of compassion, not of punishment, Blankenship. With our guidance, some of these people might forget their savage ways and become civilized."

Blankenship nods and remains quiet.

* * * * *

The ocean voyage back to Australia is uneventful for a few reasons. The First Eleven are exhausted from the endless pace of the English tour and use most of their time aboard the ship in just recovering. Harriman is much less picky about whether or not the Aboriginals have a drink or with whom they socialize. And they are not the same novelty on the way home that they were on the way to Great Britain. Their stature is assured based on their exploits abroad. They have proven what they set out to prove. They are now, more or less, taken for granted by their fellow passengers.

They have no idea what changes have been made or what may be in store for them as they all congregate in Sydney for their first get together back in Australia. It has been arranged that they will take a victory lap, as it were, playing a few more matches as a team, starting here in Sydney, then to Melbourne and to a few smaller venues in Victoria. The Albert Club hosts their first match. In the change rooms before the match, they exchange some war stories. They are all rested and in good spirits. This is their first time all together since England.

Dicky Dick says, "I kissed the ground when we got off that ship."

With a laugh, Twopenny says, "Bullocky kissed the ground too. He fell down the gangway."

Bullocky is quick to say, "I didn't have anything to drink. I just couldn't walk on land yet. It was too wobbly."

Dicky Dick asks, "Do you think you can stand behind the wicket? Or should we get you a chair?"

Bullocky smiles his one-tooth-missing smile. "I think I can stand up now. But if I don't, Unaarrimin can always take over."

Mullagh says, "No, I won't. I have to remember which end of the bat to use. Three months on that ship made me forget everything." He smiles a broad smile.

"I hate to admit this," says Johnny Cuzens, "but I actually missed seeing you brothers who came back on the other ship." He looks from one to the other. "No. On second thought, I'm already sick of looking at you again."

They all laugh. The atmosphere is what should be expected. They are like veterans who have managed to survive a war and share their unique experience with other veterans. Their camaraderie is quickly re-established. Their warrior spirit is back.

However, the weather is not so obliging. The Albert Club cricket pitch is a pond. They try to play for a short time until the futility of it is obvious and the game is called. Charles Lawrence is especially disappointed because he wanted to show his old club how his Black fellas have improved. Instead of returning to his team's change rooms after the match, he goes with his old mates to catch up with them.

The Indigenous players are on their own back in the change rooms. Johnny Cuzens is the first to comment. "It was like being back in England," he says. "I didn't like playing in the rain there and I don't like it here."

"It made me miss the old place," Dicky Dick says.

"Are you sure it is the rain you miss?" Twopenny says.

Dicky Dick shrugs his shoulders and gives a little smile.

Mullagh is pensive. "You know," he says, "we were ten thousand miles away in a place we couldn't have imagined. Think about that. Think about how unlikely that was. No elders in all our history could have imagined such a thing. And we did it. I wonder what the elders would think."

Dicky Dick says, "They would think it rained too much too!" Mullagh throws a towel at him.

"I hope we get good weather in Melbourne," Bullocky says.

* * * * *

They are in the change rooms at the Melbourne Cricket Ground preparing for a match when there is a loud banging on the door and a voice says, in language, "Open up. I'm looking for a bunch of scruffy wombats!"

Dicky Dick yells so that whoever is outside the door will hear, "Lock the door. We don't want any more white fellas in here. One is enough."

Tom Wills opens the door and walks in. The entire team crowds around him, punching him in a friendly way on the arm and pounding him on the back like a long lost brother. Everyone has a huge smile on his face. Wills says, "You blokes look terrible! Haven't seen you around here in a while. Where have you been?"

Dicky Dick says, "We got caught in the rain in some wicked place called Great Britain. It was terrible. Too many white fellas. A lot like you. None of them could play cricket either. A *lot* like you."

Looking from one to the other, Wills attempts to change the tone by saying, "I can't tell you how proud I am of what you've done. I wish I could have been there with you to see it. You made all of Australia proud of you. Welcome home, brothers."

Dicky Dick says, "Who is this white fella? Anyone know him?"

Johnny Cuzens says, "This is the Black fella change room. What are you doing here?"

"Who do you think you wombats are playing against?" Wills says. "The team I put together for this match is going to make you wish you were back in England."

Wills wasn't exaggerating. The Aboriginal team's antics are subdued for this match against one of the best sides they have ever faced in either England or Australia. Wills has assembled a team at the MCG that includes the best cricketers available from New South Wales and Victoria. This is highly competitive match. Everyone is on his toes.

It's not a surprise that for everyone at the MCG, the greatest attraction is Johnny Mullagh. Some had seen him play on previous occasions, but none of them has seen him since he won over the British cricket establishment and the British public. This created an aura around Mullagh that took him to a unique level of respect and celebrity. He is not only among the first Australian cricketers to play at the home of cricket and proclaimed as the best they had ever seen, he is also, as he put it, *a proud, Black, Jardwadjali man from Australia.* The MCG spectators know that they have an international cricket superstar performing for them now who at the same time one of their own. That is why when the time comes and he joins Twopenny at the crease, a hush settles over the crowd in anticipation of what they expect to come. In his own still way, Mullagh is also keyed up.

On the first ball, Mullagh singles. For the crowd, it might as well have been a boundary. They stand and cheer for nearly a full minute. When play resumes, Twopenny makes contact and starts racing for the opposite wicket. Mullagh sees that the ball is headed directly to the defensive player at cover with some velocity. He digs in and races toward the wicket. The defensive player fields the ball cleanly and fires it into the stumps just ahead of Mullagh's outstretched bat. Mullagh is out.

Everyone at the MCG shouts *Oh, no* virtually in unison. During his much too brief time at the crease, Mullagh scored all of one run. Even Wills is disappointed as Mullagh slowly walks back to the team's area with his head down. His own disappointment is palpable. He wanted so much to put on at least a respectable showing for the home fans. Instead, he sits down a dejected man a mere five minutes after he picked up his bat.

The competition remains fierce but a pall has been cast over the entire proceedings. Without seeing Mullagh bat for at least a respectable amount of time, no one is going to leave the MCG satisfied. It is as though he wasn't really here. Taking a wicket when he bowls is often spectacular but a good session at the crease is what they are here for.

However, later in the innings, it turns out that Peter isn't feeling well. He begins vomiting and looks pale and exhausted. He tells Lawrence that he is unable to bat. Upon seeing this, Tom Wills makes an immediate and instinctive decision that shocks, surprises and delights everyone at the MCG. He allows Johnny Mullagh to substitute for Peter and bat for a second time in the same innings. Unheard of. But generous and brilliant.

When Mullagh walks toward the crease for the second time, the MCG erupts in cheers and applause. There is a smile on every face as he taps his bat on the ground. Wills has saved the day. His action is unprecedented and paints him as a superlative sportsman. Mullagh is still at the crease when the innings ends. All the rest of his teammates have been bowled out. He stands there for another moment alone. The spectators are cheering and applauding him and calling his name. He waves his hat and strolls back to join his team with a wide smile on his face.

Back in the change rooms after the match, Mullagh is sitting to the side when Tom Wills enters the room. Mullagh looks up at him as he approaches. He has a knowing smile on his face as he nods at Wills. Wills stands there for a moment smiling back at Mullagh, nods in return, then abruptly turns and walks out again. No words are necessary.

When the room has nearly cleared out, Wills returns. He has something in mind. He pulls Johnny Mullagh and Johnny Cuzens aside. "How would you two like to come back to the MCG and play with me when this tour of yours is finished?"

"Can we do that?" Johnny Cuzens asks.

"Yes," Wills answers. "You two are legends here now. All the papers have been singing your praises since you went to England. You heard how the fans responded when they saw you today, didn't you? Hasn't anybody told you how good you are?"

"Where would we stay?" Mullagh asks.

"I'll take care of all of that," Wills says. "I'll even be able to get you jobs here at the MCG helping look after the grounds. That way, you'll have some spending money. What do you say?"

Mullagh and Cuzens look at each other.

Johnny Cuzens says, "I wouldn't mind playing cricket for a while longer. It beats working at a station."

Johnny Mullagh is thinking. Finally, he nods. "Why not?" he says. "We can show them what a wombat can do on the cricket pitch," he says smiling at Wills.

Wills extends his hand to each of them. They all shake hands vigorously. "It is agreed, then," he says.

* * * * *

With Wills and the MCG behind them, as a team, the Aboriginals play a few more matches around Victoria and are greeted as returning heroes by many of the spectators. But there is also something about these Black fellas that fans take notice of but can't always articulate. Something in their demeanor, in their stride. Something. Physically, they appear to be the same players they were the last time they were seen at Ballarat or Lake Wallace or wherever, but something is different. The team's final event is scheduled at the Hamilton Cricket ground, the place where it all really began. Many of the people who watched them that first time are on hand again this time. These people, understandably, feel that they have a special claim on The First Eleven. But as they look at the team today, there are some who resent the confidence the darkies seem to project. They don't appear to have the same humility they had before. There are spectators here who wonder if these Black fellas have forgotten their place.

    For Augustus Harriman it is a homecoming of epic proportions. He is lionized by his friends and neighbours for what in their eyes is a monumental achievement. More attention is paid to him than the Indigenous men who did the actual achieving. In his own mind, Harriman sees this as fitting. Here, the darkies are his team, not Australia's. The local newspaper, *The Hamilton Spectator*, waxes poetic about Harriman and "his" darkies and credits him, personally, with his *excellent generalship.* The paper goes on to say, *the appearance of the darkies is in every way a credit to him.* But the most profound praise is this: *They seem to have undergone a process of civilization which changed their nature thoroughly, and their conduct would compare favourably with most white men.*

Mr. Edwards is sitting with Harriman in the stands, pleased to watch his friend bask in this glory.

"You have done a wonderful thing, Gus," Edwards says. "You should be very proud. Everyone here in the Western District is talking about it. It has been in all the papers from the time you left for England."

Thank you, my friend. That means a lot to me," Harriman responds. "We could not have imagined that all this would come to pass from the little talk we had back then." Harriman smiles at his friend when he says, "I told you you should have invested a quid or two."

"So you did, Gus. So you did," Edwards smiles back. "My loss. You'll have to pop over to Pine Hills for a cuppa and tell me what I missed. Pity that the boys aren't playing today. I'd like to have seen that."

"No, we couldn't work out the details with the Hamilton club, but I'm sure you and the others will still enjoy the show my darkies are going to put on," Harriman says. "In England, it was all the talk. Some people even preferred these native games to the cricket.

An abbreviated version of their native games is performed for the people who have come to Hamilton. Dicky Dick, Charlie Dumas and Mullagh show off their boomerang skills and Johnny Cuzens goes through his routine with the woomera and spears. When Dicky Dick returns with his ball dodging show, it goes over as well as ever. But for them, there is also something indefinable about performing before this Western District audience, something different. The audience is no less attentive or appreciative. It is more a feeling among the Aboriginal men themselves. They still like showing off their warrior skills and do it with pride, but these spectators represent the same people who have denied them their culture, who brutally took over their traditional lands and then marginalized them further by putting them to work on stations. Before these Indigenous men went across the seas and had the opportunity to be acknowledged as men and not an inconvenience, they felt forced to tolerate the way these same people regarded their cricketing as an oddity at best. These people didn't think beyond wanting to see the Black fellas play a white man's game. It's as though the Aboriginals are constantly reminded of their difference here, their powerlessness, whereas there were moments at least in England when they were perceived as men. Now, to add to that insult, they have learned about the decree from the colonial government and the Aborigines Protection Board that they will be herded and corralled into missions and reserves where they will be further punished for merely being themselves, another assault on their manhood and their dignity and on their roots.

In the change rooms at Hamilton, after their performance, the mood is solemn. Hanging over everything is the fact that this is their last corroboree. Through all they have endured over the past year, they have had each other. Now, they will be scattered like dandelion pods in the wind, landing on unfamiliar soil, not on their traditional lands, not on country.

Everyone has changed out of their costumes and into their fashionable clothing for one last time, as a celebration and recollection of their amazing adventure together. But, no one knows what to say. Laughter seems forced. Smiles are strained. Everyone waits for someone else to start a conversation. It is the first time in all their lives that they feel uncomfortable in each other's company. In the midst of this, suddenly, Dicky Dick, who has been silently staring at the floor, loudly announces, "I'm on my way to the Ebenezer Mission . . . It isn't even my country . . . It will be like going to prison . . . We won't be able to leave . . . I won't be able to make any money."

None of them has ever seen him like this, so demoralized. Gone are the jokes. Gone are the smiles. Gone are the side comments that brought such great hilarity and joy. The man who always dressed in his own style, who always had a quip ready, sits there like a marble statue with his top hat next to him on the bench, staring down at the floor. There is no laughter. No smiles. No words. Nothing. Only dead silence.

Bullocky finally breaks it by saying to Johnny Cuzens, with no sense of envy, "At least you and Unaarrimin are going back to Melbourne." The comment, which everyone hears, just hangs there like fog.

Chapter Eleven – Aftermath

In the Wimmera, there is a local constable named Kennedy. He has very strong views on how Aboriginal people are treated. He believes they are being exploited and this exploitation can easily lead to huge problems for Indigenous people, like excessive alcohol use and exposure to diseases that can wipe them out. He is not among those who believe their extinction is inevitable.

One of the men he is particularly concerned with is Dicky Dick. Kennedy foresees too much potential for mischief and bad behaviour in taking The First Eleven on tour, first to New South Wales, then to England. To demonstrate his concern in a tangible way, he agrees to take care of Dicky Dick's son while he is on tour. During that time, he calls the boy Richard and gives him his own surname of Kennedy.

Dicky Dick returns to the Western District a shadow of his former, exuberant self. He has no motivation. There is nothing for him to do at Ebenezer Mission. What few opportunities he has for income barely provide enough for basic needs.

Once settled, Dicky Dick goes to Constable Kennedy to see his son. It is a touching reunion.

The boy has grown in many ways, but still has the same sense of family that binds Indigenous people. When he sees his father, he runs to him and they embrace.

Kennedy watches with a soft smile on his face. He has done his best to provide the boy with stability while his father was away. Now his father has returned and the family is happily reunited. Mission accomplished.

"I cannot tell you how grateful I am to you, Constable," Dicky Dick says.

"I have enjoyed every bit of it," Kennedy replies. "He's quite a boy. Has a lot of your spunk."

Dicky Dick ruffles his boy's hair. "I hope he is a lot smarter than his father," he says. The boy smiles up at him.

"I hope you don't mind that I call him Richard and have given him my last name," Kennedy says.

"No," Dicky Dick says, "not at all. In fact I like it. I am also going to call him Richard." He thinks for a moment and says, "I would like to ask you if you mind if I take your name too. I would like to be known by the name of Kennedy. Dicky Dick is a name that I never asked for. It doesn't seem proper. From now on I'd like to be Dicky Kennedy."

"I would be honoured," Kennedy replies.

Months pass and Dicky Kennedy's life remains relatively idle and uneventful. But, little by little, some of Dicky's old self begins to re-emerge. He starts by seeing his life in a less hopeless way. This eventually gives way to seeing things with bit of humour, with a sense of irony, sometimes. He begins smiling to himself and before long, laughing. His happy, fun loving self blossoms once again. He is conscious of having made the best of a bad situation and eventually settles comfortably into life at Ebenezer Mission. To complete this metamorphosis, he marries an Aboriginal woman named Eliza who was recently widowed. He becomes a family man again. Gone are any thoughts of his English tryst with Virginia.

One day Dicky and Eliza are chatting and he tells her about some of his cricketing exploits. Up until now, he has been guarded about speaking of those days. This is the first time he has spoken about them with humour and a sense of enjoyment. Eliza is all ears and delighted when Dicky remembers the day he almost hit a spectator. "One of the things I did for our native games was throw a boomerang toward the crowd," he laughs as he tells her. "This one day, it was a bit windy and you couldn't be sure if the boomerang would fly correctly. But we were required to put on the show no matter what, so I was as careful as I could be. I threw it and thought I had calculated for the wind, but a gust came up and forced the boomerang down toward the crowd. It passed so close to one man that it barely clipped his hat and knocked it off his head on the way back to me." Eliza smiles deep into his eyes. To her, sharing these stories with her means everything. It means he trusts her. And allows her to feel more confident about her place in his life and his in hers.

Eliza is thoughtful for a moment, then says, "Do you know what you should do? You should start a cricket team here at the mission."

To Dicky, this thought seems to have come out of nowhere, but he thinks about it. "Hmm. There are quite a few young fellas around here who might like that," he says.

"That's what I was thinking," Eliza says, smiling. Despite his reticence to talk about it, everyone at Ebenezer Mission knows who this famous cricketer among them is. Many are secretly hoping he will tell them stories of those magical days. So, when Dicky decides to form and coach a cricket team, there is no shortage of volunteers. After a week or so, he assembles the team he wants and begins drilling them the way Tom Wills and Charles Lawrence drilled him and his teammates.

"We'll start with these Swedish calisthenics," he says. "And after you are completely worn out, we will start having some cricket practice. If we do this right, you will all hate me by the end of the week." He smiles a smile that he forgot he had. He prepares the team for district competition and everyone loves it. Dicky once again feels he is in his proper place, being admired and respected, with a sense of freedom to make his wise cracks whenever he decides to, the center of attention.

But then, with lightning speed, an epidemic of measles strikes Ebenezer Mission. The epidemic spreads in no time through the entire Aboriginal community. The Indigenous people have no resistance to it. No one is equipped to deal with it. No one knows what to do to be safe from it. The disease easily finds the most vulnerable. One in five people at the mission dies from measles.

Dicky and Eliza seem to have been saved from this "white man's" disease, as King Cole would have called it. But despite his physical stamina and will to resist, Dicky begins to show signs of the disease's effect. One of the complications with measles when the disease has taken hold is potential brain damage.

All of a sudden, it seems, a normally light-hearted Dicky becomes morose and melancholy. Nothing Eliza says or does can make him happy or lighten the load he seems to be carrying. She grows increasingly concerned.

"My head hurts," Dicky says one day. "It feels like it is going to explode. I think I am going crazy."

Eliza tries to sooth him but to no avail. Soon he becomes incommunicative and shows signs of depression. She goes to one of the missionaries. "Reverend, you have to help me," she says. "My husband is not himself. These measles are killing him, making him crazy. What can we do?"

The missionary is prepared to lead her in prayer but little more. He is as unequipped for this epidemic as everyone else. "Let me talk to some of my superiors," he says. "They may have an idea how to deal with this."

More days pass. Dicky has now reached a state where he either cannot or will not speak. If they could read his mind, they would see a man who is also becoming suicidal. He loses his temper easily. He forgets things. He can't sleep. He sometimes hallucinates. Every situation leads him to conclude that life is not worth living. But no one is equipped to discover or treat this at a little Christian mission in the Western District of Victoria.

By now, the entire community is concerned. He is their star. They relate to his accomplishments as their own accomplishments. Yet, they are all as helpless as the missionaries. Finally, the people in control decide they must take action and to send him to the Ararat Asylum in hopes that someone there can help.

The staff at Ararat Asylum is aware of who Mr. Kennedy, as he is known here, is. As mental institutions go, this one is progressive. Despite the stigma attached to this condition, the nurses and doctors here use enlightened treatments that are outside the box. They promote recovery by engaging their patients in useful activities, regular routines and various amusements. Each of these things is meant to stimulate and re-orient their minds. The hope is that the slightest image may produce a recollection of a long forgotten event that will, in turn, bring them into the present.

The doctors examine Mr. Kennedy and conclude that they may be able to help, but it will take time and is largely dependent on Mr. Kennedy himself. They diagnose his condition as a brain complication that has resulted from a bad case of measles. They immediately immerse him in their activities plan. Nothing seems to work. And to make it even more challenging, he still will not or cannot speak.

Undaunted, the medical staff forges ahead, hoping one day that he will relate to something and start to come around.

"The problem," one of the doctors says to Jenny, the nurse who has been caring for Dicky, "is that these diseases caused by measles are rarely curable. And with Mr. Kennedy, the fact that he won't talk makes things even harder."

"Do you think we may have to dismiss him, doctor?" Jenny asks. And quickly adds, "I certainly hope not. He seems such a sweet man."

"We'll give it a bit more time, but it is not looking good," he responds.

One day, Jenny goes to Dicky's room. He is sitting in a chair and staring into space. This is often how she finds him but she always ignores it and treats him as if he were coherent and responsive and hanging on her every word.

She greets him in the same way each time she walks into his room. "Good afternoon, Mr. Kennedy," she says cheerfully. "It's Jenny. How are you feeling this afternoon?"

Dicky doesn't acknowledge her presence.

"I know you haven't had your lunch yet," she says. "Hungry?"

Dicky continues staring.

"Do you know what I think?" she goes on. "I think some fresh air would do you good. Why don't we take a walk down by the creek. Everyone is there. It's our annual picnic. They always have good food, especially the desserts. Do you think you would like that?"

He makes no response. He is virtually catatonic.

"Come along, then," she says and takes him by the arm and helps him out of his chair.

It is a lovely, warm, sunny day as Jenny guides Dicky toward the creek where tables and chairs are set up. Many of the patients are already there in varying states of consciousness and awareness. A few are talking among themselves. Jenny decides that Dicky would prefer to be alone and sets a chair up by the bank of the creek where he can look out at the water and listen to the birds. He seems content.

"I'll just go and fetch you a plate of food," she says. "Don't wander away now." She smiles down at him and pats his shoulder.

While she is preparing his plate, some of the men on the staff are setting up stumps and bails for their annual cricket match between patients and staff. It is one of the activities that all who are able to, look forward to with great relish.

Jenny returns to Dicky with his food. He is staring out into space as is his habit indoors or out. She helps him with his food, for all practical purposes, feeding him. It is known that he can be reluctant to eat otherwise.

After some time has passed and Dicky has eaten, Jenny says, "I'm going to leave you alone for a little while. You stay right here and enjoy nature." She pats his shoulder as she leaves to join the cricket game.

    Dicky is still lost in his unknowable, galactic vacuum of a mind when he hears a faint sound that penetrates the vacuum long enough to register as remotely familiar. He can't attempt to identify it. But it does grab his attention as nothing ever has before. Now, in spite of himself, his concentration focuses entirely on this sound. What is it? He hears it again. A little more clearly this time. He knows this sound from somewhere. Without thinking about it, he turns around toward where the sound is coming from. This represents the only voluntary movement he has made in anyone's recollection for the many months of his being here. What he sees when he turns is people playing cricket, though it still doesn't register as such. He continues to watch, straining to bring something -- he doesn't know what -- back to mind. He rises from his chair and slowly begins to walk toward the cricket game, still puzzled by it, but curious.

    By now, Jenny has noticed Dicky and excuses herself from the game. She rushes toward him. "Are you alright, Mr. Kennedy?" she asks. She takes his arm, fearing he may fall. No one has seen him walk without help since he arrived at Ararat.

    Dicky stops. Time freezes as he ever so slowly turns toward Jenny and focuses on her face. He is staring at her with a kind of concentration she hasn't seen before, as if he were truly looking. And If she didn't know better, without much effort, she could even mistake the look on his face for a slight smile. Suddenly, his eyes brighten. He looks deep into her eyes and his smile explodes light. "You are Jenny."

Tears fill her eyes as she smiles and says, "Yes, Mr. Kennedy, I am Jenny."

Dicky now looks at the cricket game in progress with the same concentration. Again, he lights up. "That is a cricket game . . . I used to play cricket," he says clearly. "I went to England and I played cricket at Lord's with Johnny Mullagh."

Jenny is beside herself with joy. "I know, Mr. Kennedy. I know," she says through tears.

From that moment on, Dicky continues to respond to people and things around him. He chats with other patients and jokes with them as in days of old. In a few months, the doctors decide he is well enough to return to Ebenezer Mission.

On the day of his departure, Jenny comes to his room. "Hello, Mr. Kennedy," she says brightly. "All packed and ready to go?"

Dicky looks at her with a very serious, unfamiliar expression and says, "Jenny, I have to tell you something. Please don't tell anyone else."

Jenny regards him with equal seriousness and concern. "What is it, Mr. Kennedy?"

"I could have left here months ago, but I couldn't leave you. I think I am in love," he says as his eyes light up with mischief.

Visibly relieved, she says, "You are a devil, aren't you? Just for that, I'm not going to kiss you good-bye."

"I won't leave until you do," he says, sitting down on the bed and crossing his arms.

"Oh, all right, then," she says. She gives him a kiss on top of the head. "Now, go home to your wife, you heartbreaker."

His return to Ebenezer Mission is a hero's welcome. Friends and neighbours flock around him as he walks home from the buggy. Eliza is standing at the door as he strolls up. She is smiling with relief and pure love as they embrace.

A few years have now passed since his illness. Then one day some of his old skills are called upon once again. A nearby local toddler has wandered away into the bush. The little girl has disappeared. No one can find her after two full days of searching.

Someone remembers Dicky's tracking reputation and seeks him out to see if he can help. His senses are as sharp and his instincts are as good as they were when he found the Duff children so many years before. He examines and searches and hunts for clues until he finds the faintest little footprints that no one else had seen, only this tracker whose vision is trained for it. He carefully follows the tracks for six miles until he spots the little girl lying down on the ground. Just as the Duff children were, she is hungry, thirsty and frightened. But she is alive. The local settlers take up a collection and present it to Dicky as a reward for this rescue, just as the others had. The name King Richard resurfaces somehow and Dicky is also given a breastplate that has been specially made to honour the occasion. Eliza looks on from the background while her husband stands smiling in the place where he feels most at home -- the spotlight.

More years pass. Dicky and Eliza are talking one day when he floats the idea of applying for a land grant. "I can ask the Justice of the Peace in Horsham to do the paperwork for me," he says. "With all I've done, it may be hard for anyone to ignore my application, don't you think?"

"It can't hurt to try," Eliza says. "It would be nice to have our own place. I could have a big garden."

The Justice of the Peace makes the application and gets a favourable response. Dicky and Eliza are delirious with joy. They are going to have a new start on their own plot of land and leave the Ebenezer Mission behind. Everything points to the future when the Justice of the Peace comes to see Dicky and Eliza one day.

"Mr. and Mrs. Kennedy," he says, "I'm afraid I have some bad news for you."

Dicky and Eliza sit down at the shock of this statement. "What is it?" Dicky asks.

"Well, everything was going along all right until the missionaries here had second thoughts," he says. "It seems they are concerned that you've had these mental bouts in the past and are afraid they might come back. They don't think you would be capable of independent living. They say it pains them to refuse you, but it is for your own good."

"I'll be able to look after Dicky, if needs be," Eliza says.

"If it were up to me, there would be no question," the Justice of the Peace says. "But, unfortunately, it isn't up to me. The mission has the final say."

As if to prove a point, Dicky is so upset by this decision that he suffers another mental episode and is returned to Ararat Asylum for treatment and care. After six months, he is released back to Eliza and Ebenezer Mission. But his constitution is broken irreparably. He will never be himself again. A short time after that, Dicky Dick Kennedy, the great tracker, cricketer and Wotjabaluk warrior, dies at Ebenezer Mission of what could be described as a broken heart. The missionaries decide that Dicky should have a proper, Christian burial. But to do that, he must be a Christian. Therefore, they baptize him on his death bed without his or Eliza's permission.

* * * * *

The Corowa Cricket ground is situated in the town of Corowa in southern New South Wales. Like all cricket grounds of the day, the local teams are made up mainly of amateur athletes who play for the pure joy of it.

One afternoon, while a match is in progress, one of the officers of the club notices a Black fella propped up against one of the sheds. He doesn't like the looks of this darkie. He finds an attendant. "There's a darkie over there by that shed. Go over and find out what he's doing here. Then tell him to get the hell out."

The attendant has seen this Black fella hanging around the grounds before. He says to the club officer, "He's been around here a few times. He is harmless. Doesn't bother anybody. Stays out of everybody's way. He just likes to watch the cricket."

"I don't care if he is harmless or not. I don't like having a dirty looking abo loafing around our cricket ground," the club officer says. "Go over there and get rid of him."

The attendant would like to tell this bloke to go over and get rid of the Black fella himself, but instead shrugs his shoulders and strolls toward the shed. He has never been this close to the darkie before. Since he doesn't cause any trouble, the attendant has always ignored him. He has enough responsibility just keeping the pitch in reasonable condition without policing harmless Black fellas who want to watch a game of cricket.

The Black fella is sprawled there, legs spread out, leaning with his back against the shed for support. From this closer distance, it appears that the Black fella could be either sick or drunk. When the attendant reaches the shed, the Black fella looks up at him.

"Sorry," the attendant says, "but you'll have to move along. The people who run the club don't like the looks of someone like you hanging around like this."

The darkie focuses on the attendant through a blur. "Oh, I just like watching the cricket," he says innocently. "I'm not causing any trouble. I just like cricket," he smiles his one-tooth-missing smile at the attendant.

Taking a closer look, the attendant thinks he recognizes this Black fella. "Say, aren't you one of the Black fellas that went to England?"

The one-tooth-missing smile broadens. Bullocky tries to reach out to shake this man's hand, but tips over instead. "I played with Johnny Mullagh," he says as he tries to straighten up.

The attendant reaches down to help Bullocky stand. "I saw your picture in the papers. I remember you. You done us proud," he says.

Bullocky does his best to remain vertical and steady. It is a challenge. The attendant changes his tone. "Listen. What's your name again?"

"Bullocky"

"Listen, Bullocky, some of these people are not too happy having Black fellas around here. If it was up to me, I wouldn't care. But they told me to chase you off. And if I want to keep my job, I've got no choice. Like I said, if it was up to me, I'd tell them to get stuffed, but . . . "

Bullocky has steadied himself to the best of his ability. This is not a new situation for him. He has often been asked to leave premises whether they are cricket grounds or pubs. He is resigned. And he is no longer hot headed about it. It is now his way of life. "No worries," he says. "I'll be moving on. But could you give us a couple of bob? Hair of the dog and all that. For old times' sake?"

The attendant reaches into his pocket and finds a few coins. "Here you go, Bullocky. Good luck to you. And let me shake your hand. I want people to know I met you."

Bullocky takes the attendant's extended hand and smiles his one-tooth-missing smile.

* * * * *

Very little is known about Jim Crow beyond the fact that he was jailed in Swan Hill and Echuca. He also ran afoul of his clan. It most likely had something to do with either adultery or running off with someone else's wife. Both of these are capital offenses according to tribal justice. Two Aboriginal men track Jim Crow down and summarily execute him.

* * * * *

"It has been brought to my attention, gentlemen, that some of our darkies have skirted the mandate that requires them to be located on missions," Chairman Morgan says. "That is why I have convened this special meeting of the Aborigines Protection Board."

"Who has been responsible for such an outrage?" Dunphy asks.

Morgan reads from a piece of paper. "A Johnny Cuzens and a Johnny Mullagh, it says here."

Blankenship can't help himself. He snorts out loud.

"What is so amusing, Blankenship?" Morgan asks.

"Is it possible that I am the only member of this body who knows who these men are?" Blankenship says, trying unsuccessfully to suppress a smile.

Morgan is not amused. "Clarify, please," he says.

"I cannot believe this," Blankenship mutters to himself. Then, aloud he says, "These two men are two of the most distinguished of the Indigenous players on the cricket team that went to England. They are now playing for the Melbourne Cricket Club. One of them has been hailed as the best cricketer playing the game today. And the other isn't far behind."

"The government's ruling doesn't have any exceptions for cricket players," Dunphy says. "They are in breach of the regulations." Morgan nods his approval.

"Gentlemen, if I may," Blankenship says, "I would suggest you pull your heads out of the sand. No politician on earth would dare carry out those regulations for these two men. The Melbourne Cricket Grounds and everyone who attends matches there would openly revolt. And that would be the least of it. This board would become the laughing stock of the entire colony of Victoria. The newspapers would have a field day . . . again."

Owens says, "I'm afraid I have to agree with Blankenship, gentlemen. I suggest we ignore that any such information has been brought to our attention." He gets a cheeky twinkle in his eye. "Perhaps we all should take a field trip to the MCG."

* * * * *

At the Melbourne Cricket Grounds, Tom Wills is talking with Johnny Cuzens and Johnny Mullagh in the change room as they are about to call it a day. "By the way, there's a member of the Match Committee that has been trying to make trouble for you boys. He has had it in for you since before the Boxing Day match," Wills says.

"What did we do?" Johnny Cuzens asks.

"As far as I can tell, the worst thing you did is you grew black skin," Wills answers. "But it's all taken care of now. I just wanted you to know that you should be careful who you are friendly with here. This bloke's name is Gerald Sampson. He is a banker who thinks he is more important than he actually is."

"He must be white," Mullagh says with a straight face.

"He must have bet against us," Cuzens says, also straight-faced.

These last two of The First Eleven have been playing at the MCG for several months and the season is about to come to a close. They have become completely integrated onto the Melbourne Cricket Club as essential to the team's success. Wills looks like a genius when all he actually did was invite them to play. The rest has taken care of itself. One or the other of them, along with Wills, always leads the team in wicket taking. And they also are always among the top five batsmen, often the top three, Wills being the third. The fans no longer see them as a novelty. They have demonstrated day after day their excellence on the local cricket pitch.

As the final days of the season approach, the two Johnnies are walking together along the boundary at the MCG. The sun is shining but there is beginning to be a chill in the air.

Johnny Cuzens looks up into the grandstand. "Do you ever think about what it was like when we first came here?" he asks.

"Every day," Mullagh replies. "All of this has been like a story somebody made up."

"You know? I think I have had enough of it, though," Cuzens says. "This has been nice but I miss country. I am probably going back to Framlingham when we finish the season. I can go back to work on the station. What about you?"

Johnny Mullagh is pensive for a moment. "Tom wants me to stay on and be available for next season. He said I can keep working here, but I'm not sure. If there's no cricket to play, it doesn't make much sense. But I don't know what else I am good for. Shearing, maybe, but not much more. I may go back to Pine Hills for a while and decide later. I'm sure they will allow me to come back and maybe look after the animals."

They fall silent as they continue their walk around the grounds. It has a feeling of finality about it, as if they have already decided that this cricketing adventure together has ended. As they approach the change room, Johnny Cuzens announces with certainty, "Yep. I'm going back to country. There is nothing Tom can offer me that will fill this need I have. It has been too long. I don't belong in a big city like Melbourne anymore. I hate to leave you, my friend, but . . ."

Johnny Mullagh puts his arm around his friend's shoulder. "We all have to do what is right for us," he says.

When the season officially ends, Johnny Cuzens announces his decision to Tom Wills. Wills says, "I'm sorry to see you go, Johnny. You are a great cricketer and we will miss you. But I understand." Then in language, he adds, "You have to keep the old ways. Cricket was just part of your story. Long life to you, my friend." They shake hands and Wills leaves the two Indigenous men together.

Johnny Mullagh embraces his teammate and friend. In a scene that neither of them expects to be as emotional as it is, through misty eyes, Johnny Mullagh says, "We have fought like warriors, side by side for a long time, my brother. I will miss you."

"I will miss you too, Unaarrimin. It has been a special adventure. I hope to see you again. Soon," Johnny Cuzens says. "Now, before we both turn into sobbing women, let me smile into your eyes and say goodbye."

Mullagh laughs and smacks him playfully on the arm. Then, they look intensely into each other's eyes with hands on one another's shoulders for a long moment without saying a word.

A few weeks after he re-settles back in Framlingham, Johnny Cuzens unexpectedly joins his ancestors.

A cricket fan from nearby Warrnambool notifies the Melbourne Cricket Club of Johnny Cuzens' death and asks that the club fund a proper burial for one of its premier players. The MCC coldly responds by saying that the club can't afford to pay for a funeral. A funeral is eventually funded by local police.

Chapter Twelve – Return to Country

Johnny Mullagh is folding towels when Tom Wills enters the change room. Mullagh smiles as he says, "G'day, Tom."

Wills doesn't smile back. "I have some really sad news," he says. He pauses for a moment to collect himself. "I just heard that our brother in Framlingham has passed away. There were no details." He goes to Mullagh and puts his arm around his shoulder. "I'm so sorry to have to tell you,"

Mullagh is physically affected by this news. He staggers as he finds a bench and sits down. He buries his face in his hands and his shoulders shake. Wills stands by him and says nothing.

After a while, Mullagh looks up. Tears have been streaming down his face. "Another one," he says simply. "Sometimes I wonder if we are cursed."

Wills sits on the bench next to him and puts his hand on Mullagh's shoulder. "It isn't a curse, mate. It's just life. You know that."

"I do," he says. "It's just that he and I were so close. We were . . . I don't have to tell you. You saw." Mullagh pauses for a moment. "He was so excited about going back to country. I am glad he was at least able to do that. But it still hurts my heart."

"I know," Wills says. "It hurts my heart too." They sit together is silence for several minutes, each lost in his own thoughts.

Wills is no less affected by this news. He thought of Johnny Cuzens, not just as a great cricketer, he was also a joy to be around. He was a friend. And each time someone close to him dies, it brings back the pain of his father's tragic death.

As for Mullagh, his thoughts are taking a turn he realizes have been simmering inside for some time without being articulated. Johnny Cuzens' passing has brought them bubbling to the surface. He turns to Wills.

"Tom," he says, "I've been thinking about this for a long time. Now I have to say it out loud. I am not sure I want to continue playing cricket here in Melbourne anymore. You have been a good friend to me and that means a lot, but I have been away from country for much too long. I have to go back to the land. I have to get out of this big city and become who I truly am again."

Wills allows this to soak in. "Are you sure that's what you want?" he asks.

"When our brother said he wanted to return to country a few weeks ago, I felt a tug I hadn't felt for a long time," Mullagh says. "He woke something up in me. I began thinking about it then. I am not a white man. This is not my place. I am Aboriginal man. Country is my place."

"Where will you go?" Wills asks.

"I will start by going back to Pine Hills," he answers. "The Edwards are good people. I am sure they will be glad to see me. And I am sure they will allow me to work for my keep until I can figure things out."

"I understand, my friend," Wills says. "But remember you always have a place to come back to if you want. It will take six players to replace you. A good wombat is not easy to find these days." Wills smiles.

Mullagh smiles back. "Thank you, my brother."

They both nod.

* * * * *

Timmy is the first to see the fashionably dressed Johnny Mullagh approach the veranda of the Pine Hills homestead. The boy lights up like a Christmas tree as he waves and shouts, "Hi, Mr. Mullagh!" Without waiting for a response, Timmy dashes into the house. "Mum, Mum, Mr. Mullagh is here!"

In no time, Mr. Edwards comes out onto the veranda. He gets a huge smile on his face when he sees Mullagh. "Why, Johnny, what a nice surprise. Welcome back, my boy."

Mullagh couldn't have imagined how good it would feel to be here again. He looks around at the buildings he knows so well as he approaches Mr. Edwards.

Edwards has come off the veranda and meets Mullagh with his hand extended. They shake hands warmly. "You are looking very fit, my boy. Let's have a look at you."

By now, Nell and her mother have come out of the house, still in their aprons. Mrs. Edwards smiles and says, "My, my, my. Who is this handsome gentleman that's come calling?"

Mullagh is caught completely off guard by this kind of attention from these people who were his employers only a year or so before. It actually creates an awkward moment for all of them. No one knows what the correct protocol is for a reunion of his kind. Everyone in the Edwards family, as always, is gracious. If this were a revered white friend who was returning, there would be hugs and kisses. But this is a new and uncharted kind of social interaction. They hold him in great affection, but at the end of the day, he is a Black fella, a widely accomplished one, but still a Black fella. Yet at the same time, it is their Johnny who has done these great things and, in their eyes, brought a sense of pride and credit to them all, which elevates him to near-family status. Hence the awkwardness.

Timmy lightens the mood and saves the day. He comes running out of the house with a cricket bat and ball. "Look, Mr. Mullagh. I got these last Christmas. Want to have a hit?"

"Don't you think it's a bit cold, sweetie," Nell asks.

Timmy looks at Mullagh with a hopeful expression. "Is it too cold for you, Mr. Mullagh?"

Mullagh sees that the boy is counting on him to say no. "Maybe for a little while," he says.

Timmy says, "Come on, Pappy. You play too." Mr. Edwards has no choice but to also say yes.

The three of them have a hit – theoretically – but actually it is Timmy who has a hit. Mullagh bowls and fields and Pappy Edwards is the wicket keeper. The boy is in seventh heaven as Mullagh lobs the ball to him. Timmy's batting skills are not quite perfected and the few times he actually makes contact, the ball dribbles back close enough to Mullagh that he only needs to take a step or two to retrieve it.

They have been at it for about half-an-hour when Jake returns from the paddock. "Got room for another?" he says as he approaches Mullagh with outstretched hand.

Mullagh takes Jake's hand and says with a smile, "We could use a fielder. I'm getting tired of bending over so much."

The four of them stay at this for a while longer, one of them having heaps of fun, until Mrs. Edwards comes out and clangs on the dinner bell. "You athletes hungry?" she calls out. She and Nell have set the table in the dining room. Chops and potatoes are steaming in bowls as the cricketers join them.

It still feels bizarre to Mullagh to be sitting at the dining room table having a meal with the Edwards family, but he has endured a year of bizarre experiences already. This is just another one, closer to home.

"So, what are your plans, Johnny?" Jake asks. "You want to come back to work here? We've always got room for you."

"We could play cricket every day," Timmy says enthusiastically.

"Now, relax, sweetie," Nell says. "Johnny may not want to play cricket every day. That's what he has been doing all the time he was away. Maybe he wants to do something different."

"Sorry, Mum," the boy says, realizing that he is being too aggressive. "Sorry, Mr. Mullagh."

Mr. Edwards asks, "What are your plans, Johnny? Have you given it any thought? I see you've been playing for the Melbourne Cricket Club. Do you intend to go back there?"

On the journey to Pine Hills, Mullagh did nothing but think about his future. His resolve to return to country remained the dominant thought. He wants to state this carefully, but definitively. "I don't want to work for a while. I need to be on the land again. What I would really like is to make a little camp for myself out by the billabong here on the property," he announces.

"Why don't you stay closer?" Jake suggests. "You can have one of the bunks here. It would be a lot more comfortable for you?"

"No," Mullagh says, "I have been in cities and hotels for more than a year. I need to be on country. I need to. For my soul."

No one knows quite what to say. Most of the Edwards family has assumed that the tour has been a white washing experience for him, so to speak. Living by a billabong in the bush seems so. . . so. . . native.

Mrs. Edwards changes the subject. "You know that Mr. Buckingham, over at your old station, died, don't you?"

"Yes," Mullagh answers.

"Alice is running the entire station now," Nell adds.

Jake says, "And she's doing a pretty good job of it too."

Nell says, "I know she would love to see you. She has told me how close you were as children."

"If you want to go visit," Mr. Edwards says, "take one of the horses, Johnny. Take Thunder."

Jake says, "Listen, Johnny, if you want to think about coming back to work here, we are always open to that. Why don't you go see Alice and think about it. You can let us know later."

This has come out of nowhere for Mullagh. Without question, he wants to see Alice. Just not now. Not yet. He has had her in his thoughts without pause since he was run off Mullagh Station. Her handkerchief has never left his possession. It has been a talisman for him. But he needs to think about what he wants to say to her and how he wants to say it. It is too important.

The idea of going right away actually frightens him. But on the other hand, he likens the situation to seeing a cricket ball rocketing toward him at a perfect speed and in a perfect location. He feels that he must quickly adjust and seize the opportunity or it may pass. It could be a sign.

Mullagh stills himself before saying anything. He doesn't want to sound too excited. He says, "I may take you up on that, Mr. Edwards. It would be nice to see Alice, especially now that she has so much responsibility. She might be glad to see a friendly face."

"I am sure she would," Mrs. Edwards says. "That girl has been through a lot. Old friends always come in handy at a time like this."

"Why don't you bunk in here for tonight," Jake says. "You can get an early start tomorrow."

"Thanks, Jake. I'll do that," Mullagh replies.

For the rest of the evening, Mullagh fields questions from Jake, Mr. Edwards and Timmy about playing cricket in England. He regales them until Mrs. Edwards comes into the lounge room and says, "All right, all you overgrown boys, that's enough cricket talk for one night. Let the poor man get some rest."

* * * * *

Mullagh takes his time saddling Thunder. He knows this horse well and bonds with him again while brushing him and combing his mane and patting him and pitching some hay into the stall and talking with him. It is also a way of procrastinating. In his mind, Mullagh has been playing and re-playing, editing and re-editing the conversation he has wanted to have with Alice since hearing of Buckingham's death and learning that she is now running the station. When he can't put it off any longer, he puts on Thunder's bridle, throws on the blanket and saddle, cinches the saddle in place, adjusts the stirrups, grabs the reins and mounts. He allows Thunder to set his own pace. Mullagh has left early enough that he can dawdle along the way and give himself time to do more editing and re-editing.

It is a cold, bright day. No threat of rain but a definite need to rug up. Mullagh had to borrow some winter gear for this journey. He would like to have shown up at Mullagh Station in his finery, but in addition to looking out of place, those togs would do nothing to mitigate the cold weather, as he found out the hard way yesterday when Timmy wanted to play cricket.

Thunder plods along in no hurry until they arrive at the stream where so many memories linger.

Mullagh dismounts and lets Thunder munch on grass while he stares into the stream for a while before taking a drink of the cold, fresh water. As he gazes into the ripples, all the old stories and memories return, like being here with his father and learning that his totem is the Black Cockatoo and the time he learned to throw a boomerang and the day he was run off Mullagh Station. Today he gazes into it like a crystal ball, hoping to be able to see into the future.

A little snort from Thunder interrupts Mullagh's reverie. "All right," he says out loud. "I'm coming."

Mullagh Station is in sight and Mullagh is tempted to turn around and go back to Pine Hills. "Why am I so scared?" he asks Thunder. Thunder doesn't even grunt a response. "Thanks. I suppose I'm on my own."

As he gets closer, one of the Aboriginal workers spots Mullagh, waves and calls out to him. "Unaarrimin!"

Mullagh waves back. But the worker quickly disappears behind a shed. In a moment, he hears Alice shriek, then her magical laugh. She comes out in rugged farm clothes, hair barely under control beneath her father's old felt hat that is so pinched it has a hole in it. Her hands and face are grimy. But she has no regard for her appearance.

She half laughs and half yells, "Unaarrimin! You're here!"

Mullagh dismounts as Alice runs toward him with a smile that rivals the sunshine. She throws her arms around his neck and hugs him close for a long moment. Mullagh happily takes her in his arms.

This tender spell is broken when Alice pushes away from him, looks up into his face, punches him hard on the shoulder and says, "You bastard!"

"What?"

"Look at me. I've been slopping hogs."

Mullagh sniffs. "Yep, I can tell."

She punches his shoulder again. "Watch yourself. You are addressing the manager of Mullagh Station, I'll have you know.

"So I've heard," he says.

"Why didn't you let me know you were coming?"

"I didn't know I was coming until yesterday."

"Yesterday?"

"I stopped at Pine Hills and they suggested that I come to see you."

"You weren't going to come and see me if they didn't suggest it?"

"Of course I was going to come and see you. Just not at this moment."

She looks at him while she decides if this is a satisfactory response. She quickly realizes that she is so happy to see him that it doesn't really matter who suggested it or when. "Well, why don't you have a cuppa while I try to make myself more presentable," she finally says.

"That's a good idea," Mullagh says, then flinches when Alice balls up her fist. "I meant the cuppa. The cuppa sounds like a good idea."

Mullagh is sitting in the kitchen having his tea when a little while later Alice joins him. She is wearing a dress and has a ribbon tied around her freshly washed hair. She has also put on some perfume which precedes her into the kitchen. Mullagh looks up and sniffs. "Where did the hog smell go?" he says.

"You like it?" Alice asks. "It's Mum's. It came all the way from Paris, France."

"Beats hogs," he says.

Alice pours herself a cuppa and sits down at the kitchen table with him.

"Where is your mum?" Mullagh asks. "Looking for the shotgun?"

"She's in Melbourne," Alice answers. "She goes there as often as she can. I don't know what she does, but she likes it. She always hated station life, so it's perfect for both of us. Come on. Finish your tea. I want to show you what I've done with the station." She slips a thick, wool jumper on over her dress, a long, heavy coat, her dad's hat and a pair of old, muddy boots.

"Very stylish," Mullagh smiles.

Alice makes a fist and threatens him. Then smiles. "Come on," she says and grabs his hand.

The sun is nice and warm but the breeze has some Antarctica in it. They ignore the chill as they stroll around the property for the next half-an-hour or so and Alice points out her improvements. Then she says, "That's enough about Mullagh Station. Tell me. What was London like? I can't believe you were actually there. It must have been exciting. How did the women dress? Are the shops nice? Is it expensive? Did you see all the interesting sights?"

"Slow down," Mullagh says. "Too many questions all at once."

"Sorry. I'm just so excited to see you. I want to know everything. I read all about your tour. It was in the papers. They say you are one of the best cricketers they've ever seen. Is that true?"

"It's what they said," Mullagh answers.

The way he answers her and his tone make Alice think that this may be embarrassing for him. She decides it can all wait for another time. They continue walking. Occasionally, another of the workers shouts a "G'day" at Mullagh and he responds.

"Tell me. How are you really doing here?" Mullagh finally asks.

Alice perks up immediately. She takes his arm. "Oh, Unaarrimin, I have never been so happy. All the men stayed with me after Dad died. They loved him so much and they wanted me to succeed. They're more like family than employees. All of them." She reflects on this for a few seconds. "Thanks to them, we've been keeping up. Making a bit of money and staying ahead of the bank. I made Mum promise to let me have a go for two years and so far, so good."

Mullagh takes this in. "It's a bit chilly, don't you think?" he says. "Maybe we should get you out of the cold."

"Oh, I forgot. You world travelers aren't used to our sneaky cold climate in the Western District," she says. They start back toward the homestead. "I'll fix us something to eat and we can talk in the house."

Once they are back in the warmth of the lounge room, Alice asks him to tend to the fire in the fireplace. She leaves him there as she goes to prepare some food. Like being at the Edwards' dining table, this feels awkward for Mullagh. Not that he hasn't been in the house before, but because he doesn't have to sneak in and out this time. He is welcome.

He gets the fire flaring again and watches the flames shoot up the chimney. It's like staring into the stream. Old memories return. His childhood with Alice and their closeness, their inseparability, play on his mind. All those years. And now here he is, tending to the fire. Without thinking, he reaches into his pocket and takes out her handkerchief, trying to decide if this is the right time to make his edited and re-edited speech. Everything in his past two days seems other worldly. It is all untrodden ground. Nothing is clear cut. Eventually, he puts the handkerchief back in his pocket and stills himself. *I don't have to make any decisions. The decisions will make themselves.* He relaxes.

Alice comes in with a bowl of lamb stew in each hand and a loaf of homemade bread pressed against her side with her elbow. "Let's eat in here. It's warmer," she says. She hands him one of the bowls. "There's a spoon in my pocket."

Suddenly sitting in front of the fire with Alice, eating lamb stew, feels like the most natural thing in the world to Mullagh. More untrodden ground.

They eat in silence for a little while, each seemingly lost in thought. Alice breaks the silence. "What do you want me to call you? Johnny? Unaarrimin?"

"You asked me that before. Do you remember?" he says.

She thinks. "Oh, right," she says. "I do remember. All right, Emu, I have an idea that I've been thinking about for a long time that I'd like to talk to you about. Don't answer until I've said everything I'm thinking."

Mullagh's mind immediately travels to his edited and re-edited speech. *Could she have been thinking what I have been thinking?* He makes every attempt to remain calm. It is not easy.

Alice begins. "We grew up together on this station. We were separated through no fault of our own. In the meantime, we have each achieved things we couldn't have dreamed of back then. In our own ways, we have experienced a lot while we've been separated, you and me."

Mullagh nods calmly while inside he is spinning.

Alice goes on. "No one knows me better than you do and I doubt anyone knows you better I do. Without ever saying it, we both knew we wanted to be together again, this time on our own terms. Mum takes no interest in the station beyond enjoying the fruits of its success. And, it goes without saying that you and I aren't getting any younger. So, here's my plan."

These words fill Mullagh with a joy that he can barely contain, but he still shows nothing.

"What I'm thinking is we *should* be together, that you should come back to Mullagh Station and work with me here. It is really your home as much as it is mine. You belong here. And we have always been family. It will be like old times. If you want to go off and play cricket sometimes, that is all right too. So, what do you say?"

Mullagh is silent. He is waiting for more.

"I mean," she continues, "this way we can be together without interference from anyone – meaning Mum – and I can look after for you."

These words stun Mullagh. This is not the more he had in mind. At least not these words. This speech is not the one he wanted to hear or the one he wanted to make. His silence goes on for far too long leaving awkwardness in its wake.

"Well, Unaarrimin, what do you think?" she repeats.

He finally finds his tongue. He looks into her eyes. "You want to look after *me*?"

Alice's face lights up with a smile. "Yes," she says.

"I want to look after *you*," he says with some emphasis.

"That's right," she says, still smiling. "We'll look after each other. Just like in the old days."

Mullagh looks into the fire. He must still himself. This is not the scene he has played over and over in his mind. Time seems to freeze. Eventually, he looks back at Alice. Instinctively, he realizes It is now or never. He reaches into his pocket and takes out a small purple velvet jewelers' box.

Alice looks at the box and then into Mullagh's eyes. "What's that?"

"Something I bought for you in London with the money I was awarded for playing cricket. Open it."

"Is that a ring?" she asks, incredulously.

"Yes," he answers, and smiles broadly.

Alice is immediately aware of what the box signifies as she reads Mullagh's face. He is glowing. "Unaarrimin, I think you misunderstand me. I want you here with me forever, but not in that way.

You are the best friend I have ever had, my brother, but . . ."

"But you don't want me to be your husband." Mullagh finishes her sentence for her.

"No. Not my husband. I don't want a husband. I don't want a man I have to answer to. I'm too independent for that. Mum has been trying to marry me off since I was sixteen. I don't want that. I have never wanted that. But I do want you to be here with me."

Mullagh is speechless. This is all he has dreamed of since he left Mullagh Station, that one day he would return and ride off into the sunset with Alice, that they would defy all customs and norms, that they would be legally what few people could imagine or acknowledge: husband and wife. He was so sure of it that it became the truth for him and has motivated everything he has achieved. It is the foundation of his entire being.

Alice knows him too well. She knows she has hurt him deeply, in a way she would never have intended, but in a way that was unavoidable. "I'm sorry, Unaarrimin," Alice says softly. "I love you and I have always loved you. And I will always love you. Just not in that way. Can you understand that?"

The silence becomes painful as Mullagh sits there looking into the fire with the velvet box in his hand.

Alice reaches out and puts her hand on his arm. She says, "I want you here with me with all my heart, just not in that way. Please understand." The fire crackles. Again, she asks, "Do you understand?

Mullagh looks away from the fire and into Alice's eyes. Her expression is soft. His is unreadable until he says, "No, I don't understand." He puts the velvet box on a little table and rises. Without saying another word, he puts on his jacket and slowly walks out of the door and out of Alice's life.

* * * * *

A few years have passed. Unaarrimin has made a comfortable little hut for himself and his three dogs by the billabong. Jake and Mr. Edwards have worked out an arrangement with him whereby he does a few chores around station in exchange for basic rations. Dinner with the family has given way to trapping and fishing and a life so far removed from society that it has become a distant memory, or perhaps even a dream. It suits him perfectly. Being on country has healed him and centered him. Timmy is now Tim and has grown into a promising young man but he still idolizes "Mr. Mullagh" and frequently visits him, the only person who does so on a regular basis.

One day, Tim calls out, as is his custom when he comes for a visit. "Hey, Mr. Mullagh. Are you around?" Mullagh is busy skinning a possum. He looks up and waves Tim in.

"How are you, Mr. Mullagh? Tim asks.

"I'm about to have some possum. You want some?"

"Yes, sir," Tim says. "But I should tell you that you have a visitor."

"You mean, besides you?"

"Yep." No sooner does he say this than Tom Wills steps into the open.

"Got enough for one more?" Wills says.

"Here," he hands the possum and skinning knife to Tim. "You finish this," he says, rising to his feet and going toward Tom Wills. "If I'd known you were coming, I would have cooked a wombat." He pulls up some grass and wipes the blood off hands with it as he strides toward Wills.

"G'day, my friend," Wills says grabbing Mullagh by the shoulders.

"You get lost?" Mullagh says.

"No, I'm just looking for cricket players," Wills says.

"Yep. You got lost. No cricket players around here," Mullagh says.

"That's not what I hear," Wills says. "They tell me you've played a bit in Harrow."

"Oh, that," Mullagh says. "That's just to keep from forgetting how to hold a bat."

"Well, I've got a proposition for you and I guarantee you'll have to remember how to hold a bat for this one," Wills says.

Tim feels privileged in the company of these two sporting heroes and looks back and forth from one to the other as he goes about his skinning chore.

Mullagh raises his eyebrows to indicate he's listening.

"The Brits are coming here for a tour and the first thing they asked is if you were going to be playing with us," Wills says.

"I hope you told them I'm retired," Mullagh says.

"I told them you couldn't wait to remind them who the best cricketer in England is," Wills says.

"I don't know," Mullagh hesitates. "Who'll look after my dogs?"

"I will," Tim practically shouts.

Wills laughs and winks at Tim. "Well done, Tim." He looks back to Mullagh. "So?"

"For how long?" Mullagh asks. The idea of it is very tempting.

Wills realizes that the hook is set. "For as long as you want. Melbourne and Sydney would be nice for a start. What do you reckon? I'll even throw in a hotel room and some tucker, unless you want to camp in a park in which case I'll personally catch your possums for you.

Mullagh smiles. "How could I say no to such a generous offer? When does this tour begin?"

To no one's surprise, Johnny Mullagh's performance at the MCG in March of 1879 is outstanding. He has lost none of his amazing skills at both batting and bowling. His British opponents praise him, as do the local fans. It is a triumphal return. And even though he enjoys this moment of nostalgia, it does nothing to change his mind about choosing between cricket and country. After the Brits leave, he returns to his billabong.

* * * * *

More years pass. On rare occasions, Unaarrimin becomes Johnny Mullagh again for a cricket match in Harrow, but for all practical purposes, his cricketing days are behind him. He is content to live on the banks of his billabong with his dogs and the occasional visits from Tim. The two have truly bonded and Tim looks on this as his responsibility, to make sure Unaarrimin is safe and well cared for. In return, Unaarrimin teaches Tim on the ways of survival in the bush, where to look for tucker, what is edible and what isn't and how to a trap and set fishing lines.

On one such visit, the two friends are sitting by the fire, watching their freshly caught fish cook.

Three sharp, penetrating screeches echo from high in the canopy of gum trees.

"Do you know what that is?" Unaarrimin asks without looking up.

Sounds like some kind of parrot," Tim answers.

Unaarrimin searches through the trees. "Look up there. See?"

Tim looks where Unaarrimin is pointing.

"Oh, yes. I see it now," Tim announces proudly.

"That is my totem," Unaarrimin says. "The Black Cockatoo."

"Your totem?"

"My totem is my connection to the dreaming, to the history of my people, to the history of the whole of Life. We all look out for each other. It's a way of saying that all Life is connected."

"Is that why you always pat a tree when you pass it?" Tim asks.

"Yes. The tree is like a friend, another living thing. We are all one. Plants. Animals. People. One earth. One Life.

"I wish I had a totem," Tim laments.

* * * * *

One day, Tim is about a mile from Unaarrimn's camp looking for duck eggs. He spots a tall tree trunk about fifteen feet high and remembers Unaarrimin telling him that ducks often use a place like this for their nests. He climbs up the trunk and looks carefully into the hollow. No duck nest is there. But surprisingly it is filled with wool. Tim wonders about it but thinks little more of it. He is looking for duck eggs! Nearby he sees another likely tree trunk candidate and climbs it. When he looks in this time, and sees it is also filled with wool, he decides he needs to tell his dad about it.

It is late afternoon when Jake rides up to the homestead from checking the boundaries. Tim waits until he has taken care of his horse and comes into the house before going up to him. "Hey, Dad, you'll never guess what I found in a tree trunk out on the property."

Jake smiles and says, "You rascal. You found us some duck eggs, didn't you? Good boy."

"No, it wasn't duck eggs," Tim says. "It was a sheep or some sheep skins, I couldn't tell which, but it wasn't duck eggs."

"Are you sure?" Jake says.

"Dad, I know the difference between a sheepskin and duck eggs," Tim says.

Just then Mr. Edwards joins them.

Jake says, "Tim found some sheep skins in a tree trunk out on the property,"

Edwards looks at his grandson. "Are you sure?"

"Pappy, I can tell the difference," Tim says. "I was looking for duck eggs and I climbed two different stumps and there was wool in both of them."

Edwards says, "I think we have to have a look, Jake. Let's go out tomorrow. Tim can show us where they are."

The next morning, the three of them return to the place where Tim made his discovery.

"You think you can climb up there and throw that wool out?" Edwards asks his grandson.

"Yep," Tim says and climbs the tree trunk effortlessly. He leans into the hollow of the tree, hauls out a bundle and tosses it on the ground. It is a perfect sheepskin with the grass cut out of the stomach, the head rolled up in it and the legs tied.

"There's more," Tim says and continues throwing out these bundles until the ones at the very bottom are too decayed to take hold of. Tim goes to the next tree trunk and does the same thing.

"I wonder if someone is duffing our sheep," Jake says.

"If they are, why would they hide the skins out here in a tree trunk?" Edwards wonders.

"What do you reckon?" Jake says.

"I think I'll have to have a chat with Carter," Edwards muses.

"Who's Carter?" Tim asks.

"He's the local constable in Harrow, son," Jake says. "He knows pretty much everything that's going on around these parts."

The next day, Constable Carter has joined them. He takes one look and says without hesitation, "This is a Black fella's work. No white man done this."

"Black fella?" Edwards says. "There aren't any Black fellas around here."

"Except Johnny," Jake says.

"Yes. Except Johnny," Edwards agrees.

"Who's this Johnny?" Carter asks.

Tim answers. "It's Johnny Mullagh, the greatest cricketer in the world."

Edwards quickly volunteers, "He couldn't have anything to do with this, Constable. We give him regular rations. He has no need of mutton."

"Well," Carter says, "I don't know about that, but I do know that a Black done this. No question about it. Do you mind if I have a word with this fella?"

The four of them go to Unaarrimin's camp where they find him sewing a patch on a pair of trousers.

Tim says, "G'day, Mr. Mullagh."

Unaarrimin looks up. "G'day, Tim. G'day, Jake. Mr. Edwards. G'day, officer. What can I do for you? Care for a cuppa?" He reaches for the billy and sets it on the fire.

Carter gets right to work. "This boy found some sheepskins in tree trunks about a mile from here. You know anything about it?"

Unaarrimin looks into the distance for a moment. He turns toward Carter. "Yep," he says.

Mr. Edwards and Jake look at each other in disbelief. Tim stands there as if he were frozen.

"Just what do you know?" Carter continues.

"I know my dogs were hungry and I needed tucker for them," Unaarrimin says innocently.

"You killed some of my sheep for your dogs?" Edwards says. He is incredulous.

"Yes, sir, I did," Unaarrimin says matter-of-factly, without remorse or hesitation.

It takes a long time for all this to come into focus for everyone except Carter. He looks from Mr. Edwards to Jake. "Do you mind stepping over here for a minute," he says as he steps away from the camp. Edwards and Jake follow him.

"What do you want me to do?" Carter asks. "This is not something we tolerate around here. You know that, of course."

Edwards says, "I know full well, Constable. Let me think about his for a minute." Edwards is in a place that no one would wish on an enemy. He has known Johnny Mullagh for years. He knows him to be not just a great athlete, but also an upstanding man. He knows him to be honest and forthright. He has never seen him any other way. This admission is shocking to him. On the one hand, it is against the law, but on the other hand, Edwards understands Mullagh to be innocent of malice. Finally he says, "Let me deal with this Constable. I don't want to prosecute."

Carter is a by-the-book law officer. His only position would be to take Unaarrimin in to the lockup. "Are you sure that's what you want to do?" he asks.

Edwards looks at Jake. Jake nods. "Yes, Constable. We'll take care of it. Thank you for your time."

Carter mounts up and trots away. Edwards returns to Unaarrimin. "Why would you do such a thing, Johnny?" he asks.

"I didn't mean you any harm, Mr. Edwards," Unaarrimin says. "I just needed meat for my dogs and the sheep were easy tucker."

"How many do you reckon you killed?" Jake asks.

"I couldn't say," Unaarrimin says. "But I can take you to another tree trunk where I put some more skins. It's just over there." He points to a similar sized trunk a short distance away.

Edwards is quiet for a few minutes, thinking. "Johnny," he says, "I have a great deal of respect for you, you know that. But this is something that I just cannot allow. I don't want to throw you off my property so I have a proposal for you. If you get rid of these dogs, you can stay where you are and we'll forget the entire affair. Understood?"

Unaarrimin nods.

A few days later, Tim is feeling guilty about being the one who exposed his friend and mentor. He decides to ride out and try to make amends. When he arrives at the billabong, there is no sign of anyone living there anymore. But there are tracks. He follows the tracks through the boundary fence and onto crown land. In the distance he sees smoke rising near a copse of gum trees.

As he draws closer, he sees Unaarrimin's three dogs lazing around a little fire. "Hey, Mr. Mullagh. Are you around?" he shouts. The dogs look up as he approaches. When they see it is Tim, they go to him and start wagging their tails.

Unaarrimin comes out from some brush and waves Tim in. "G'day, Tim," he says. "Like my new camp?"

Until Tim gets this apology off his chest he is uncomfortable. "Mr. Mullagh, I just want you to know how sorry I am for what I did. If I'd have known why those skins were there, I would never have said a word."

"You did the right thing, Tim," Unaarrimin assures him. "That was wrong of me to kill those sheep. I just took the easy way to feed my dogs."

"Well, just the same, I'm sorry," Tim says.

"I've got some roo cooking. Want some?"

"You're not angry with me?"

"No. We're friends. Friends don't get angry at each other. Want to stay and have some tucker with me or not?"

"Well, in that case, yep, I'd like to stay. How'd you get the roo?"

Unaarrimin goes through all the details of his kangaroo hunt and Tim sits on the ground, listening in awe. When he finishes his saga, Unaarrimin says, "Sheep are easier," and laughs.

With their friendship restored, Tim asks, "Do you want me to say anything to my dad or Pappy about where you are now?"

"This is crown land and I'm not killing anybody's sheep so tell them whatever you want. But I saw your dad the other day when he was riding along the boundary. He gave me some tobacco. So your grandpa probably knows too," Unaarrimin says.

The kangaroo has been cooking in a pit and is perfect when Unaarrimin rakes away the coals. He and Tim feast on the succulent meat and munch on some bush veggies. Unaarrimin says, "I ate food in

England that they said was the best in the world, but you can give me bush tucker any day."

"This sure is good," Tim says, wiping his mouth with his sleeve. As they get stuck into their meal, the dogs are gnawing on kangaroo bones. When they've had their fill, Tim says, "I better get going back." He rises and goes to his horse. "I'm happy you're not cross with me, Mr. Mullagh. Is it all right if I come out and visit you here like I used to?"

"Anytime, Tim," Unaarrimin says. He gives a salute as he watches Tim mount his horse and trot away.

* * * * *

One day, a few weeks later, Tim is riding home to Pine Hills and decides to visit his friend on the way. As he approaches, he calls out, "Hey, Mr. Mullagh. Are you around?" When he gets closer he sees Unaarrimin sitting by the fire. He doesn't look his usual, vibrant self.

Tim dismounts and observes Unaarrimin a bit closer. "Are you feeling crook, Mr. Mullagh?" he asks. "You don't look too good."

"Aw, I'll be alright," Unaarrimin says. "My side hurts is all."

"How bad is it? Can you get around?" Tim asks.

"It hurts pretty bad, but it'll go away, I reckon," Unaarrimin says.

"You don't look good," Tim repeats with some concern. "I'm going to send my dad out and see what he thinks, if that's all right."

"If you want to," Unaarrimin says. "But it'll probably be right in a few days."

A few days later, Jake rides up to Unaarrimin's campsite and finds nothing there but some cold ashes where the fire had been. He is shocked at the sight of two of Unaarrimin's dogs lying near the ashes, stone cold dead. Jake immediately looks around for tracks, finds some and follows them for an hour or so. They lead eventually to another cold fire next to a tree. He sees that someone has been lying down on the crushed grass nearby. He continues following tracks. About one hundred yards further, he finds another camp, and then another one beyond that one. He is no longer on crown land. Then, up ahead, he sees a dog standing by a tree. Jake kicks his horse and gallops up to the tree and sees Unaarrimin propped up against it. He looks very bad.

"Johnny? What's the matter with you? What's wrong?" Jake asks.

Unaarrimin is unable to speak. He can only hold onto his side. Jake sees that Unaarrimin is shivering. He takes off his jacket and puts it over him. "You don't look too good, Johnny," he says. He packs some tobacco into Unaarrimin's pipe, lights it and then puts it up to Unaarrimin's lips. He doesn't even have the strength to draw on it. "I'm going to go back to the station and get some help. You just relax here until I get back." Jake gallops off at top speed.

When he gets to Pine Hills, Jake jumps off his horse and runs immediately to find Mr. Edwards. "Johnny is sick as a dog out there in the bush," he tells his father-in-law.

"Do you know what's wrong?" Edwards asks.

"No, but he's holding onto his side like he's trying to keep it from exploding," Jake says.

"Let's put a mattress in the buggy and get out there," Edwards says.

They waste no time dragging a mattress off one of the bunks and onto the buggy. Tim sees the activity. "What's going on, Dad?" he asks.

"Johnny is pretty crook, son. We've got to get out there in a hurry," Jake says.

"I'm coming with you," Tim announces. His hat flies off as he runs for his horse. He ignores it and jumps into the saddle.

Edwards is already cracking the whip and the buggy lurches ahead with Jake right behind him.

Tim kicks his horse and quickly catches up. The three of them are racing toward Unaarrimin at top speed. They sense instinctively that this is very serious and every second counts.

Soon they arrive at Unaarrimin's tree. He is still leaning against it as he was before, his hand still clutching his side. Tim calls to him, "Hey, Mr. Mullagh."

Unaarrimin makes no response. The three men walk closer. It isn't clear whether or not Mullagh is breathing. His dog is curled up on the ground next to him. They are now standing over him. "Oh, my god," Edwards says. He looks at Jake for confirmation. Jake nods. They have arrived too late. Unaarrimin, Black Johnny, Johnny Mullagh, has breathed his last breath. Jake and Mr. Edwards remove their hats and bow their heads as they look down on what was once a vital, phenomenal, even iconic human being. After a moment, they pick up his lifeless body, carry it to the buggy and carefully place it on the mattress for the ride back to Pine Hills. Tim is weeping.

As his father and grandfather start back toward the homestead, through his tears, Tim says, "I'll be home later." As the sound of the horses' hooves fade, he just stands there staring at the tree for several minutes. Unaarrimin's dog is whimpering next to him. Tim feels an obligation to do something to somehow commemorate and immortalize this moment and acknowledge his friend. He continues staring at the tree, at the same time absentmindedly scratching the dog's head. Slowly he nods to himself, takes out his pocket knife and painstakingly, with moisture still in his eyes, carves these words into the trunk of the tree:

This is the tree where J.M. died.

As if Nature, itself, had ordained it, this tree is on Mullagh Station property. It is on Unaarrimin's traditional, ancestral land. He has returned to country. His story is complete. His essence has blended into the Dreaming.

Tim looks up instantly when he hears three sharp, penetrating screeches coming from the tree tops.

The Black Cockatoo flaps its wings.

The dog barks.

ACKNOWLEDGEMENTS

I have a mantra that says, "Timing is always perfect." Whether it's true or just my own little myth doesn't matter. I say it and mostly believe it. On three separate occasions in my life in Oz, when I was creatively stagnant and frustrated, Adam Zwar said to me, "You know what you should do?" The first time resulted in four cabaret shows I wrote, produced and performed in at The Butterfly Club in Melbourne. The second time I was stagnant and frustrated, a few years later, Adam said, "You know what you should do?" That resulted in *The Chris Wallace Chronicles,* my Audiobiography. I would never have thought to do those podcasts, but for Adam.

Which brings us to *The Dreaming Team*. Adam followed me through the maze of circumstances that led to this book. At no time was the idea of writing this book on anyone's radar. My involvement with the story had been marginal until suddenly it wasn't. Then things took an unimaginable turn which left me stagnant and frustrated once again. And once again, Adam said, "You know what you should do?"

So, thank you, Adam, for telling me what I should do at the perfect time, each time, and also for all your excellent counsel and caring friendship.

ABOUT THE AUTHOR

Chris Wallace is a naturalized Australian citizen whose creative career began in the United States, taking him from St. Louis to New York to Hollywood and then to Melbourne. His professional background and achievements are listed on his website: **www.olentangymusic.com** and include being an actor, producer, writer, composer, lyricist, singer, cabaret artist, podcaster (***The Chris Wallace Chronicles***) and now an author. ***The Dreaming Team*** is his second book, but the first under his own name. His previous book, ***Hollywood Mosaic***, is under a pen name, Pete Joseph, and is available on Kindle.

Made in the USA
Middletown, DE
08 November 2023